NO HOLDS BARRED

Catching me harried and unaware, Leroy slammed his head backwards and nailed me in the lip. I let go thinking that at least one of my teeth was buried in his skull as my mouth went numb.

Somebody gripped my left ear and was slowly ripping it off my head. Leroy twisted around and decided my right ear would make a splendid cufflink. I should have been more alert.

I sank my teeth into his forearm as deeply as I could. Even that didn't release his grip.

But suddenly Leroy let go. I stopped moving. The people in the room all backed off another five feet.

Four inches from my temple a guy held a .357 Magnum. I was too close to see whether or not it was cocked.

Other Avon Books by
Earl W. Emerson

NERVOUS LAUGHTER
THE RAINY CITY

POVERTY BAY

EARL W. EMERSON

AVON BOOKS  NEW YORK

POVERTY BAY is an original publication of Avon Books. The work has never before appeared in book form. This work is a novel. Any similarity to actual persons or events is purely coincidental.

AVON BOOKS
A division of
The Hearst Corporation
105 Madison Avenue
New York, New York 10016

Copyright © 1985 by Earl W. Emerson
Published by arrangement with the author
Library of Congress Catalog Card Number: 84-91255
ISBN: 0-380-89647-8

First Avon Books Printing: March 1985

AVON BOOKS TRADEMARK REG. U.S. PAT. OFF. AND IN OTHER COUNTRIES, MARCA REGISTRADA.

Printed in Canada

UNV 10 9 8 7 6 5

All men must escape at times from the deadly rhythm of their private thoughts.

—Raymond Chandler

Chapter One

IF THEY HAD meant to hire a sexy receptionist, the law firm of Leech, Bemis and Ott had screwed up.

The brass nameplate on her desk said "Beulah Hancock." She weighed a good hundred pounds more than my 180. It took all my will power to keep from ogling her berry-colored blouse, an enormous thing that would have made a fair pup tent.

"May I help you?" she asked, flashing me only a fraction of a brokenhearted smile.

I gazed into her Technicolor-blue contacts and said, "Kathy Birchfield, please."

She got all bubbly and I began to like her. "Kathy's only been here a week, you know. We're all so happy to have a female in the firm. Is this about the Oppenlander will?"

"Couldn't tell you. She called an hour ago and told me she needed a private detective."

Something sad and unused behind the Technicolor said she had been gorgeous once, ages before she had ballooned to her present proportions. She was all atwitter.

"It's really something. The Oppenlander will. All that money. And he was in here twice. He's not . . . one of those hoity-toity snobs. He's considering loaning me some funds to start a boutique. It's really an idea whose time has come. Lingerie for the big woman. Don't you think?" I nodded and grinned.

"Miss Birchfield was in a hurry. Could you buzz her?"

"Certainly." After speaking into her telephone, Beulah Hancock turned and began stabbing her fat fingers at the plastic keys of her machine.

I had gone only about two steps when she half-twisted around, her swivel chair protesting in a raspy screech. She made a peculiar, grimacing face at me. "You're Kathy's friend?"

"Yes."

"The detective? You're her detective friend?"

I nodded.

Like a frantically boiling stew that had been rescued from the burner, she simmered down. She then assumed a secret and somewhat bemused look of curiosity and of titillation.

"Did Kathy say something about me?"

Beulah Hancock only smiled and rolled back to her typing.

The Grueman Building was situated in the Montlake area below the University of Washington, just north of and out of sight of Husky Stadium. A moody Muzak inundated the place, saturating my thoughts. It was one of those modern office complexes, long, low, and filled to capacity with waxed plants, smelly new carpets, and tagged regulation fire extinguishers. The pretty secretaries tiptoeing down the corridors were all dressed like the sleekest models in the "career clothes" section of the spring Spiegel catalogue.

Kathy Birchfield's door was the second one on the left in the Leech, Bemis and Ott wing. When I shoved on her half-open door, I discovered Ms. Birchfield thoughtfully staring at a nearly bare desk top, a pencil butted up against her lip as if it were a gun barrel and she were contemplating suicide.

A stunning brunette, she had violet eyes, a lithe body and an engaging manner that gave one the impression she was not aware in the least that she was attractive.

"Good morning."

She said, "I want you to find fifteen million dollars."

I whistled. "Somebody lose their wallet in the john? You check the wastebaskets?"

"A twenty-five-year-old man has disappeared. At least, according to his father he's disappeared. He's the heir to the Oppenlander fortune."

"The father, or the guy who disappeared?"

"The young man who disappeared is the heir."

"What'd you tell that receptionist out there about me?"

"Did you meet Beulah? Isn't she sweet?"

2

"She's a regular pot of honey. What did you tell her about me?"

"Tell?"

"Don't bat your baby blues and give me that why-would-I-tell-a-fib look. You told her something and I want to know what it was."

The beechwood desk was about a mile wide, with a creeping fig plant dangling off one corner of it. For a few moments, she rolled about in her swivel chair describing small and ever-tightening concentric circles, giving me a fishy stare.

"Me?"

"Yeah, you. I remember when you told that beefpot, Iris, that I had only four months to live and couldn't face it, and the one thing that would make me die happy was to have a torrid affair with her and her roommate, the lady wrestler."

"You three were great together."

"Very funny. I had to change my phone number."

Kathy wore a long-sleeved white blouse that had a high, stiff collar and, just over either breast, a broad band of lace running down the front. Even though it was new and chic, it had an old-fashioned look. The pleats of her charcoal-gray slacks were so sharp she could have whacked off slices of French bread with them. Her nails were a soft coral. The throat of her high-necked blouse was held together with a gold pin, inlaid with mother-of-pearl. Her long, full hair was worn loose, brushed back on one side. She bore the look of success with pride and a certain panache.

Continuing to assess me with narrowed eyes, she bobbled the yellow pencil between her fingers and said, "His father thinks something might have happened to him."

"And you don't?"

"I don't know."

I plopped onto the front edge of her desk, one leg cocked up and the other bracing myself against the floor. I grinned my hardest, striving to be an insolent bastard.

"Give me the details."

Kathy Birchfield sat rigidly upright and fixed her pooled violet on me. "Leech, Bemis and Ott is handling a case, an estate case. A gentleman back East by the name of Rufus F. Oppenlander died and left his fortune to a grandson. All except a pittance to each of the others. The family had no hint that he would do anything that drastic. They're not wealthy people. They figured, at the very least, to share even-steven. It was quite a shock."

"So the rest of the family is a little piqued that they didn't get what they thought was their rightful chunk of the pie."

"Precisely."

"And now somebody's missing?"

"The one who inherited it all, the youngest son, Lance Tyner."

"How long has he been gone?"

"His father hasn't been able to get in touch with him for a week or so."

"How big is this family?"

"There's the boy who inherited the money, his brother, a sister and their father. They don't have any other close relatives. The father thinks he should have gotten all of it. You see, it was *his* father who died, Lance's paternal grandfather."

"People wait years for these old geezers to croak. It's a major disappointment when they don't come up with some hard cash."

"Don't be flip. We're trying to reach some sort of settlement, divide up the money a little more equitably. The court battle is over. The son won. It's his legally. Now we need to negotiate privately, if he's amenable. And we think he is. We can't do that until we find him."

"That's where I come in?"

"That's where you come in. You find him."

"A guy inherits fifteen million dollars and his family has to take him to court to get any?"

"From what I gather, it's a rather peculiar situation. But our client believes we still might be able to dicker. So do we. Even a fraction of the total would be significant. Will you do it?"

"Why not? Who's your client?"

"His father. He's in the other room. He's almost hysterical, thinks his son is going to run away or get murdered before he can get this thing settled. He's almost more interested in the money than in his son. Let me go get him."

"Wait a minute. Murdered?"

4

"Frankly, I think he's being melodramatic. Perhaps we had better let Mr. Tyner fill you in."

Kathy Birchfield rose, sauntered around the mile-wide desk and walked toward the door. I liked the way she walked. I turned my gaze in time to avoid the deft look she cast over her shoulder, her long hair whirling with the turn of her head.

Chapter Two

Moments later Kathy led a tall, pale, elderly man into the office. "Martin Tyner, this is Thomas Black."

"Mr. Tyner."

"Martin," said Tyner, gripping my hand in a bear squeeze and pumping it long and hard, testing. "Call me Martin." His voice sounded like a rusted motor.

Squeezing my hand until his teeth gritted and made audible crunching noises through his thin cheeks, he gave one last painful clasp, then tossed a disdainful, yet faintly interested glance toward Kathy's rear end as she navigated back around her desk.

Tyner wore an undistinguished gray suit with a tie that lay on his bony chest like a lizard mashed under a truck tire. His elephant ears waggled when he thought. His dim gray eyes bulged slightly. His dirty-white hair was combed straight back, revealing a widow's peak. To some, he would have been an imposing figure.

"How do you know your son is missing?"

"I call his boarding house every couple of days. Nobody there has seen him for over a week. Can't tell me where he is."

"Maybe he's just . . ."

"He's missing."

"Tell me about your son."

"Lance could have gone anywhere, that bumbling idiot. Not an ounce of common sense. I've had three children, Mr. Black, and I'm proud of all of them, even Lance." He stopped, as if considering what he had just said. "He's just strayed, that's all. Went off track a long time ago. What the hell can you do?"

"What do you mean, 'off track'?"

"He just started hanging around with *them*. I guess it was partially my fault, pushing him into sports like I did. Both the boys. These days, they're in every sport. He didn't really take to sports, Lance didn't, but I think that's where he first got hooked up. When he was a freshman in college, God forbid, he even took one to a dance, a school dance. I mean, where does a kid learn these abominations?"

"You're not making a lot of sense, Mr. Tyner."

"He went through two years of college, mostly on scholarships. I still don't know how. He's not half the student Babs is, but still, he seemed to do all right. Whistled right through two years."

"You said he was hanging out with *them*. Who do you mean?"

"The blacks. Where you been?"

I looked at Kathy Birchfield and then back at the old man. "Do you have a picture of your son?"

Martin Tyner rolled onto one hip in his chair and dug a wallet from under one of his skinny buns. Sorting through several plastic-encased photographs, he carefully selected one and jabbed it at me. He was tentative, and at the last second he almost did not release it. He was a man who counted his change twice, kept the extra when there was a mistake in his favor and raised holy hell if the error was to his detriment. "I'll be wanting that back," he announced.

"I figured you would."

The wrinkled two-by-two-inch photograph in my fingers revealed a slender young man who looked much like his father must have thirty or forty years ago. He had the long, angular face, the widow's peak and was attempting, not very successfully, to grow a beard.

"The peach fuzz is gone," said his father, watching my eyes on the photograph the way any proud father would have. "Scraped it off. That was during his welfare phase. He worked in a government office for two years handing out welfare. Can you believe that? *My* son worked in a welfare office."

Exchanging amused looks with Kathy, I said, "Life can be cruel."

Unexpectedly, she commiserated, "We all pull down our share of misery."

"That's for damn sure," said Martin Tyner without perceiving the sarcasm, combing a claw of a hand through his dirty-white hair. "Lance has been nothing but a headache since his second year of high school. First he became a Marxist, then an atheist, then he decided he wanted to devote his years to world peace. You ask me, he needs psychiatric help. I don't understand it either, the other two kids being so good and all. Not a bit of trouble from either." A vein ballooned to life and began dancing on his forehead.

I said, "Do you have an address for him, Mr. Tyner?"

"What?" He was staring at the floor, wondering what other foul dishes fate had yet to ladle up.

"Do you have an address for your son?"

"Oh, yes. Of course. Lives in a goldanged boarding house over by the university. Crashing, I think he called it. We call it living. They call it crashing. Tells you something, doesn't it? Not far from here, actually." He gave me a street number and I scrawled it down in my notebook.

"Have you looked there for him?"

"Me? I tried. The landlord is a little . . . difficult. He's not really the type of man you can deal with." Tyner shot me an oblique look, trying to decide if I were the type of man he could deal with.

"Where does your son work, Mr. Tyner?"

"Work?" he scoffed. "Lance hasn't worked in years."

"He's been living off the inheritance?"

Kathy interceded. "He got the first of the money only last month. Most of it was tied up until then. He won't receive the entire estate until it has all been liquidated back East."

"How long do you think?" Martin Tyner asked, anxiously turning his attention to Kathy Birchfield for the first time since her rear end had entertained him.

"A couple of months, at the very least," she replied. "He'll be receiving the funds in rather small doses as each transaction is completed in New York. Your stepfather was very fastidious. He knew exactly what he wanted done and he had good attorneys to do it."

"Fastidious? Hell, the old fart was senile! We all knew he was senile. The only reason we never did anything about it before was because we didn't realize how far he had actually gone round the bend. The poor old poop was senile. This is a sorry joke he played on me, giving it all to

Lance. Poor Lance, he'll go bankrupt inside of five years, if he lasts that long."

"Oh, I doubt that," Kathy Birchfield said, trying to reassure her client. "That would mean he would have to squander three million dollars a year."

When Kathy put it into words like that, into stark figures, the sudden realization of what destruction his son could wreak hit home for the first time. What she had hoped were words of comfort only allowed Martin Tyner to visualize the impending travesty more fully. The Dumbo ears waggled, the face pinked up and the vein on his forehead squirmed. He looked as if he were going to break down and weep.

"What makes you think he won't last that long?" I asked.

"They'll be all over him when they find out, if they're not already."

"Who will?"

"*They* will."

"You mean the blacks?"

"You bet I mean the blacks."

"You really believe that?"

"Assuredly," he said, dismissing my question. "Who knows what they'll do when they find out how much he's worth? I'm surprised he hasn't bought the farm already."

I looked at Kathy, who, unbeknownst to me, had been staring my way. She smiled tightly. Martin Tyner was not her cup of tea.

The *they* he kept referring to were the blacks, the Negroes, the colored folks. It was a recent and more dehumanizing attribution. I had been hearing a lot of rednecks who foolishly considered themselves upper-crust abusing the word recently, using it as the Germans had against the Jews back in the 1930s. They.

"Do you have any names for me, Mr. Tyner?"

"Names?" He presented me with a strange look.

"Your son's friends? If you could give me a few names it would be a big help."

"Naw," he said, shaking his head as if I should know better than to ask such a fool question. "We haven't been that close. Not for years. Lance has got too many problems. All I know is that address there. Tell you the truth, I don't think he has many friends."

"And you don't know where he works?" I caught his look and corrected myself. "Or worked?"

"Just the welfare office. But that hasn't been for quite a spell. They tossed him out for giving away too much of the government's good money." He snorted angrily.

"How about his car? You know what he drives?"

"His sister tells me he bought hisself one of those fanciful Jap sports cars, but I haven't seen it."

"A Datsun?"

"Hell, that's the one. A Z-car, they call them. I buy American. I fought the goddamn slants in '44. Took a goddamn Jap bayonet to my keister. People seem to forget the war. Not me. I never forget anything."

"I can see that."

He was a tall, stoop-shouldered man, though not as tall as I was. His lean cheeks and the narrowness of his shoulders made him look taller. His brow and face were furrowed with worry lines. Sixty years of hard living and scrabbling had chiseled a lot of pain into that mug. Every hurt and insult he had ever endured was etched in the face, stamped into his memory with a branding iron of imagined humiliations and unfulfilled revenge.

"You don't believe me? I never forget a thing."

"We believe you, Mr. Tyner," said Kathy Birchfield.

Martin Tyner gave me addresses for his daughter and for his other son, then Kathy ushered him out of the office and into a nearby waiting room. When she came back, she closed the door and leaned against it, sighing heavily.

"Quaint old racist," I said. "We need that sort of old-fashioned bigotry, don't you think? Peps things up for the rest of us. Maybe when things get rolling real good, he can run one of the ovens."

"Thomas!"

She walked over slowly, bellied up to me, and reached up to cradle my face in her cold hands. On tiptoe, she kissed me lightly. Then, in a businesslike march, she traipsed back around her desk and plunked down in her swivel chair.

Chapter Three

"WHAT WAS THAT for?" I asked.

"You really should wear a suit and a tie. It's no wonder you don't get the big accounts. The firm has enough cases each year to keep three detectives scrambling and you slump in wearing jeans and a sport coat. Honestly, Thomas."

"I don't want any big accounts," I said.

"But a tie, Thomas? A simple little thing like a tie?"

I fished a blue-striped hunk of polyester out of my coat pocket. "I keep it for snobby restaurants and in case I proposition a pretty lady lawyer and get rebuffed. Then I can hang myself on the lamppost."

"I'm glad you came."

"How are they treating you?"

"I'm the first female attorney this firm has ever had. Ever. I feel like I'm assaulting a bastion. They open doors for me and stare at me, and when anything challenging comes up, they hand it to one of the male staff members. I landed this case because it was next to hopeless. Almost everyone here has had dealings with Lance and his father, and nobody wants to muck with it. I have a job. A desk. They installed a snazzy electric pencil sharpener. It sort of hums when I use it. I can't quibble."

"You like it here, then?"

"Of course, all I'll get for a while is the dregs, like this case. The kid's a nerd. And Mr. Tyner tried another attorney before us. He wore that attorney out. The kid has a way of infuriating people, too. Bemis tried to deal with him several months ago. You think with fifteen million bucks hanging in the balance they'd hand the case over to me if it wasn't already a total washout?"

11

"You're a realist."

"Thank you."

"How much do you make?"

"Don't be cute. You'll get your silver. The firm pays its bills."

Nine months earlier Kathy Birchfield had graduated from the University of Washington Law School, passing the bar exam with flying colors on her first attempt. Now she was toiling for one of the most prestigious law firms in the state. In one sense, I was proud of her achievement. But there were other things. She had packed up and moved out two weeks earlier. The basement apartment was empty, awaiting another tenant, a tenant I could not bring myself to seek out.

"So what do I do when I locate this missing nerd?"

Tapping an index finger to her lips like a salute, Kathy warned, "Please don't let anybody hear you call him that. I shouldn't have either. I've never even met him; Mr. Bemis was handling the case before I got here. Ideally, you could find him, then come and fetch me and his father and take us to him. That would be marvelous. But you'll have to work that out, depending upon the circumstances."

"Why isn't old man Bemis in charge? Fifteen million?"

"Lance spat on old man Bemis."

"Seriously? Spat?"

"H_2O. Right in court. All over his toupee and a new suit. Bemis was furious."

I laughed. I met the pompous elder Bemis once while working on a case and I would have paid good money to have seen the ruckus with Lance Tyner. "Why can't you get in touch with Lance's lawyer? Handle it through him?"

"Lance doesn't have a lawyer. He's set up an account with the attorneys back East. They dump it all into a bank here as they liquidate the holdings in New York. He writes checks on the account."

"Fifteen million dollars? It's that simple?"

She nodded.

"Have you been in touch with the bank?"

"Bemis spoke with them this morning. He has a contact there. Lance hasn't withdrawn any money for two weeks. Up until two weeks ago he wrote checks almost daily. But he's spent very little. For a twenty-five-year-old man who's just inherited a fortune several times over, he's doing pretty doggone well. I doubt I would have that much restraint."

"I *know* you wouldn't," I said, smugly.

She gave me one of her goggle-eyed clown looks. "The unofficial word is that he's spent about twenty or twenty-one thousand. Mostly for his car. He paid cash for it."

"But he hasn't written anything on the account in two weeks?"

"That's the way we understand it."

I got up and moved to the door. "I'll be in touch."

"What do you think, Thomas?"

"It's too early to think."

"I'll be having a housewarming at my new apartment when I get the rest of my furniture. Be there?"

"Wouldn't miss it," I said, trying to keep the melancholy from oozing into my voice.

For the last four and a half years she had lived in my basement, leasing the apartment the former owner had built. She had been my periodic breakfast partner, always platonically, and I considered her one of my best friends. Most people who knew us figured we were lovers, or ex-lovers. Such was not the case; never had been, although I doubted if either of us could put a finger on the exact reason. Son-of-a-bitch, I was going to miss her.

I strolled out past the behemoth with the Technicolor contacts, and wandered out of the building into the June haze. It was muggy, shirt-sleeve weather, but the sun was nowhere to be seen. Overcast. The Northwest had basked in a balmy, snowless winter, then enjoyed an exciting and exceptionally fair spring, so it only made sense that the climate in June, July and August would be soiled with clouds and constant drizzle.

The job was almost a joke, a fiasco, a regular debacle. Martin Tyner could have unearthed his son in an hour. A one-eyed taxi driver with a wooden leg and no sense of humor could have cracked the case.

Chapter Four

I DROVE STRAIGHT to the boy's boarding house, a dilapidated affair that I pegged as a place he must have been too busy to move out of. It was on Fifteenth Northeast, a few blocks north of the University, not far from my own digs. These places were always chock full of student types. I wondered how Lance Tyner had landed there. He hadn't been working. Had he been in school?

Parking was skimpy and I had to run my Ford truck four blocks up before I found a spot roomy enough.

The boarding house was three stories, set up from the street on a small hill. Peeling paint, lopsided house numbers, and squeaky, cracked stairs all contributed to the general rundown look. I tried the knob and found it locked. No doubt each of the tenants had his own key. A faded, hand-lettered note was taped to the glass window beside the door. "You come in after 9 p.m., you be descreat." The students in the place must get a big kick out of the landlord's spelling.

A crone in a baggy, misshapen housedress answered the door. Her cotton-candy hair was peppered with tiny black dots, sand, or maybe hordes of dead ticks. I displayed my license and asked for Lance Tyner.

"He ain't here," she blurted, trying to slam the door. The door bounced off my shoe and back at her.

"Could you call him?"

Curling her lip and shooting me a disgruntled look, she clenched her yellowed teeth and shuffled to a staircase. Making a sound like a hunk of sheet metal being torn in half, she squawked up the stairs. I had to assume she was yelling Lance's name. I couldn't decipher anything else.

14

Waddling back to the door, she said, somewhat hoarsely, "See. I told ya. Ain't here."

"When was the last time you saw him?"

"What? You think I'm some sort of memory expert?"

"Mind if I talk to some of your other boarders?"

"Talk away, smarty. But you don't wait in *my* house, Mr. Fancypants. I ain't gonna be robbed blind by some mealy-mouthed private dick. You think I believe all that TV baloney? I know what you fellas are like. My sister used to date a dee-tick-teeve. Bunch of thieves. Now move your goddamn foot before I call a patrolman."

Slamming the door, she trudged back down the hallway and disappeared through a doorway that apparently led into her private quarters. Peering through the window, I saw a pay phone in the hallway, several scraps of paper taped to the wall alongside it, lists of instructions similar to the note on the window. I was too far away to catch the bungled spellings.

Passing up the wooden porch and its wicked-looking slivers, I put the seat of my pants to the concrete steps down by the sidewalk. It was 10:20 A.M. With luck, some of the other boarders would return for lunch. Or perhaps some of them had not left yet.

Watching the traffic, an occasional coed hurtling helter-skelter down the sidewalk, and bicyclists whistling down the street, their knapsacks crammed with books, I waited thirty minutes before I heard somebody rustling around at the back of the house. Garbage cans banged and I heard the sound of breaking glass. Then a muffled kawump. A few seconds later, another kawump.

I got up and sidled alongside the house, which was long and deep. Neighboring houses were crushed in on either side. Only ten feet separated the buildings.

Squeezing past two evergreens draped with dew-soaked spider webs, I discovered a weathered garage on the alley. In front of the garage a '53 Hudson was parked. It was no collector's item. It had the look of a rusted oil burner. One cracked tire was a whitewall. The other was a bluewall. Kawump. Kawump.

Inside the garage, a man I took to be the landlady's husband was pulling aluminum cans from a green plastic sack and flattening them between a pair of two-by-fours on a hinge. Kawump. Kawump. He bounced on the two-by-four,

15

crushing the cans with his body weight. Judging by the size of the sack, he would be there for a spell.

"Morning," I said.

He scratched one thigh, stood straight, stretched the kinks out of his back, and gave me the once-over. He looked near eighty. He wore a dingy, sleeveless T-shirt and baggy trousers. His slippers had holes in the sides so that his little toes poked out. He had not shaved in days. His arms, once strong and powerful, now hung slack, fat and atrophied muscle jouncing in tune to his labors. He had a beer gut and a lazy-looking face that sported reddish spiders across the cheeks and nose.

"Who are you?" he asked. Kawump.

"Thomas Black," I said. "I'm trying to locate Lance Tyner. I understand he lives here."

"You must be the private heat Myrtle told me was bugging her."

"That's me."

"Guy named Lance lives upstairs, first door on the left. Don't know if his last name is Teener, or whatever you said. Myrtle takes care of the checks and deposits and whatnot. I just know him by his first name. Went to Canada a couple of weeks ago." Kawump. "Just got back this morning."

"Is he here now?"

Kawump. "I doubt it. You heard Myrtle calling him. He's got this girlfriend. He expects a lot of phone calls from her. We've just got the one pay phone in the hallway. Myrtle likes to keep it free. But he comes a running lickety-split when you call him. He don't wanta miss one of them phone calls. Don't blame him myself. She does sound sweet, his girl does. And awful young."

"When do you think he'll be back?"

"Couldn't say." Kawump. "Maybe not for a while. He took a little trip up to Canada, like I said."

"How do you know he got back this morning?"

"His room is directly over our bedroom. I heard him banging around this morning. Must a been four or five o'clock."

"He always get in that late?"

"Sometimes. This young gal he's been dating's got him on a short leash. Spends most of his time over there."

"You know where there is?"

16

"Haven't the foggiest."

"You've never seen her?"

"He had kind of a heavyset woman visit him a while back. Pretty face, but fat as a blimp. But I don't know. She didn't sound like the girl I hear on the phone. He's been away quite a bit of late. Had something to do in court. Never did get the whole skinny on that. Think he was in some kind of trouble."

I grinned. Lance had inherited fifteen million bucks and this guy thought he was in trouble. One month's interest on Lance's inheritance would set up this old gummer for life. He'd never have to flatten another Sprite can. But Lance hadn't told him. I wondered if Lance had told anybody. I wondered if I could have inherited that much cash and kept it a secret.

"I guess I'll just have to wait out here then," I said, moving toward the front yard. "Maybe one of the other roomers knows where he might be."

"Sure," said the old man. Kawump.

"By the way, you know why he went to Canada?"

"How the hell would I know a thing like that?"

"Catch you later."

"Might be he's gone up to Dash Point," said the old man, almost under his breath.

I stopped in the doorway to the garage. Behind me in the house one of the venetians wavered and a large gray eyeball appeared in the opening. Myrtle was keeping her jaundiced eye on the private heat. "What makes you say that?"

"This morning he asked me directions on how to get there. Don't know what he'd be doing there. But he took his pack and a sleeping bag and such."

"Dash Point State Park?"

"Yeah. It's between Tacoma and Seattle, south of Federal Way . . ."

"I know where it is. Thanks."

"Uhyep."

Chapter Five

I PHONED KATHY from my house. "Do you want to come fetch Lance Tyner with me?" I asked. "I'm reasonably sure I know where he is. He was at his boarding house this morning."

"I'll telephone his father."

Locating Martin Tyner turned out to be a cumbersome and time-consuming task. Our calls back and forth, Kathy's and mine, whittled away the overcast afternoon. Eventually, she got hold of him by phone and arranged a rendezvous in the parking lot of Leech, Bemis and Ott. Upon his insistence, we drove in Martin Tyner's Mercury.

It was 7:30 when we reached Dash Point State Park. Whether Tyner was being evasive, or merely thoughtless, it had taken Kathy seven hours to locate him.

As we drove up in the gentle dusk, a tall ranger decked out in khaki, smile wrinkles ambushing his eyes, was just swinging a gate across the blacktop road leading into the park.

Martin Tyner pushbuttoned his power window down, leaned his head out and yelled, "Shitferbrains! Get your goddamned hands off that lock!"

Bewildered, the ranger said, "What did you say?"

"Shitface. Get your child-molestin' mitts off that lock or I'll stuff it up your ass."

Uncertainty staining his features, the ranger looked us over. Wrenching sideways, I grabbed the collar of Tyner's lightweight jacket, yanked his shoulders and head back inside the car, then reached across and raised his electric window.

"Kathy," I said.

She knew instinctively what I meant. She sprang out of

the back of the Mercury and approached the ranger, consoling him as if he were a bear with a thorn in its paw.

"What the hell did you say that for?" I asked Martin Tyner. I had been on the case for ten hours and I was getting a mite grumpy myself.

"Bastard was locking us out. Trying to lock me away from my only son . . . my son."

"You mean, your only son with *money*. He's twenty-five years old, for godsakes. If you don't see him tonight, you can see him tomorrow."

"My *missing* son . . ."

"Nobody was ever missing. I explained that all to you."

"Goddamned rangers. Think they own the goddamned woods."

Uttering nary a word on the drive down, he was now in a paroxysm of rage. His face was flushed pink and the veins in his skull were all throbbing like cooking noodles. Something was bothering Martin. It didn't make any sense to me, but then I didn't have fifteen million worries on my mind.

Kathy appeased the ranger somehow and he swung the gate wide for us, swapping a concerned look with Martin Tyner's maniacal face as we wheeled past. Kathy had to lunge into the back seat of the car while it was still rolling, for Martin, sniffing his prey, wasn't stopping for anything or anybody. Not now. I wondered how much cab fare back to Seattle was going to run.

"Number twenty-one," said Kathy. "The ranger said there's a party under the Tyner name at campsite twenty-one." We snaked through the campsites on a narrow macadam roadway.

The park consisted of small, rolling knolls, the campsites spaced evenly. In the daytime very little sunlight would pierce the tall fir trees, their trunks four and five feet across. Their shadows cast a premature nightfall over the area.

Devoid of both people and cars, camp number twenty-one consisted of a wooden picnic table, a small iron-walled fireplace and a two-man tent. The fire was cold. The royal-blue tent was zipped up. That's how you lock things in the woods: a zipper. The last domain of the honest and the free.

Scrambling out of the car, Martin Tyner thrashed through the dusk toward the tent. I slid the transmission

19

into park, set the emergency brake, shut off the motor, and confiscated the keys. The old man had unzipped the tent and was floundering around inside like a hungry maggot swimming in a dead bird. A minute later he hustled back to the car and dug a five-cell flashlight out from under the seat, then began a thorough search of the tent and several bags inside it. So much for the last domain.

Across from twenty-one, a family consisting of three adults and about seven kids was growing a little concerned about Martin's savage attack on the tent.

Kathy and I moseyed over, making conciliatory nods and gestures and wondering how we ever got tied up with this flake.

Under her breath Kathy said to me, "I've got a real bad feeling about this whole thing." I looked across at her. She had a sixth sense sometimes and I had never seen it fail her.

The family across the road gathered closer together as we approached. They had been dawdling around a snapping, smoky blaze, swatting at mosquitoes and swallowing scorched marshmallows off the tips of crooked coat hangers. I spotted Iowa plates on their station wagon. A heavily bearded man in a down vest greeted us. He looked like the father of the brood.

"Care for some dinner?" he asked, peering over my shoulder at Martin's antics in the camp behind us.

"Thanks, but no," Kathy said, patting one of the tykes on the top of the head.

I handed the man my card while the seven ragamuffin children flocked around to ogle us. They all knew what private detectives were and several of them tried to sniff out my weapon, frisking my pants and tugging at my shirttail. Their mother halted the game with a sharp rebuke, dispatched in flat midwestern tones.

"We're trying to locate a young fellow named Lance Tyner. That's his father over there. The campsite's registered under his name."

"He steal something?" asked the washed-out-looking mother, in a blowzy sweat shirt and loose jeans. She had red hair and a pair of faded blue eyes that were too close together. Her eyes were replicated in the tykes all around the campfire. Her body hung slack and spent, worn out from years of replicating.

20

"He hasn't stolen a thing," said Kathy Birchfield. "He's inherited something. Quite a bit, actually."

"Oh, how wonderful," said the red-haired woman, sounding genuinely glad for somebody else's good fortune. Behind me the old man was still tossing the campsite. He had dismantled the tent and was turning out pockets in some clothing.

"Three of 'em," said the bearded man. "Three young guys. Two of 'em were nice and polite and then there was the one ornery one. Believe they went down to the beach a while back. Probably clamming. They're not big, but they're mighty tasty. We've got a pot all steamed up right here. Care for some?"

"Thanks, but no," I said. I had smelled the fishy, humid aroma of cooked clams earlier and I was tempted, but then I remembered what the beaches were like in this area. Commencement Bay had recently been named one of the ten most polluted spots in the country. Although a red tide had not been declared yet this season, I looked around to see if any of the children's lips had turned blue. "The beach, you say?"

"Much earlier," chimed in his wife. "But then two of them came back on foot and left, whole kit and caboodle. You just missed 'em. I guess the other's still down at the beach."

The family explained how to get to the beach and we wandered back to twenty-one to see if Martin Tyner was through playing white tornado.

Exasperated, Tyner slowly revolved the light around the eyesore he had generated, then sighed loudly and said, "Sheeeeit."

"Find any money?" I asked. "A million or so?"

Shooting me a sour look, Tyner surveyed the belongings he had flung around the campsite. "Afraid I made a sorry mess. I thought he would have left something around that would tell me where he was. Tell the truth, I half expected to find him in the tent with his throat slit. Bet he was out here shacking up with some of *their* women. All that money and the boy's too cheap to go to a motel . . ."

"You find any women's clothes?" I asked.

"Naw."

"That where you go with *their* women?" I asked. "Motels?"

21

Martin gave me a look he might give someone he wanted to horsewhip.

Waggling her eyebrows meaningfully, Kathy began picking up the chaos.

I said, "He was here with a couple of men."

The old man didn't think that needed a response, so he hunkered on a log and ran his hands through his white hair, hair that took on a strange luminescence in the dusk, under the fuzzy shadows of the tall firs.

When Kathy and I had put the camp back in order, I jangled the keys over my head and said to Tyner, "Come on, big guy. Let's go look for your kid."

"What? You know where he is?"

I grinned. "Come on, big guy. I'll show you."

"Why did you fritter away all that dad-blasted time? What the hell are we paying you for if all you're going to do is sit around and look smug. Fiddle-faddle, where is he?" Martin Tyner was snapping at my heels like a starving puppy after a scrap from a deer carcass. With that much money at stake, it was hard to blame people for getting panicky.

We clambered into his car, he in the passenger seat, I driving, and Kathy in the back.

Oddly enough, the park was split by the highway, with the beach and the day camping area situated across the road. We drove out of the campground, crossed the highway and found the beach road.

Tacked to the state park sign was a white paper plate, painted in red, written in Chinese. An arrow on the Chinese sign pointed down the hill toward the beach.

A two-lane road curlicued downhill for almost a mile through a tree-lined gulch to the beach. The ravine spilled out onto a tight little strip of sand that was only a couple of hundred yards across at high tide. Tonight, with the tide sucked low, the beach ran out of sight around the point on the south and past the steep bank to the north.

When we got out of the Mercury I looked around and spotted a gunmetal-blue Datsun 280-Z a hundred yards away in the lot. Though it appeared to be spanking new, it may or may not have belonged to Lance Tyner. I had no way of knowing without jimmying a window and going through it.

"I don't see him," said Martin Tyner, eyeing me.

22

"We just got here," said Kathy. "Give it a chance."

Through the haze the brilliant sun was setting like a giant peach viewed through gauze. The low tide exposed hundreds of yards of flat, damp, dimpled sand. The area was serene. Only a few Orientals were scattered along the beach, chattering in foreign dialects. Their children chased sand crabs excitedly, splashing in the shallow tide pools in their noisy flapping sandals.

Chapter Six

"WHERE THE HELL is he?" Martin Tyner kept mumbling, sometimes to himself, sometimes to anybody who would listen. Kathy and I walked in front, treating him like an unwanted stepchild.

We scoured the picnic area near the road and I passed the photograph of Lance around to clumps of Oriental men. Several of them did not understand enough English to know what I was saying. Eventually a woman in her early twenties, her face framed in glossy black bangs, pointed north, toward Poverty Bay.

Tromping through the dry, fluffy sand, we headed in that direction, keeping to the high-tide line along the base of the bluff. A half mile out in the shipping lanes, the Sound was five or six hundred feet deep, so it was hard to believe the beach was shallow enough for a three-foot tide to bare this much sand. But it did.

The tide line was speckled with pools a foot or two across, speckled with mounds of sand, rocks and broken shells where people had been clamming and neglected to police the holes afterwards. The pools looked like dozens of miniature graves awaiting miniature burial parties.

Across the water we could see Vashon Island. To the south was Tacoma and its famous smelter stack, though it was too murky and too distant to see the trail of poisons it injected into the atmosphere. To the north were the low hills jutting up from the water that comprised West Kent, Des Moines, and parts of West Seattle.

In the shipping lanes a rusty Japanese freighter churned north, heading toward Canada.

"Gonna run outa goddamned beach purty soon," said Martin Tyner, huffing behind us, dropping back periodi-

24

cally to catch his breath and mop the perspiration off his face with a balled-up, checkered bandana.

"Keep your pants on," I replied. "If he's down here, we'll find him. Maybe he was planning to sleep on the beach." Even as I said it, I recalled the mummy bag back at the campsite. It was unlikely that Lance had hauled two of them to the park.

The old man was right as rain. Another ten minutes of brisk hiking and we would run plumb out of beach. A mile down the shoreline I could see houses on the water, private docks and a few rafts moored out in the flats, left high and dry by the low tide. The park ended this side of the private houses.

"What's that?" said Kathy, pointing out toward the tide line. Among the mounds of sand and castoff shells was a lump that looked larger than the others. In the distance and the faltering light it was difficult to discern what it was. We headed out, noting our spot along the hillside in case we had to resume there.

Halfway to our destination, I spotted a wet hundred-dollar bill pasted to the sand by the damp. Twenty yards later I spotted another. And another. All in all, we crossed paths with ten or eleven of them, most pasted flat, glued to the surface of the world, waiting for the tide to lick them free and wash them to Coos Bay, or Ketchikan, or Borneo.

Kathy and I ran the last two hundred yards across the packed sand, our footsteps thumping rhythmic and drum-like at the moist earth.

We found him in the clam beds. He was face down, dressed in a cobalt-blue T-shirt and neatly hemmed cutoff jeans. He was sprawled in the sand, one leg floating in the incoming sea water, rising and lolling in tune to the waves from the Japanese freighter.

Though his teeth were full of sand and the hair on the back of his head was matted in dark blood, he was breathing. I located a pulse in his neck and another much weaker one in his wrist. Using a finger, I spooned the gobs of wet sand out of his mouth and quickly checked him over for latent injuries. He was cold, no doubt suffering from hypothermia. I could find no wounds apart from the mushy, blood-covered spot the size of a steak tomato on the back of his head. The tide was coming in fast. In another few minutes he would have drowned, ironically within sight of us.

"Is it Lance Tyner?" Kathy asked.

"I thought you could tell me."

"I've never seen him."

"I thought you went to court with him."

"I told you—that was before I was with the firm."

"The guy who used to change his diapers will be here in a moment," I said.

"You were a policeman," urged Kathy. "You should know this identification business. You saw his picture."

"So did you. But I didn't know him. There's a difference."

When he finally reached us, Martin Tyner had no trouble making an identification. It took him several efforts, but he finally gulped enough air into his lungs to gasp out, "Lance. Lance. What have they done to you?"

Lance was showing signs of waking up. I was reasonably certain he was not dying. It gave me enough leeway to put my foot in my mouth.

"Maybe somebody shot him with a clam gun," I said. It was a tired joke between Kathy and me, stemming from a case I'd handled several years ago.

She chewed her lip and gave me a look of pure disgust.

Hunched over, hands and dirty money braced on his knees, Martin gasped a few times and said, "Clam gun? What's that? Is it bad?"

Kathy and I exchanged looks. We both knew instinctively that he was not a native Northwesterner. Everybody knew a clam gun was a hollow tube that you screwed into the wet sand to suction out clams. Every Northwest garage had one tucked away in a corner wrapped in cobwebs.

"Just a bad joke," said Kathy. Then she turned to me. "What are we going to do? What's the best way to handle this?"

"Watch him," I said, dragging him carefully up the beach, trying to keep his spine aligned. "Don't move him except to keep him out of the tide. If he comes to, don't let him move. I saw a state truck back by the restrooms. I'll jog back and fetch some help."

"Shouldn't we pick him up?" Martin Tyner asked. He was finished being obnoxious. Now he only wanted what was best for his boy, kneeling in the moist sand, patting his son's blood-matted hair with one arthritic-looking hand. "Shouldn't we carry him up the beach? We could do it."

"Sure," I said. "If you want a paraplegic on your hands. There's no telling what sort of spinal injuries he's got. When you have a head wound like this, you always treat the patient for spinal injuries."

Martin Tyner looked down at his unconscious son with new eyes.

Kathy had rolled up her pants, shucked her shoes and was wading in the shallow water, searching for something. Whatever it was, she would probably find it. Her intuition rarely failed.

It was about a thousand yards. I ran the whole way, no jogging, just running, the sand kicking up from my shoes and sailing over my head, raining into my hair. I could feel minute globs of oozing mud striking and clinging to the back of my shirt. When I found them, the park rangers were swabbing out the restrooms, doing a surprisingly thorough job of it.

"Got a guy down on the beach, unconscious," I gasped. I heaved and caught my breath. I was in good shape, but I hadn't paced myself. "He's been in the tide and he's got a head injury. We need a vehicle and a spine board. Some blankets."

The frizzy-haired ranger looked up from his mop and bucket in the dim yellow light of the restroom and said, "I'll get Marsha. We've got it all in the truck. You come with us. It'll be faster."

Their green park department truck stood beside the women's restroom. On the short hop across the beach the frizzy-haired ranger told me his name was Bill and asked, "You an EMT?"

"I was," I said. "I let my card expire."

"You a fireman, or what?"

"I was a cop."

"I tried to get on with the state patrol," he admitted, his words forming a sort of half-assed bond between us. We were both straight arrows, both civil service nitwits. Marsha sat rigidly in the front seat, sweating and hyperventilating, the transition from mopping to lifesaving too much for her.

Lance was only semiconscious when we got there. We rolled him onto a spine board, taped him down, wrapped him in blankets and hefted him into the back of the truck. Martin Tyner rode with his son, a look of pure pathos on his face.

Kathy and I trudged up the beach on foot. We would meet the rangers at the top of the hill where a county ambulance would take Lance to the nearest hospital.

As we walked across the beach behind the speeding park truck, Kathy pulled a piece of wet pipe out from behind her trouser leg. It was three-quarters of an inch in diameter and about ten inches long. It would have made a good weapon.

"What's that?" I asked.

"Pipe," she said.

"Where'd you get it?"

"In the tide."

"Why did you look out there?"

"One of my feelings."

"You think that's what he got hit with?"

"I know it is."

"Who hit him?"

"I've got some remedial ESP in my bones. I'm no wizard."

"It's a bad business," I said, mimicking a line from an old movie I'd seen on Channel Thirteen that week.

"What do you think happened?" Kathy asked.

"Somebody hit him with that piece of pipe," I stated, flatly.

"Very funny."

"All that money lying around. It looks a bit like he got mugged, doesn't it?"

"You think he did?" Kathy asked. "Right out here in front of God and everybody?"

"That would be my working hypothesis."

"His friends?"

I shrugged.

"But his wallet was still in his pocket."

"Was it?"

"It was in his pocket," said Kathy. "But it was empty. I checked."

It wasn't quite dark as we waited at the ranger's living quarters at the top of the hill, listening to the distant whining siren as it slowly worked its way nearer. The sky was the color of champagne and the evening had the tex-

28

ture of air in a desert bat cave. Though Lance hadn't come to, he seemed to be in no serious danger of dying within the next few hours. He was warming up under the bundles of blankets and his pulse was stronger. For the first time I noticed a black eye on the young man, an old wound, almost healed, a battering that must have happened a couple of weeks ago. Beat-up, coldcocked, all of his luck was not good.

Tyner was enormously worried over his boy, tears sparkling in his eyes when he clambered into the back of the ambulance without unfastening his clawlike hands from the aluminum frame of the stretcher. Oddly, I felt sorry for the skinny old man. Some families never got close except through crisis. The Tyner family seemed to be one of them.

Martin arranged for his other son to meet him at the hospital and Kathy and I drove back to Seattle in the Mercury, marveling at how the woods had filled up with houses and condominiums and golf courses.

"It won't be too long," said Kathy, sadness infusing her voice, "before they chop down every tree in the state."

"Not too long," I said. "Couple of weeks, maybe."

"Where are all these people coming from? My father used to hike out here and hunt pheasants. Now it's just wall-to-wall houses."

"I think they're coming from inside the earth," I said, making a feeble joke. It was typical of me to wisecrack about things that scared me. We passed the beginnings of a new development the dozers and big cats had just scraped raw. The ochre earth reminded me of graves. Everything tonight was reminding me of graves.

Chapter Seven

NOBODY EVER FOUND OUT who slugged Lance Tyner and dropped him into the tide, or why. The King County Police never spoke to me about it. I had been a policeman myself long enough that it didn't bother my sense of social symmetry to think that it might never be solved. Most crimes never were.

Lance Tyner wasn't injured as severely as we had feared. In fact, after twenty-four hours in the hospital, they tell me he returned to his own complicated little affairs.

After I mailed them a dismally typed report, Kathy drove out one evening with a check from Leech, Bemis and Ott.

I heard nothing further about the incident.

A week after the Tyner fiasco, I followed a woman for her embittered husband, a woman the man called a trollop. He was suing for divorce and he needed some dirt on her. I don't usually opt for cases like that. But I took it before my better sense rescued me. There was something about her photograph that I began to hanker after, something foreign and entreating. Shades of *Laura*.

That was me, Thomas Black, the ultimate professional, infatuated with a Polaroid, hankering. Always hankering. I was a sucker for a pretty face, an upturned nose, or a fairy tale, flopping down in front of the tube with a gargantuan bowl of popcorn every time Dana Andrews and Gene Tierney went through their charade.

I blew three days huddled in my truck down the street from her house—watching, waiting, focusing binoculars, doing bladder-stretching exercises, falling hopelessly in love with her, keeping precise track of her harmless movements in a spiral-bound journal with greasy thumbprints smeared across its cover. I would prove to her paranoid hubby that he was nuts. Hell, she was practically an angel.

Two-thirds of a block up the street from my quarry, I sat ensconced in my truck until late at night, crumpled against the driver's window. One evening around eleven o'clock, something tapped sharply on the glass on the other side of my brain.

I snapped awake and twisted to see what it was. A man I recognized as one of the lady's neighbors was standing next to the truck. Aimed at my face was a gun slightly larger than a sewer pipe.

Little shocks. Life was full of them. My life was suffering a glut.

Savoring the tiny squeaking sound the window handle made, realizing it might be the last sound I ever heard, I carefully cranked the window down.

"Evening," I said.

"What the hell are you doing out here?" he asked. He wasn't irate. Not much. I knew if I sneezed, his Gesundheit would send about a hundred and eighty grains worth of my brain out the opposite window.

"Just doing my catechism," I said.

"Don't give me that crap. You've been here three nights runnin'. What the hell are you up to? Casin' the neighborhood?"

The jig was up. People were getting the jump on me right and left. A month ago a guy I had been tailing sneaked around the block and rearended me.

"I'm a private investigator," I said, slowly plucking my billfold out of my pocket and displaying my license with a wary grin.

"So what are you doing? Ralph Hargrove send you after me?" The pistol glided closer, edging toward my nostrils, so close I could no longer smell anything except the deadly aroma of gun oil.

"I don't know any Ralph," I said, beginning to feel the sweat seeping out of my hide, the droplets popping out individually. "I'm watching the woman down on Cherry Lane. Her husband's divorcing her and needs to get the goods on her or she'll take him." I was as close to stuttering as I'd come in a long while. People didn't die with

31

sense, for noble causes; it was always purposeless misunderstandings, hideous aberrations like this one.

"The brunette with the big hips down in the yellow house?"

I nodded and the gun gradually ebbed out of my face and disappeared into the man's pajama bottoms. He was wearing a raincoat over Winnie-the-Pooh pajamas, pajamas with a drop seat that must have been a joke gift. "The one with the great legs?"

"That's her."

He scratched at his scalp, his pallid face contorting in disgust.

"Gee, what a tramp. We never seen anyone in the neighborhood like her before. Been quiet the last few days, though. Things'll perk up in a bit. The wife says she must be on the rag. Come on in. I'll tell you all about her. Gee whillikers, a real tramp. Sorry about the gun. These days, you can't be too careful. Did you know about the slow-pitch softball team she had there . . . Two whole days."

He was talking about my future wife. Little shocks. My days were full of them. I received enough of them during the course of my job that I preferred my private life to be as dull and humdrum as possible.

We were enjoying one of our first sunny days all summer. I was playing a ho-hum Kareem Abdul-Jabbar to about nine excited five-foot Filipinos in one of our weekly contests. I was the only Caucasian in the game. At six-one, I was the tallest player by an easy eight inches.

It was a school court several blocks from my house, hot and deserted, glimmering in the summer heat. Basketball on the public playground. It gave me a great sense of what it must feel like to be seven feet tall and to play with a bunch of ordinary mortals.

I did not notice her at first. She appeared at the game, a gamine, her spit-polished black hair tied back into a bun at the nape of her neck, wisps floating around her ears and at the base of her throat.

Her skin was like oiled mahogany.

Pretty and slight, she stood tranquilly in a light cotton dress, and when I got very close during one of the timeouts she spoke to me almost in a whisper.

"Mr. Black?"

I turned around and gave the timid Afro-American a cursory glance. She was about seventeen or eighteen, nineteen at the outside. She looked like a model, though she was probably too short. And a shade too black for the Madison Avenue types who outlined beauty for us. She carried herself with the grace of someone much older, someone in old age, actually. But still, it was an *élan,* a serenity that one rarely observed.

"Yeah," I said, hawking, spitting, wiping a slug of sweat off my brow. It was 2:30 in the afternoon and the sunshine in the clear blue air had heated up the macadam court like bricks in an oven.

"May I talk to you? It's about your work."

"Yeah. Sure thing. Can you hold on here? The score's awful tight. Two hundred and twelve to thirty-one." Oblong splashes of sweat stained the pavement in various stages of evaporation. "I think we're just about to blow them out of the water."

She stepped meekly out of our way.

Several of the Filipino players suddenly began exerting themselves under her gaze, chattering like a roost full of hot chickens. The game took twenty more minutes. After I waited in line, drank, splashed my face at the concrete fountain, and had flung a couple of miscellaneous shots at the hoop, I sauntered over and plunked down on the grass beside the court, ready to supply my autograph or whatever else she desired.

The Filipinos wandered off, shouting, "Next time, jabber. Next time." They called me "jabber," after Abdul-Jabbar.

"So how did you find me?" I said, looking the slim young girl over carefully and noting now that she was dangerously close to tears.

"Lance told me you were the one who saved his life on the beach."

Her tone was so muffled I could barely make out her words. Even though the Filipinos had evacuated the premises by now, their nattering drifted to us from the other side of the playground like part of a mirage. Behind us in the sunshine, Scotch broom seeds popped in the heat and whizzed twenty feet away like missiles fired from children's pea shooters.

"I found him, yes. It wasn't hard, really."

"Timely, though. He said he might have drowned if you hadn't gotten there when you did."

"What's this about?"

"Lance."

"Listen, I never even met Lance. The last time I saw him he was riding in an ambulance."

"He's gone again." Tears welled up in her long-lashed, brown eyes and sluiced down the mahogany cheeks.

"He wasn't really missing the first time," I said.

"I know that. I was with him."

"*You* were?"

Chapter Eight

"WE WENT TO CANADA, just him and me, as a sort of celebration. You know, about him inheriting all that money and such? His father was giving him so much trouble, calling every day—he just had to get away. Had to give himself a chance to think."

Her sobbing became more voluble, more animated. She sank to the dry sod beside me, mopping up the tears with her thin, dark hands, pulling her light cotton dress tightly around her knees.

"You are Lance's girlfriend, then?"

Weeping noiselessly, she nodded, her head seesawing on a long, elegant stem of a neck.

I found myself envying him. She wasn't gaudy, she wouldn't cause any accidents in the street, but she was special. She had style and she knew it, though her tears were nibbling away at the illusion.

"I'm sorry," she mumbled into her fists. "I'm so awfully sorry . . . Lance has never done this before. P.W. and D.W. saw him last night, and this morning we were supposed to go downtown together and get a marriage license. Only he never showed up. That's not like Lance. I know something hideous has happened. I just know it."

"Who are P.W. and D.W.?"

"They're my brothers, my younger brothers, Austin and Halprin."

The initials didn't fit, but I let it slide. "Exactly how long has he been missing?"

"What time is it?"

"Three o'clock."

"Seven hours. We were supposed to meet at my house at eight. Believe me, I was worried sick at 8:10. Lance is

35

never late. Never. Who knows how much longer he was gone before I knew about it?"

"What do you mean?"

"I mean if he didn't show up at eight, it was because he couldn't. What if our appointment had been at seven this morning, or six? Would he have been there? P.W. and D.W. said he came by last night before they went to bed, but I was at choir practice. As far as I know, that's the last time anybody saw him."

"Chances are he just went out to celebrate and got carried away." It sounded lame, even to me.

Knuckling her eyes, she took a deep breath, looked at me sheepishly, and spoke, her voice thick and milky with crying. "I just know something bad has happened."

"We have to have something more to go on than feelings. What makes you say that?"

"I just know it. Lance and I have been together for six months, since just after Christmas. We don't let a day go by without spending time together. And this was the day we were planning to get our marriage license. I know something has happened."

"You try his boarding house? Does he still live in that firetrap?"

"His landlady says he hasn't been in all night. That's not like him."

Sponging droplets of sweat off my face, I propped myself up on one elbow, suddenly very tired, mired in my own thoughts. When a young man vanishes and he's got thirty dollars in his pocket, he's after a change of scenery. When a young man vanishes and he's got fifteen million crackers, there's a rat in the barn.

"Most police departments don't generally take missing persons seriously until they have been misplaced a full twenty-four hours. A lot of sorry experience and misspent hours back up that policy. Why don't you just hold on for another day or so?"

A rustling bird crashed into the dry sod at my hip. It was a wad of wrinkled bills the girl had fished out of a small, ruby-colored handbag.

"There," she said. "That's all I have. Fifty-five dollars." I picked up the paper-clipped wad of bills, mostly fives and ones, the faces on the dirty, wrinkled denominations all neatly aligned in the same direction. It bespoke a mind more orderly than I had anticipated. "Will you find Lance for me?"

"This isn't enough," I said, sounding gruffer than I wanted to sound, the school bully extorting lunch money.

"Lance'll pay you more when you find him. You know about his grandfather's will, don't you?"

"I know."

"He'll pay you." She was pleading and it sent a sickly-sweet feeling rippling through the pit of my stomach, like a heat wave. "I promise."

"I'm sure he'll pay." I looked away, trying to ward off the sadistic, almost sexual thrill her imploring created in me. "Thanks, but there are too many things your boyfriend could be wrapped up in. This just isn't my kind of caper."

"Please?"

The guy probably got cold feet at the last minute. Marriage was a big step. And theirs wasn't exactly going to be a conventional one, no bed of roses for either of them.

"Supposing I don't find him? Who would pay my fee then? Fifty-five bucks won't even cover my expenses."

"You have to find him."

"It's not enough," I said. "I don't want to get involved in it."

"Why not?"

"It's got a bad smell to it."

Abruptly, she darted her eyes to the ground, picked up the money she had thrown at me and stood, taking it as a personal, perhaps a racial slur. Her movements were graceful, artfully choreographed. She was a dancer, or had been one.

Chapter Nine

SHE WALKED TEN FEET before I called to her. "Your boy-friend inherited millions," I said. "How come all you have is fifty-five bucks?"

She halted, pivoted, and gave me a careful, searching once-over. "Grandfather Rufus left the money to Lance. Not to me."

"You met him? Grandfather Rufus?"

"Once when he flew out here. Without the others. Lance didn't think I should meet the rest of the family just then." If there was a remembered affront in her thoughts, she didn't reveal it.

"Didn't Lance share the wealth? Nothing to his family? Nothing to you? Sounds a little stingy."

She struggled with her reply, grasping the small purse in her hands tighter and tighter, like a nervous starling fixing itself to a sun-hot wire. "He wanted to. But I wouldn't let him. That car. It cost eighteen thousand. He wanted to give me that, but I wouldn't let him."

"You don't like cars?"

"I don't drive. Besides, it wouldn't be right. It would taint our relationship. He had to know that I loved him for him, just the way I had to know that he loved me for me."

"Did he?" I asked.

"What?"

"Did he love you for you?"

"We are going to be married."

"How do you know he hasn't shown up between the time you left to find me and now?"

"I phoned his boarding house at a pay phone. A half hour ago. And I called my brothers, P.W. and D.W. He hasn't been seen by anyone, not since last night."

"Could be he's sick. Maybe he went home to his dad because he was just too sick to do anything else."

"If Lance were sick, he would come to me."

I heaved myself up, wobbling on blistered feet. I dribbled the ball twice on the bumpy grass, extended my hand, and shook with her. "My name is Thomas Black. I'm a licensed private detective. I'll find Lance for you."

"But I don't have . . ."

"A guy will do a lot for fifty-five dollars," I said, lifting the paper-clipped wad of bills out of her slim hand. "This will do as a retainer. We'll talk about the rest later."

"Lucille Ida Peebles. I don't like the Ida, but everybody calls me Lucille Ida. I can't get away from it."

"Happy to meet you, Lucille."

"My close friends call me Lucy."

She told me she had hopped a bus across town to reach me, then braved my batty neighbor, Horace, to learn that I was probably down at the school playing ball. Horace called me a shiftless bum to my face and I shuddered to think what he had called her to her face. The old bigot rarely minced words.

"It's really not a very long time to be lost," I said.

"I know. I know. That's what everyone keeps telling me. My sister, everyone. But I *know* he's in trouble."

"You have ESP, or something?" I inquired, genuinely wondering. But Lucy misinterpreted my question as solid sarcasm. She gave me a look that was equal parts hurt and reprimand, a pinch of disappointment sprinkled across the top of the concoction. I let it go. It would take too long to explain.

Thumbing through some magazines in my living room, Lucy Peebles bided her time while I showered and dressed.

The air was too hot and muggy for a jacket, so I put on slacks and a striped dress shirt, open at the neck. I limped into the living room. She was at the window, the afternoon light filtering through the wisps of dark hair at her slender neck. Even in her distress, a tranquility clung to her that was almost palpable. I prayed that I wasn't falling into my wounded sparrow syndrome again.

Before we left, I scribbled out a receipt for the fifty-five dollars, picked up the notes I had made on the Tyner case three weeks earlier, and telephoned Kathy Birchfield at Leech, Bemis and Ott.

"Kathy, Thomas here. What's the latest on Lance Tyner?"

"I know he had an appointment this morning at ten, but he didn't make it."

"Appointment for what?"

"We're negotiating an agreement with his father. He's going to divvy up some of the money."

"He call you?"

"No, he just failed to show up."

"Is that customary with him?"

"No. Why?"

"His girlfriend is here with me. She thinks he's missing." There was a long pause on the line. "Kathy?"

"I thought she might get in touch with you. She called me. I gave her your address. You don't mind?"

"Not at all."

"Thomas, I'm getting a real bad feeling about this whole affair. What does his girlfriend say?"

"They were supposed to pick up a marriage license this morning."

"Come on over, Thomas."

"Will do. Maybe I'll check his boarding house on the way."

Neither of us spoke during the junket. It was 3:45, a weekday, and the roads were congested in the U district. We parked the truck three blocks away and hiked to Lance's boarding house. Lucy kept to my pace without seeming to strain.

The crone was in the midst of beating mashed potatoes for the evening meal, stirring them in a huge dented aluminum pot she carried jammed against her hip. Blotches of mashed potatoes hung in her hair like artificial snowflakes on a stage actress.

I pushed the front door of the boarding house open and barged in past her. Swanlike Lucy, petite and serious and law-abiding, remained on the stoop. The old woman shuffled after me, a whiff of the foul smell of her underarms chasing me up the stairs.

"I'm here to see Lance," I said. "It's important."

Bounding up the stairs, I located the first door on the left at the top of the flight, the one the old man had told me was Lance's. The place smelled musty—like mothballs, potted flowers and high, unseen dust. I rapped loudly, then twisted the rickety knob. It wasn't locked. The crone was hot on my heels.

"You can't go in there. These doors are locked. You want me to call the police?"

Like a grizzled cloud, she loomed in the doorway. The room was like a long box, cramped and sweltering, most of the space blotted up by a bed and a large desk. A Windsor chair stood next to the bed. The cubbyhole was neat and spartan.

"He move out?" I asked, thinking aloud.

"Did he? That bugger. He's paid till the end of the month. I'm not giving him any refund. He thinks I'm handing out refunds, he better think again. This ain't the Goodwill."

I pulled open the closet door. It was about a third full of clothes, mostly starched chambray work shirts on hangers, a jacket or two. In the bottom on the floor was the blue tent I had seen in the state park, bundled up and brushed clean. A pair of heavy hiking boots with Vibram soles sat beside it like soldiers at a memorial. He hadn't moved, not yet. The desk was bare except for a calendar, two empty note pads, and a business card. I picked up the business card and slipped it into my pocket.

"I'm going to call the police," said the old woman in the doorway, threading her best evil eye through the back of my head. One could only stand so much abuse. The funny thing was, I liked her. She reminded me of my Aunt Mildy.

"Sure, go ahead," I said, trying a door behind the spindle-back chair. It was stuck, no doubt painted shut. "Call the electrical inspector while you're at it. You're not up to code, lady. This is going to cost you a bundle. None of this wire is code." I pointed at the bare overhead light and she stared up, her flabby white neck flattening out like a cobra's hood.

"Electrical inspector?" she snapped, her voice breaking.

"What's behind this door?"

"There's no wires out there. That's a sun porch. My son's got some storage out there. It's not heated. It's not really part of the house."

I shambled out past the old lady and descended the stairs. Lucy was still waiting demurely on the porch. A tanned, blue-eyed young man lounged in the living room downstairs, paging through the afternoon *Times*.

41

"You know Lance Tyner?" I asked.

He glanced up at me. "Sure," he said.

"Where is he?"

"Couldn't tell ya. He hasn't been around since . . . supper yesterday."

"He come in last night?"

"I don't think so. My room's across the hall from his. I usually hear him."

"He taking classes?"

"Naw. He's just here 'cause it's cheap."

"You good friends with him?"

"Not really. He keeps to himself. Has a couple of grubby-looking pals visit him once in a while. And one woman. But he never talks to us much."

"What's the woman look like?"

He was noncommittal, nodding. "Nice."

"She young? Old? White? Black?"

"White. Not too old. Heavy. Real heavy."

Chapter Ten

"THE ELECTRICAL INSPECTOR?" shrieked the landlady, making her teetering way down the stairs, using the railing as a crutch.

"I can get him, you know," I said. "You give me trouble, I can get him. He's a personal friend of mine." I glanced down at the tub of mashed potatoes she had abandoned on top of some mail on a stand. "Maybe I could drag my uncle, the health inspector, down here too."

I left her nonplussed, shooing a noisy fly out of the mashed potatoes, glowering at me through the glass door. I glimpsed her husband in their apartment, napping on a cluttered couch, an enormous gray Persian cat curled up tight against his face.

On the way down the stairs to the street, I told Lucy what I had found and showed her the business card. It belonged to an attorney named Jack Thomas.

"You know this guy?" I asked.

Studying the card, she shook her head. "Lance didn't keep secrets from me. I don't know who that could be."

"It was in his room."

"We never kept secrets."

"Maybe it was a surprise."

She shrugged. I gathered they never surprised each other either. No secrets and no surprises. What a deal.

The lot of the Grueman Building was so full that if I hadn't spotted an angry lady in a Mercedes just evacuating her place, I wouldn't have found a slot. We trotted in past Beulah Hancock, who stunned me by smiling. She looked as if she had gained about twenty pounds since I'd seen her three weeks ago.

Kathy was in her office. "What'd you find?" she asked.

"Not a whole hell of a lot," I said.

Remembering my manners, I introduced the two women, the one who had lived in my basement for the past five years, and the one who was marrying a missing fifteen million dollars. They exchanged anxious smiles and polite, evaluating looks.

"Don't worry," said Kathy. "If anybody can find Lance, Thomas can. He's the absolute best there is."

Kathy wore a pin-striped business suit that had padded shoulders and a goofy-looking russet cravat tied into multiple bows at her neck. She went around behind her desk and sat down. Lucy took the green seat Martin Tyner had used several weeks before. I remained on my feet.

"I just spoke to Lance's father," Kathy began. "He's worried, too. He and I and the younger Bemis were all supposed to meet this morning for a final thrashing out of the agreement. I believe we were very close to a settlement that will please all parties. He wants you to drive out to his place, Thomas. He said he might have something to help."

"You know this guy?" I said, handing Jack Thomas's card to Kathy.

She perused the card. "Where'd you find this?"

"In Lance's room in the boarding house."

"That's really funny. We've been talking almost every day and he never mentioned another attorney." Kathy swung her chair around and sprang out of it in one smooth bounce. "Let me take this to the younger Bemis. Peyton knows just about everyone in town. Be right back."

It wasn't until Lucy looked up at me timidly that I realized she hadn't said a word since I had introduced her. She had one of those sinking personalities that could get absorbed by the woodwork. Even so, the fancy building and office did not seem to affect her. I had the sensation nothing much flustered her. She could have bided her time through a riot.

Flouncing back into the room, Kathy said, "Bemis doesn't know much about him. He's got an office up by Northgate."

"That's what the card says," I volunteered, cheerfully. Kathy gave me a slightly reproving look. I raised my hands as if being arrested, and said, "Just commenting."

"You want me to phone him?"

I nodded. She made the call on a speaker so we could listen. The man was with a client, but Kathy told his secretary who she was and that it was vitally important. She sounded good on the phone, very professional.

"Jack Thomas? Katherine Birchfield here, of Leech, Bemis and Ott, in Seattle."

"Sure." He knew the firm.

"Sorry to spoil your meeting. I've got a private detective here in my office. He's looking for Lance Tyner." She let it hang in the air, the three of us awaiting some mystical pronouncement from the speaker box.

"Yeah, yeah," Jack Thomas, finally said. "I know him. I didn't realize he was in any sort of trouble. You want me to give you the address I have for him? It's in the U district somewhere on Fifteenth."

"That's not it," said Kathy. "He's missing. He's inexplicably skipped two appointments today and one of them was to get married." She glanced at Lucy who squirmed slightly in her chair. "We're afraid something might have happened."

"I'm truly sorry. But I don't know anything about it. Is there anything I can do to help?"

"Tell us what you were working on for him."

The line went silent and stayed that way.

Finally Kathy said, "Mr. Thomas?"

"You know that's privileged information, Miss Birchfield."

"I also know that a young man got clear title to millions of dollars a few weeks ago and now he's missing. He was attacked and left for dead the first of the month. Did you know that?"

"Miss Birchfield, I cannot reveal my client's affairs. But I assure you I do not know where he is. Nor do I have any information that would help you find him. I really don't."

"What did you do for him, Mr. Thomas?" Kathy asked, firmly.

Two beats went by before he answered. "I drew up a will, that's all. Two wills, actually. Alternate wills. He couldn't decide which one he wanted."

"Do you have copies?"

"You know I do. But I don't know which one he endorsed. We set it up so he could go either way and tear up the one he decided against. I have no idea which he kept.

45

He was a little eccentric. He was going to come in later and tell me."

Kathy wasn't fazed by the information. I wasn't too surprised. But Lucy was dumbfounded. She spoke for the first time since she'd come into the office.

"A will? No. No. Somebody writes a will, they're thinking about dying. Lance wasn't thinking about dying. I don't believe it. He didn't write any will." She was resisting, but somebody was trying to put it to her—the whammy.

Chapter Eleven

IN THE PARKING LOT, amidst the heat and stinking gusts of diesel exhaust, I handed Lucy one of my dog-eared cards and told her to call me.

"Pardon?"

"Call me. I'll be in touch. I'll keep you apprised of my progress. Where do you live? I'll drop you off."

She looked down and spoke as if reading a speech off the tops of her pumps. "No, no. You don't understand. If you're going to see Lance's father, I'm coming too."

"There's no need for that."

Her eyes were suddenly large and very winsome. "You don't know much, do you?"

"What do you mean?"

"Don't you know why he wants to see you?"

"Why?"

"He's going to try to hire you away from me."

"Naw, he won't."

"Course he will."

"So what if he does? You hired me."

"No, no," said Lucy. "I'm coming with you. I want to be there."

"He's not going to hire me away," I said, nearly uttering something about rampant paranoia. But a black friend of mine had once explained, and reasonably I had thought at the time, that only whites were ever paranoid in the sense that they were suffering delusions. When blacks suffered those same symptoms, they were merely being observant.

"I'm coming," said Lucy.

Speaking to Tyner would be a perfunctory part of the search, at best. She wouldn't disturb my work.

"You'll be bored," I said, amused. It was the last thing I thought she would do, get tough.

Martin Tyner lived south, surprisingly close to Dash Point State Park, where I had found Lance trying to drink his share of the Puget Sound. I wondered if Lance hadn't gone there to do something other than clamming.

The southern sky gloated with menace, charcoal clouds moving swiftly. The entire southern hemisphere was roiling like smoke from a burning city, obliterating another summer evening. We drove down past Three Tree Point to the Redondo, Lakota area. Raindrops the size of marbles spattered against the windshield, pecking at the hood of my truck.

"Gosh," said Lucy. "There are so many new houses. I can hardly believe it. Where do people get so much money to buy all this?"

"It's about forty miles from Seattle to Tacoma," I said. "I used to make jokes about the entire forty miles being paved. Now it almost is. One day the entire state will be concrete and houses."

"But the money. Where do they get all the money?"

I shrugged. "Mom and Dad help with the down payment. The wife and husband both work. The kids spend their days in school and with baby sitters. It's a wonderful life at 320 Sycamore Lane."

Her look turned defensive and a wee bit indecipherable. "I had a job. Worked in a drugstore. Been laid off for four months now. I've been taking care of my younger brothers. Mother's been . . . sick."

The Tyner homestead was a sixty-year-old house on one of the few pieces of sizable undivided real estate left in the region. Everything else was tract housing thrown up on quarter-acre lots. From the air, it would look like a marathon Monopoly game some unregenerate kids had been playing.

We drove in over a bumpy private driveway, past a mailbox with Tyner painted in fresh black lettering. The old farmhouse, a three-story edifice, was surrounded by a small apple orchard, hundreds of Granny Smiths glistening in the wet. Overlooking the water, the house boasted an unspoiled view of the Sound. The rusted wire fence around the property enclosed ten or twelve acres.

The slate-gray slab of water below us was called Poverty

Bay. It had a greenish hue, the dark sky tinging it the color of bad meat.

When we got out of the truck, the air was ten degrees cooler. Before we reached the house a torrent opened up, drenching us both. It was like being squirted with a garden hose. We jogged through the yard to the front porch, past a yapping dog that looked disappointed enough with life to bite on a whim. As we cowered on the porch and shook ourselves off, the raindrops tattooing the roof over our heads, Lucy laughed at our plight. People who laughed at their troubles were few and far between. Lance, I thought, had better hold on to her.

The screen door to the porch was unlocked, the front door wide open. "Mr. Tyner?" I shouted, leading Lucy in by the hand. From deep inside the house I heard a muffled reply.

"Mr. Tyner?"

"Enter." He had appeared in a room three doorways away, a room to my left. "Get yourself in here. We got things to talk about, son." He hadn't seen Lucy yet. She hung back in the doorway, waiting for him to spot her, to reject her. It was an old house and he was renovating it. Tools, sawhorses and building materials were everywhere.

"Who's that?" he asked, squinting down the corridor at Lucy. "Pick up a hitchhiker?"

"Her name is Lucille Ida Peebles," I said. "She's engaged to your son."

"Lance?"

"Yep."

"Engaged to do what?"

"To be married."

Stealing another quick look at her, Martin Tyner's face fell and his skin slowly began to turn roseate. "A dad-blamed jigaboo?"

"Can it, old man. You're already on thin ice."

"Lance ain't engaged to that." Tyner glared at me, throttling me with a look of antipathy. "She ain't engaged to him."

"I'd say she is."

Tyner wheeled around and stared at Lucy. He was a strong man, with a personality to match, and I guessed he would be hard on the kids he raised. He knew no other way. He glowered at her so intently that I turned around to see what the matter was. The shower had soaked her cotton dress through to the skin, pasting it to her shoulders, stomach, and thighs, revealing all the gentle, sweeping curves of her young body. When she moved, the light from the doorway silhouetted her legs through the cotton print dress.

I examined the contours of her mahogany face. "Maybe you would like to wait in the truck."

She gave me a searching look, then turned and walked out. Tyner didn't take his eyes off her until she had vanished.

"Don't have that normal goof-ball body most of their women have."

I stared wordlessly.

"You know what I mean. They look like pogo sticks. Big ass. The big tits. Match-stick legs."

"The only big ass around here," I said, "is standing in front of me."

"Listen, you eggsucker," said Tyner.

"No, you listen! You called me here. You need me. I can leave any time I want. We play by my rules."

Tyner squinted. He didn't want a rumpus, but he sensed that I would go as far as I had to. Suddenly he sighed and combed his fingers through his hair. We had crossed a line. Now we understood one another and nothing further would be said about Lucy. Outside, the rain hammered at the house. Out the living room window on the other side of the house, I could see the squall racing over the Sound, playing cork-in-a-bucket with a two-masted schooner below us. Several smaller boats scurried toward their chosen havens.

"Anyway," he said, attempting to salvage our feeble alliance, "she don't look so bad."

"Forget it."

"Like the house?" Tyner asked. I let the question sag and fall of its own weight. "When I finish with it, it's all going to be just like it was forty years ago. Be worth four times what I paid for it. Four times, easy. It's what I do for a living. Real estate. Buy cheap. Fix it up. Sell high. Want the tour?"

I said, "I'm going to have to find out some things about Lance. I figured to start with your other son and your daughter. You gave me addresses for both of them three weeks ago. Are they still good?"

"Moved," he said, beginning to travel around the house. "Barbara moved." When we got to a small, burnished phone stand, he thumbed through a personal directory and read her address to me, holding the book at arm's length, too vain to wear glasses. I penned her street number in my notebook. She was staying in a resort area in the Cascades.

He bragged up the whole house, towing me around to see each room. He did nice work, but I didn't bother to bolster his ego by saying so. Downstairs he was replacing wallboard and taking up the floor in several spots. The plumbing in the kitchen had been uprooted. Upstairs, there were four bedrooms and a gabled study overlooking the Sound. Only one room was complete, and he had decorated that with unremarkable carpets, some antique furniture and a Remington print over the stone fireplace. I noticed that a scrap of the white pile carpeting near a bookcase was inexplicably razored and peeled up, gone.

"What happened over there?" I asked.

"Damn dog puked on my new carpet. Had to take it up this morning. Always keep one room the way the rest of the house is going to look," said Tyner, picking up a hammer he had misplaced, sheathing it in a loop of his Farmer-Brown overalls. "Keeps the finished product in my mind. Also gives me someplace to go and relax when the clutter begins to bog me down. A man can't live in this clutter all his life. I get done with this, I'll start another one. That's one of the things drove the wife bughouse. She couldn't abide a mess. Kicked me out in '67. But it didn't change my bowel movements any."

"What did you want to see me about?"

Steering me away from the completed section, he took me into a room from which we could view Lucy through a set of rattan blinds. The rain had abated and she had picked a handful of nasturtiums out of the weedy yard and was stooped over, cooing at the dog, trying to get him to cross the rainsoaked yard to the porch. The suspicious pooch was having none of it.

"You're looking for Lance, right?" Tyner said. "You're looking for my boy."

"That's the main idea."

Tyner turned from the window and scrutinized the muscles of my shoulders through my wet shirt. It was hard to tell what the old man was thinking, but it had to be

51

something bad. I had the feeling the last time he had smiled F.D.R. had been in office. Correction. He probably smiled when the A-bombs dropped on Japan. The Truman administration.

"You working for her?" He jerked his head stiffly toward Lucy.

"I'm working for her."

"I'll hire you," Martin Tyner said, shaking a lock of his dirty-white hair out of his eyes. The room we were in must have been his office. It had a TV small enough to throw, a desk, and a cot, along with several changes of clothes scattered over a straight-backed chair. I recognized the suit he had worn the first time I met him, wrinkled and thrown across the foot of the cot.

Marching stiffly over to the peeling desk, the old man opened a drawer, pulled a checkbook out and began scribbling in it. His hands were speckled with beige paint. "What sort of retainer do you need?"

"Put the pen away," I said.

Tyner looked up, deflated.

"We're ready to settle. I have a good notion that egg-sucker is going to go thirds with us. Quarters, at the very least. That's almost four million dollars. I'll be willing to give you a hundred thousand of that if you find him safe and sound."

"I've got a client."

Baffled, Tyner glared through the rattan blind at the unsuspecting Lucy. The raindrops from the broken gutter tinkled and splatted in the rockery, a xylophone in the puddles. "How much she paying you?"

"Fifty-five dollars," I said, barely able to contain my smirk.

Tyner's jaw dropped. "A measly fifty-five dollars? Are you stupid? Did you hear what I offered?"

"You know a lawyer named Jack Thomas?"

Tyner still hadn't recovered from my refusal. "A hundred thousand dollars. You deaf?" He pronounced it deef. "Tell you what . . . I've got about eight grand in my account. How about I write you a check right now for three grand?"

"Save your money. I'll find Lance. What does it matter who I'm working for?"

A tiny smile crept across the old man's liver-colored lips,

the kind of smile dead cats along the highway retained long after the Chryslers that sent them to their doom were garaged and cool. "Don't you understand? If Lance is in any sort of bind, it's because of them. What the hell do you think a bunch of jigaboos are gonna do when they sniff that sort of money? Eh?"

"Make damn fools of themselves," I said. "Same as you."

"You're blind and deaf and stupid besides. I'll bet a million to one her purse is full of food stamps and welfare coupons."

"You offering her a job?"

Tyner glowered. His look could have poached eggs in their shells.

I walked out to the porch, took Lucy by the arm and headed across the damp yard to my truck. Tyner stomped onto the porch behind us. "You're a fool, Black!"

"Tell me something I don't already know," I said, under my breath. I turned and faced him. The dog wandered over beside the old man, keeping a respectful distance, just out of boot range.

"Jack Thomas," I said. "You know him?"

Knotting up his jaw muscles, Tyner said, "Hell, yes, I know Jack Thomas. He's been my lawyer for years. He's the one who recommended Leech, Bemis and Ott for this courtroom business and negotiation with Lance. He said they was snooty, but good."

We got into the truck and mucked through the damp, dirt road to the highway.

Lucy said, "He tried to hire you, didn't he?"

I laughed. "That he did."

Chapter Twelve

EGG-SIZED RAINDROPS blitzed the road in front of us, pelting the roof of my truck like fingers drumming on it.

On the freeway we were immediately hemmed in by a traffic tie-up—generated, according to the blasé radio announcer, by a truckload of mayonnaise spilled onto the roadway near Southcenter. Thousands of vehicles came to a dead stop.

"I guess he offered you a lot of money," said Lucy, looking at the blurred landscape.

"Some."

"How much?"

"It's not important." But it was important. Now she trusted me implicitly. Before, we had been acquaintances. Now we were something more. Her eyes glowed like buttons.

Our clothes were still damp and the humidity inside the truck filmed over the windows. I cracked my wing open to dissipate some of the fog, letting in wisps of exhaust from motorists too hobbled by haste to shut their engines off to relax and relish the thunderstorm.

"I don't get out of the CD too often," Lucy admitted. The CD was the Central District. "Lance takes me places, me and D.W. and P.W. Lance has always been so nice."

"Tell me about this guy who slugged him on the beach," I said.

"Lance never would talk about it. He only said he went to the park with a couple of his old friends, a couple of guys he knew before he met me. I think they were bums."

"Bums?"

"He had a rough time of it the last couple of years," she

explained. "Until a month ago when he got the first of the money."

"Was he in trouble with the law?"

"I don't think so."

"Just on the streets?"

"Something like that."

"How did he pay for that room he was renting?"

"Last few months, he worked part time cleaning our church, Tuesdays and Fridays. It didn't pay much, but it kept him alive. That's how he got his room and the bus fare to visit me. I think Pastor Jeremiah got a kick out of giving charity to a white boy."

"Why didn't his father help him out? Never mind . . . stupid question."

"He liked the U district, to be close to all that learning, even if he wasn't enrolled. He'd go and audit classes. Lance said, when you're poor, education is all you've got. He even took me a few times. To the library, I mean. I want to take some college one day." She gazed out at the horizon, dismally calculating the probability of that ever occurring. "And he used their reference library. Spent days wandering through the stacks. Especially after he found out he was going to get the money."

"Used their library for what?"

"All sorts of things. He was trying to figure out the best way to help the world, to aid mankind."

"You're kidding!"

"No. Lance felt an obligation with all that money. He wanted to help as many people as he possibly could. He researched all the possibilities."

"The last idealist," I said.

"He's not the last," she exclaimed.

"Did you have some ideas, too?"

"A few."

"Such as?"

"Founding a company that would hire a lot of people." Her voice altered, became animated. "People need jobs so badly these days. Starting a foundation like Kurt Vonnegut wrote about in *God Bless You, Mr. Rosewater*. You ever read that?"

"I've read it."

She seemed startled that we had the book in common. "He wanted to give it all away at first, but I convinced him

55

that would be a waste. If he invested it and only gave away the interest, then he could keep on giving for the rest of his life."

"What did he say to that?"

"He liked it."

"You have the names of any of his friends? Anybody he palled around with."

"I really don't know. I think there was somebody named Billy. Or something like that."

"Know any last names? Or where they work? Or what they do? Ever see any of them?"

She shook her head. "Lance didn't mention his life much. We talked about other things. I didn't even realize Grandfather Rufus was that wealthy until Lance asked me to go to court with him."

"Did you go?"

"Once. I sat in the back."

"So today wasn't the first time you met any of his relatives?"

"Yes, it was. Except Grandfather Rufus. He was nice. A gentle old man. I saw his father and brother and sister in court, but I don't think they knew who I was. There were a lot of people there, you know, just to gape. I suppose they attend for the spectacle, like people running down to the corner when there's an accident. But I didn't like it. I didn't like the way Lance's father and brother stared at him, as if they wanted him to sink through the floor and just keep on sinking."

"They ever threaten Lance?"

"I don't believe so. But that's the sort of thing he wouldn't tell me. We were close, but he kept many things to himself."

"You never got any of the story about what happened down on the beach?"

"All I know is that Lance promised to help Billy or Joey or whatever his name is, and Billy was real mad because he hadn't done much yet. Billy figured Lance was going to hand over a bunch of money and he wondered what the delay was. Lance's ideas were more along the line of training them in a profession, getting their feet on the ground so they could take care of themselves permanently."

"You don't know why they were down at the beach?"

"Free clams? Fishing? The campgrounds were cheap. A

56

lot of guys who are bumming use campgrounds in the summertime. They mooch food off the tourists. I don't know. Lance said Billy used to steal a lot of stuff, too."

"Billy used to steal? He ever conk anybody and steal a wad of hundred-dollar bills?"

Lucy shrugged. "His father gave them back to him. He only lost a couple of hundred. I don't know why Billy or whoever conked him. Might have been to rob him. Might have been."

"Then you think it was his friends who left him on the beach?"

"Lance never said. Maybe a group of guys attacked them all."

I considered that. If there had been an out-and-out gang fight, though, somebody most likely would have seen it.

To the east, out over the Kent Valley and the Boeing complex, we could see black clouds rumbling. From time to time jagged streaks of lightning illuminated the sky, hocus-pocus from the heavens. Lucy oohed and aahed, caught up in the wonder of it.

I had misjudged Martin Tyner. I'd been virtually positive he was going to hoard all that money for himself, to steam the bills into the binding of a dictionary. But he had returned the money to his son, a son who never would have missed it. I had underestimated the old man.

It took an hour for the choked freeway to cough itself clear. During that time Lucy and I gradually got acquainted. I rooted out the story of how she and Lance had met and fallen in love, a story most women love to tell. Her words and the corkscrewing symmetry of her speech patterns captured me. Lucy and Lance had met in Bible study. They had been attracted to each other at once and he had begun phoning her. She found out later that Lance, broke and on the road, had been using phones in vacant offices at the main branch of the public library.

I kept thinking about that insane basketball game that afternoon and all the worries she had stored up, and how she had smiled meekly and waited. I had acted like a buffoon, and she like a minor-league saint.

When they met, Lucy was working in the drugstore in the Central District, and Lance would wander in and flirt. She was attracted to his shy, deprecating manner and his concern for the world at large. She also admitted that she had never had a white boy chase her. Gazing across the cab at her chiseled ebony features, I found that hard to believe.

Neither one of them had much money, so their dates consisted of long strolls through the city parks, bus rides to the zoo, or field trips dragging her two younger brothers to the aquarium or the rose garden at Woodland Park.

Leapfrogging from subject to subject, Lucy told me about her family. Though she had had a hard time, she was candid, and not a bit swamped in self-pity. I sighed, wondering if time would change her outlook the way it had mine. Time had a habit of raping hope.

Her mother had been a heroin addict, using the needle when she was carrying Lucy's twin brothers, D.W. and P.W. As a result they were born with severe problems: hearing difficulties, sight problems, and both had been adjudged mildly retarded. Their mother had been in and out of hospitals for the past three years. Lucy had an older step-sister who drank and stayed out late and who liked to slap her two younger brothers across the room.

There was no father in the picture. The four children had been sired by three different men. Life was a bitch, I thought, listening to Lucy's cheerful talk about distinctly uncheerful subjects, listening to her unreel her life like a spool of gossamer black thread.

"How does your family feel about Lance?" I asked.

She sighed wistfully. "My mother doesn't pay too much attention to what goes on. My younger brothers like him. He used to take care of them sometimes when I was at work and Mother was ill. But Cleata almost yanked his ears off one night." She grinned at me, as if telling an old and favorite fable. "P.W. and D.W. sicked the dog on her."

"Cleata ever hit you?" I asked.

Lucy hesitated. "When I was younger. I fixed it so she doesn't mess much with me anymore."

"How'd you do that?"

She was reluctant to elaborate. "I lost my cool one night, that's all. It's nothing to brag on."

"Sure," I said. The freeway cleared slowly, and we began driving, eventually plodding up to fifty-five.

Lucy and her family lived in a tall, old, rundown house not too far off Rainier Avenue in the south end of the city.

I watched Lucy swing up the slanting, unpainted steps and disappear into the monster of a house, idling my Ford at the curb until I was sure she was safely inside. At one time this part of town had been the cat's meow. All these rundown hulks had once been the homes of Seattle's high society. Important decisions had been made in them. Lawyers and judges and senators had been born in them.

It was seven o'clock, but it seemed like another century. Lucy's nattering had held me mesmerized. I liked the girl and I felt she was concealing a lot of hurt.

As soon as I arrived home, I knew I was leaving again right away. Once I got started on a case, I couldn't sit still. That was one reason I took so few.

As a cop I had always assumed that being my own boss would be hunky-dory. I could set my own hours, come and go as I pleased, goof off till the cows came home. I would no longer have the Seattle Police Department straitjacketing my every move. On my own, though, I drove myself harder than I ever had for the department.

I let Kathy's phone ring twelve times before giving up. Then I dialed the number of the pay phone in Lance's boarding house. One of the students answered, a television tweeting in the background. No, he said, Lance hadn't been around yet. I wasn't surprised, but I needed to exhaust my alternatives.

After fueling up the truck, I headed for the highway. I wanted to speak to Lance's brother and his sister. I decided to get the sister over with, since she was farther away.

Barbara Tyner was leasing a ski lodge up near Snoqualmie. It would take an hour or two to reach it. If I had to wake her up, so be it.

Motoring east up into the mountains, I pondered why I couldn't go home and hit the sack like everyone else, why I had to keep hammering away at things until I either solved them or dropped from fatigue. Single-minded. That was me.

I had owned a dog like that once. He used to chase rats— Seattle is a great town for huge, cat-killing dock rats, and that little bugger never gave up until he had one. He was easily as single-minded as I was, taking a squiggling rat into his teeth and shaking until the little beast was limp and broken. Our traits were so very similar, the pooch's and mine. I took vicious things into my teeth and shook them limp, too. Where was he now? Buried under my roses.

One dark and stormy night somebody crept into my yard and clubbed him to death.

Chapter Thirteen

FOLLOWING INTERSTATE 90 across Lake Washington, I wended my way up into the green foothills.

Dusk had not yet descended when I located Barbara Tyner's lodge, just this side of Snoqualmie, off a small, private road that intersected the highway. The lodge was new, two stories tall, a poor replica of a Swiss chalet. Fourteen autos were scattered helter-skelter around it.

Walking up the hill to the lodge, I stumbled into the pungent, singed-rope odor of marijuana.

A dewy-eyed woman of about nineteen squatted on the wooden steps, sucking hard at a roach no longer than her fingernail. Her piercing blue eyes met mine. Though it was a tad chilly, she wore khaki shorts, pockets low on the thighs, a halter top, and nothing else. She looked as if she had just stepped out of a sweatbox.

"Hi," she said, sudden knots of tension denting her bare shoulders.

"Evening. Does Barbara Tyner own this place?"

"Who?"

"Barbara Tyner?"

"You mean Babs. Sure. She's right up there. But she doesn't own this place. Rents it."

"She throwing a party?"

"Naw. It's always this way. Babs likes to have a lot of friends around. And right now she's got more than she can count."

"Her brother here?"

"Tony? No. But I think he was up a couple of days ago."

"Not that brother. Lance."

She gave me a quizzical look. "I didn't realize she had

two brothers. He hasn't been here, at any rate. Not that I know of. And I came up two weeks ago."

"You rooming with her?"

"You have to understand Babs. Anyone who can keep up with her head trips can stay, gratis. Food, laundry, entertainment, it's all on Babs. She came into some money a while back."

"I knew her brother had inherited money. But I thought the rest of the family got axed out of the will."

Inhaling deeply on the acrid smoke, she said, "Naw. She got ten thousand dollars." She held the smoke in her lungs long enough to assure me of her pluck and sophistication, then expelled it slowly.

"Doesn't sound like it's going to last long."

"I wouldn't be surprised. Last summer she inherited some moola from one of her aunts. Flew me and three others to Europe with her. Paid for everything." She made a big production out of pursing her lips and sucking on the joint. "We had a blast."

I stubbed up the stairs to the house and rapped on the huge front door.

"Hell, go right in," she urged. "Nobody'll answer."

I stepped into the smoke-filled menagerie. In one corner five people chattered excitedly over a backgammon game. Next to them a garish jukebox that didn't fit the decor of the room blasted out a Michael Jackson tune. On a balding bearskin rug two young women arm-wrestled, goaded on by a chorus of chuckling men who slopped beer onto the rug from tilting cans. The place was too hot. In the stone fireplace five logs the size of fire hydrants smoldered, barked and broke into flame when I looked at them. Black and his magic.

Removing my jacket, I plowed across the room and up to the next level to another open area. Scanning the room, I checked all the young women against a photo I had seen at Martin Tyner's house, a touched-up graduation picture. In the photograph, Barbara looked intelligent, wholesome, plump and a trifle flighty.

This level of the chateau was packed with arcade-style video games. A man, older than most of the others, stood with his back to me, wobbling his narrow buttocks as he played a car racing game. His thin, muscular arms wrenched the steering wheel expertly from side to side. He wore boots, dirty jeans and a sleeveless T-shirt the color of crushed raspberries. On his right shoulder was a tattoo of a swallowtail butterfly.

Everyone was having a rollicking good time. Babs was quite the magnanimous hostess.

It wasn't long before I spotted her, caroming from guest to guest, babbling like a magpie. She looked to be in her mid-twenties. Her dark brown hair reached her shoulders and looked as if she were between styles. She was dressed all in black, her wide shoulders and hips, thick thighs and generous bosom swathed in black velvet. Her face was wide and amiable, wide enough to write notes on.

She draped a bare arm over the shoulder of the racing game player, kissed his ear, and addressed him as Lee.

He reached out and hugged her, called her Babs, and began sweet-talking. When he turned his head, I could see a hollow-cheeked face riddled with acne scars. There was something a little odd about his chatter, like a farmer conniving a calf into a slaughtering pen. He was ten years older than anyone in the room—anyone except me. The game vacuumed him back into its orbit.

Catching Barbara Tyner's eye, I signaled and moved to a relatively quiet corner of the room beside a maniacal teenage boy who manhandled the control knobs on a game of Donkey Kong. Barbara disengaged herself from the race car driver and slouched toward me. Everything about her was broad—her smile, her shoulders, her hips. "Hi," she said, as if we were old and fast friends.

"My name is Thomas Black. I spoke to your father this afternoon. I'm looking for your brother. I'm a private investigator."

"Not Lance?" Her dim blue eyes were reminiscent of her father's, though one false eyelash was askew.

"Lance."

"What happened to him?"

"I wish I knew."

She hunkered down on the horizontal face of an electronic table game. A speck of food was jammed between her lower incisors.

"Gosh, that's just terrible. Do you have any idea where he went? You don't think something happened to him, do you? I mean, Lance isn't exactly one to jump into trouble, but then, he hasn't been avoiding it either, has he? What do you think? What'd my father say? How long did you talk to him, anyway? Say, as long as you're here, wanta play some games? It's really fun. I mean, you might think it's a bit juvenile, but it really is fun. It'll relax you. And what about Lance?"

I grinned. I envisioned her stomach all stacked up with little colored pills. She had the look of someone on a rampage, always thinking of five things at once, and talking faster than you could listen.

"What about Lance?" I prodded. "You have any idea what might have happened to him?"

"It's all so weird. Our whole lives are so weird. I mean, look at me. I could have had all my grandmother's jewels. Do you have any idea what she had in her collection? It was unbelievable, stuff that's been in our family for over a hundred years, junk straight from Germany.

"And then Grampop gives it all to Lance. Lance? I mean, I hate to say this about my own brother, but Lance is a dip. He never . . . Grampop should have dumped it all in Tony's lap. Tony would know how to handle it. It's just sort of ironic. Don't you think?"

"Tony and Lance get along, do they?"

"Lance never got along with anyone, except Grampop Rufus. He's a brown-nose." I sensed a vein of bitterness. "I mean, here I am studying my ass off to get my philosophy degree, Dad's always working, and Tony. Tony! And Grampop hands the whole boodle over to Lance. I mean, Lance was a fucking hobo, for godsakes. A hobo." She was a social swearer, using the words and simultaneously watching for her listener's reaction.

"How do you know that?"

"What?"

"That Lance was a hobo."

"Everybody knew. Last summer when I got that stash from Aunt Ethel, I gave him three hundred dollars. And what does he do when Grampop kicks off. He pays me back the three hundred dollars. No interest, no nothing. He's just a dip. Tony tried to talk to him. Lance always looked up to his big brother, so we thought Tony would be able to talk some sense into him, but it was no go. Lance even took a poke at him. Can you believe that? At Tony?"

"How long ago was that?"

"I dunno. A month?"

"What happened?"

"I guess you don't know Tony. He polished Lance off. I mean, Tony's an athlete. He probably could have been a top-notch fighter if he'd wanted. Mostly he played basketball and football. Baseball in the spring. Now he's a golfer. And he bowls. He does it all. And Lance tried to slug him. What a joke. You ought to see Tony hit a golf ball. Smooth?"

"You all three got cut out of the will. Any idea why?"

She brushed her straight hair off one shoulder. "We'll get a fair division. Father's working on that right now."

"He can't work on it if Lance is gone."

Her voice squeaked, evolved into a high-pitched whine, and I suddenly knew what she had sounded like as a little girl. "How can he be gone? I talked to Father yesterday. He saw Lance yesterday."

"Yesterday is yesterday. Nobody saw him today."

"He'll turn up. Wanta play some games? We've got it all here. I rented all these machines. Pretty nifty, huh?"

"Yeah, real nifty," I said. "Is Tony the one who gave Lance that shiner? He had a black eye when I saw him a few weeks ago."

"Yeah, that was Tony."

Babs Tyner surveyed the room appreciatively, tallying her friends, toting up all the love in the world with her name on it. The man at the race car console looked away from the screen for a second and levered his eyebrows in recognition, his eyes hardening when he spotted me. He was a tough customer, no doubt about it. From the look of him, I figured he had done some hard time.

"Who's that?" I asked.

"Lee. He's just been everywhere and done everything. Do you know he used to work for Barbra Streisand?"

"Yeah," I said. "Fancy that. I had a great-uncle once,

used to follow Buffalo Bill Cody's horse with a shovel. You know where Lance lived before he moved to Fifteenth?"

"Nobody ever knew where Lance was living or what he was doing. He just never cut the mustard in our family. I mean, I've had straight A's since first grade. And Tony was all-state. He played semi-pro basketball for two years. Poor Lance. He never really made the grade."

"He's younger than both of you?"

"Tony's the oldest. Lance is just a year younger than me."

A teenaged boy in one of the other rooms yelled raucously, then called, "Babs! This thing's on the blink."

"Excuse me," Barbara Tyner said, spinning herself around on the face of the console and hopping off. The pale opening between the back of her blouse and her black velvet pants went all the way down to the crack. She was a heartbreaker.

One thing I had noticed about all the people in the place, including the woman outside on the steps, was that they all had a special look to them. They were all tinted in one hue.

Last winter I had investigated a cult for a group of concerned parents, trying to get the lowdown on whether their kids were really happy with cult life. When the parents hired me, they showed me a photograph of about sixty young people clustered together, all members of this particular religious cult. Studying the photo, I realized they all had one thing in common. They looked like life's losers—jilted suitors, the people panhandlers invariably begged from, the people who foolishly signed up for and flunked Latin III without having taken I or II. They had the sad demeanor of people who couldn't hack the vicissitudes of life.

Barbara Tyner was playing hostess to all of them, each one looking a little down on his luck, a day late and a dollar short, perpetually watching his or her shoelaces getting sucked into escalators.

On a hunch I sidled across the room and sat down on a sofa next to a sloe-eyed woman. She had been casting withering looks at the man running the car race console ever since I came in. It took her a few moments to snap out of her reveries and realize she had company.

66

When she turned and gave me an icy look, I said, "I'm looking for Babs' brother."

"Tony? Why would anyone want to find that creep?"

"Not Tony. The other one."

The woman was about twenty and a pouter. She had long dark hair parted in the center and curled around her face as if a cold wind had frozen it that way. Her expressionless eyes were so dark they were all one color, no pupil and iris. When she spoke she was careful to move her lips only enough to make the sounds come. She strove fitfully to keep expression out of everything. I wondered who had soured her on life.

"Are you staying here?" I asked.

"Maybe."

"Have you known Babs long?"

"Long enough."

"Ever meet Lance?"

"Yeah, I've met him."

"And?"

"He's a pretty naive guy, if you ask me."

"In what way?"

"He just is."

"You didn't like him, then?"

"I liked him all right. He's just naive. He thinks he's going to change the world. He's not going to change beans."

Much as I wanted to disagree with her, I had a sneaking suspicion she was right. "How well did you know Lance?"

"Mostly I listened to him telling his sister what was wrong with the world. He knew it all. Years ago, he belonged to about six of those protest groups. You know the ones. He blocked trains that carried nuclear warheads. He was in some sort of fish protest. He's been arrested dozens of times."

"When was the last time you saw Lance?"

"I dunno. Six weeks ago?"

"Who's that guy over there?"

"Who?"

"The guy you've been staring at all night."

She traced my gaze across the room to the man with the

tattoo. "Some dude. Babs picked him up a few days ago. He's a cretin."

"He bothers you?"

She thought about whether she wanted to admit to it. "She just met him, for christsakes, and they make out like they've known each other for a hundred years. I don't understand that. I really don't."

"She sleeping with him?"

The sloe-eyed woman shrugged. "Don't know. Don't care either." She was still staring at him when I left.

Chapter Fourteen

IT WAS DARK when I plodded down to my truck.

The case reminded me of something that had happened long ago when I was still on the force.

Eighteen years old, pretty, popular Eve Tiffany had vanished one night driving between the grocery store and her parents' home in Bellevue, a distance of three miles. Every cop in the state had kept his eye peeled for her car, a restored MG her brother had left her when he died in a football accident. There would be no mistaking that vehicle. The newspapers ran her photo; rewards were posted.

The months dragged on and the posters on the shopping mall walls grew tattered and obscured by spray-paint graffiti. Every cop I knew had it pegged as a homicide, probably a sexual psychopath.

Some bug-eyed psycho had skulked up to the car at a stoplight, jumped inside with her and forced her to drive up into the foothills, then afterwards, murdered her. No two ways about it. It would only be a matter of time before some petty hoodlum would confess, before somebody would rat on a partner, or hunters would bumble into the rusting car in the foothills.

Two years later they found her off the side of the Mercer Island Floating Bridge in ninety feet of water, car intact except for some scratches. They found her when some workmen accidentally sank a large piece of expensive equipment into the lake and divers went down to hook a line onto it. She was alone in the auto. Since it was miles out of her way, nobody ever figured out why she had been on the bridge. The medical examiner failed to pin down a definitive cause of death, but, still in her seat belt, it was assumed she had drowned.

Each time I took a missing persons case, the Eve Tiffany story ran through my mind. The episode had taught me a lesson about assumptions. Eve Tiffany had been on the bottom of Lake Washington while we moved heaven and earth trying to locate her. Perhaps she had been ghoulishly laughing at us the whole time?

I wondered if Lance Tyner was laughing.

It was an hour before midnight when I got home. I showered, my body still feverish from Babs Tyner's overheated chalet. I dragged out the telephone book and dialed every hospital within reasonable traveling distance, including the one Lance had been ambulanced to the night we found him on the beach. It took forty-five minutes. Nobody knew anything.

The next morning it was an idea that woke me. I should have been looking for Lance Tyner's car. It was new and expensive, and the police machinery in the state was much more adept at locating autos than it was people. At least if we knew where his car was, we'd have a jumping-off point.

I telephoned Kathy Birchfield.

"Oh, Thomas," she said, moaning the sleep out of her voice. "It's not even seven o'clock yet."

"You used to be up at six."

"Sure. In school. This is the real world, Thomas. People don't get up until at least . . . 7:15. What's going on? You sound as if you're getting your second wind on the case. Have you found him?"

"No, but I've got some ideas."

"I can tell that by your voice."

"His car. I'm going to find his car. That should be a lot easier than finding him."

"Brilliant."

"You must have been sleeping pretty hard." Even as I spoke, I heard a man's voice on the other end of the line, then the muffled sound of the receiver being smothered with a palm. She had a man with her. Sure, that was all right. Kathy and I had no claims on each other. If it was okay, though, I wondered why my stomach suddenly felt as if I had swallowed a quart of warm grease.

"What was that? What were you saying, Thomas? The cat just knocked something over." She didn't own a cat. It was an old code we used with each other.

70

"Sure. Your albino cat. I wanted to ask you about the negotiations between the Tyners. How are they going?"

"If you want the god's-honest truth, I don't know how they are going. Lance is really an oddball. Lance hasn't promised a thing. We go in there and it seems more like some sort of family counseling than legal jostling. Lance and his father have been at each other's throats for years."

"Funny. The old man tried to hire me yesterday. He told me you had almost reached an agreement. He was talking about a quarter or a third of the whole shebang."

"What?"

"A quarter or a third, he said."

"I don't know where he got that idea. The only concrete offer I ever heard Lance make was five thousand a year after his father reached seventy, and that won't be for a couple of years."

"The old geezer offered me a hundred thousand to find Lance."

"I doubt he's got it."

The line was silent for a few moments. I mused about the identity of the man in Kathy's bed. "Lance ever say anything about how he spends his days?"

"Not a peep. He just shows up for the meetings. We do most of the talking."

"Never said a thing?"

"He hardly talks at all. Lance sits there and listens and daydreams. When his father isn't running off at the mouth, we make proposals. The queer thing is, Lance always appears genuinely interested in our submissions. I don't think he is, but he appears to be. It keeps us hopping, and hoping. I suppose he's just toying with us."

"Do you know why he's still living in that sleazy boarding house?"

"I couldn't even guess."

"Later, then."

"Thomas?"

"Yeah?"

"I miss you."

"Yeah, I'm sorry I called. I didn't mean to wake you." Who she was sleeping with? The younger Bemis? There had been a time, and recently too, when she would have volunteered the information, maybe not right now with

71

him listening, but eventually. I sensed we were beyond
that time.

"Thomas?"

"Huh?"

"I said I miss you."

"Sure."

I phoned Smithers but he eluded me, having just left the
precinct station minutes before my call. Smithers and I
had mustered into the Seattle Police Department together
and occasionally he would do favors for me. He saved me a
lot of time and trouble. The young woman cop who answered the phone told me he probably wouldn't be back until change of shift at noon. He was working a double shift.

Then, I recalled the notebook I had kept the first time
Lance disappeared. For every case I kept a separate notebook and I had all of them, from day one. I retrieved the
small journal and meticulously paged through it. I had
scribbled two license numbers into the book: Martin Tyner's Mercury and the Datsun I had spotted on the way
down to Dash Point, the car we had assumed was registered to Lance Tyner.

Copying the Datsun's license number, I dressed and ped-
alled my ten-speed the mile and a half to Lance's boarding
house. Fifteenth was a busy street and the traffic shooed
me along as I scanned the parked vehicles, searching out
Datsuns.

I sprinted from block to block when the early morning
traffic permitted. This was probably the closest I would
come to a workout today, so I wanted to make it good. I unearthed green Datsuns, white Datsuns, black Datsuns and
even a Datsun with a roll bar and the headlights broken
out of it, but I didn't blunder into Lance Tyner's Datsun.

After a bit, it occurred to me that because of the parking
crush in the neighborhood, many student car owners
leased garages. I started in the alley behind the boarding
house.

Within minutes, I discovered a dirt-floored carport housing a gunmetal blue Datsun. The license number was identical to the one weeks ago at Dash Point. The odds of this
being a car other than Lance Tyner's were monumental.

Tilting my bike up against the paintless wall, I walked
into the bumpy-floored carport, my legs slightly rubbery
from a half hour of heavy cycling.

As I expected, the car was not locked. The registration was wedged under a clip on the visor. According to the Washington State Bureau of Motor Vehicles, Lance Tyner was the owner. I slid into the driver's seat and pawed through his meager belongings. In the glove box I found a well-thumbed copy of Thoreau's *Walden*, a paperback copy of Edna St. Vincent Millay's poetry, a paperback Bible, a compass, an accident kit, and half a dozen snapshots from a nearby drugstore camera department. I shuffled through the snapshots with deliberation. They had all been taken in Canada, scenic shots or photographs of Lucy and Lance clasping hands like newlyweds. Neither one of them was much of a talent with a camera. Lance looked much more handsome and well-integrated in these photos than he had in the one his father had loaned me. I pocketed them.

When I got up from the seat I realized I had been sitting on several oblong splotches. The stains were dark, almost black against the baby-blue fabric. They could have been blood. Or ketchup. Or a lot of things: motor oil, a tomato drink, glue, paint. Blood. Blood.

Slowly I wheeled my ten-speed up the alley toward Lance's boarding house, listening to the echo of the gear cluster as it ratcheted loudly. It was five to eight. Clipping a padlock and chain onto the rear wheel, I locked the bicycle to a telephone pole.

My guess was that a man who owned a brand new sports car didn't trek too many places without it. He might saunter down to the corner drugstore for a packet of Tums or the latest issue of *The Environmentalist,* maybe even pick up a fruit-colored condom, but I doubted if he was riding the bus across town. Lance probably wasn't far. Not far at all.

The blotches on the driver's seat could have been anything, but a little voice in the back of my brain kept telling me that they were blood, Lance Tyner's blood.

In the back of the boarding house, under the kitchen window, I could hear the clatter of dishes and the metallic whisper of pans being scrubbed. Myrtle's voice carped, but the sound of rushing water drowned her words.

I thumped on the back door.

She answered in a lather, soapsuds creeping up her arms and spotting her apron, her bloodshot eyes taking me in

73

like I was a smelly old tomcat that had been missing for a year.

"You?"

"I talked to my uncle the electrical inspector," I said. "I think I can get you out of the jam if you let me look the room over again."

"I thought your uncle was the food inspector," she said, eyeballing me suspiciously.

"Listen," I said, "Lance Tyner is missing. I'm a private investigator and I've been hired to find him."

"He ain't been around here. The boys is having breakfast right now, and he ain't with 'em. I tell ya, he's long gone."

"I don't think so. His car is parked less than two hundred feet from here."

"Don't tell me your problems, I've got enough of my own. The boys say I burnt their toast. I ain't never burnt no toast. They just want to cost me money." We both peered down at a trash can on the porch, topped off with eight or ten stiff, incinerated slices of Wonder Bread.

"I need to go up and see his room," I said, producing a five-dollar bill from my wallet. "It won't cost you a thing. You want to come up with me, fine. I'm not going to take anything."

Before I could spit, the five-dollar bill disappeared into the folds of her apron. She started to lead me through her living quarters, then thought better of it, blocking my progress with her stumpy body.

"Meet in front," she said. Suddenly we were collaborators in some sort of spy masquerade.

In the communal dining room, four clean-cut male students cocked their heads away from the black-and-white Sylvania when Myrtle led me up the stairs, no doubt viewing me as a potential boarder, another partner for gin.

I flipped through his books, searched inside the rolled-up socks in his underwear drawer, even felt under the mattress. One desk drawer was filled with brochures on fish farms and soy bean agriculture. Another was littered with notes from the classes he had been auditing, mostly social studies and history courses. His closet was, as I remembered it from yesterday, filled with work shirts and neatly aligned boots, a tent pushed into the corner.

Eyeing me, Myrtle heaved a sigh, her lungs rattling like

paper. "I ain't got all day to dither around. Some of us work for a living."

I handed her another five-dollar bill. She snapped it in her strong hands with a sharp report, and made her wobbling exit. I closed Lance's door behind her and sat on the bed. Idly, I wondered what Lance Tyner had thought about as he lay on this bed, what jaunty sprites had romped through his brain, pondering how to squander fifteen million dollars.

The sassy razzle-dazzle of a bluebottle fly began irritating me. I dug the pillow out from Lance's bed, ripped the pillowcase off, formed it into a whip and snapped it expertly several times. The pillowcase sounded like a gunshot in the tiny, cramped room.

Shooting into the wall, the bluebottle crashed and spun downward onto Lance's desk, ludicrously buzzing around on its back.

"Thomas Black sends another one to the boneyard," I said aloud.

It wasn't until I went to replace the pillowcase that I realized it, too, had stains on it, black-purplish-red stains that matched the smudges in Lance's car.

Ripping the bedspread off, I discovered a slew of stains on the sheets—light, smudged stains as if someone had undergone a surgical operation and the dressings had leaked. Yet there was something odd about the blemishes. Blotches like this always ran from fresh to not quite fresh, to older, to oldest. To my regret, I had recuperated from bloody wounds in bed before, and the history of my sleepless nights was indelibly imprinted in the sheets. The blots on Lance's sheets were all of one tint, had all, to the best of my deductive reasoning, been put there at about the same time, as if he had climbed into bed, then risen shortly thereafter, never to return.

Painting the room with new eyes, I found a dried splash in the closet next to the neatly aligned shoes. I located several more tiny dried drops on the hard wooden floor next to the bed. Yet there was no evidence of bloody clothing, no soiled handkerchiefs. I upended the tiny metal wastebasket onto his desk and sorted through the contents. Several Kleenexes, none of which were bloodied. Some sooty pencil shavings. The wrapper from a Granola bar. Two pairs of movie ticket stubs. And one uncrumpled aluminum pop can. I mangled it in my fist.

Perhaps Lance Tyner's injury was merely a bloody nose? People got those all the time.

Dropping to my hands and knees, I scrutinized the pattern of droplets on the floor. Under the bed I found nothing but dust balls. I found more splotches by the door, a few by the bed, and then some more over behind the spindle-backed chair beside the door I had assumed was painted shut. The trail of speckles led under the door.

I tossed the Windsor chair aside and jerked hard on the knob, then again, until the door rumbled and popped open. I stepped onto the low-roofed sun porch.

Bloody noses didn't kill people.

Lance Tyner lay flat on his back staring up at me. Eyes don't come any deader than that, a milky film dimming their blue, a boredom beyond all boredoms infusing their depths.

He wore white socks, blue jeans that had faded from a hundred and one launderings, and a sleeveless white T-shirt; at least it had been white at one time. Now it was piebald, splotched black and white. His right shoulder had a hole in it, not a particularly large hole, but large enough to kill a man. A gunshot wound.

Chapter Fifteen

I STUMPED DOWNSTAIRS and squared off with the boxy black pay phone. A sign tacked to the wall said "No Canadian Coins." Punching a Canadian quarter into the machine, I dialed the number Lucy had given me.

A strident female voice answered the phone. I had to concentrate to decipher what she said, which was, "Peebles residence. Cleata at your service." The mumbled phrases were polite, the pitch and inflection were anything but.

"Lucy, please," I said.

"Ain't no Lucy here," said Cleata. She hung up the phone precipitously. I stayed on the line and kept the connection unbroken, listening to the silence. A few seconds later the phone was again picked up, and the new voice was a trifle sweeter.

"Hello?"

"Lucy?"

"Oh, Mr. Black. I'm sorry about that. Cleata likes to do her little jokes."

"Is she still in the room with you?"

"Sort of."

"I'm afraid I have some bad news. I wanted to come over and tell you myself, but I'm going to be tied up for a while."

"Not Lance?" She breathed heavily into the receiver. I had the feeling her sister Cleata was lurking in the background, eavesdropping, ready to mock and jeer at whatever she could.

"Lance died," I said, as gently as I knew how.

I could hear Cleata in the background, moving away, yammering exuberantly at somebody else in the house.

The line fell silent except for the stereo babble of television sets: The TV at Lucille's house was tuned to the same channel as the one in Myrtle's dining room. The effect was unsettling.

"Lucy," I said. "Did you hear me?"

"He couldn't be deaaahd," she said, slipping into dialect and sounding more like her sister.

"Somebody shot him. He died up here in a cubbyhole behind his room. I'll give you the details later."

"You at his boarding house?"

"Yes."

"Who would do that?" she asked, her voice a blur of disbelief.

"I don't know who. Listen, do you have somebody you can be with, somebody who can give you some emotional support?"

"Sure. P.W. and D.W. are home from school all summer. They're here watching the morning news right now." Her two retarded brothers and the college boys at Myrtle's were all fastened on the same broadcast. What a deal.

"Good. I'll get over there as soon as I can. It might be a couple of hours."

Myrtle shuffled out of her quarters, shoveled up an armful of dirty breakfast dishes and edged past me in the narrow hallway, squinting disdainfully. "That's my personal phone," she barked. "I don't like outsiders using it without my permission."

"I put a plumber's slug in it," I said.

The crone snicked the door to her living quarters behind herself like it was a giant clamshell.

"Lucy," I said. "Are you still there?"

The blathering from the televisions bruised my brain. "Lucy?"

A tiny voice crackled on the line. "I'm just thinking."

"Are you all right?"

"You're sure he's . . ."

"Positive."

"He's so young."

"So are you. I know it feels like the world is caving in on you right now, but you've got a lot of years in front of you. Lance would want you to go on, to succeed." I could have kicked myself for saying something so trite.

78

Although I could hear nothing, I sensed she was weeping.

"Lucy, are you going to be okay?"

Her voice was choked with sobbing. "I think so. You're such a nice man. Thank you very much for calling me and telling me."

"Take care."

Next to the phone I noticed a faded sign which read, "Absolutely no smoking on these premises by order of State Fire Marshall." Lance had been smoking upstairs, secretly. That was why he had sneaked onto the sun porch. He didn't want the stink of cigarettes to permeate his room. Yet smoking did not seem a likely vice for Lance Tyner. Save the whales. Save the trees. Save the world. Surely he would want to save his own lungs. But people weren't always logical.

I called the cops, not bothering to advise Myrtle that her boarding house would soon be bristling with guns, badges and the musky smell of working men.

Bounding back upstairs, I mused about the curious paraphernalia next to Lance Tyner's body: matches, a packet of Camels, an ash tray with a simulated picture of Brooke Shields' heavy-browed face imposed over someone else's naked buttocks. In the obscene glass tray lay several butts, smoked right down to the nubbin.

I stood over the corpse and gazed down into his milky eyes.

Wounded, he had driven home, skulked into his room, attempted sleep, then come out here for a fitful smoke, and died. What had he been thinking about? He must have had a thousand chances to get help.

Though his abdomen was beginning to distend, the stench in the room was not yet noticeable. I lifted up one arm and sawed it back and forth easily. Rigor mortis had come and gone. He was cold and clammy, like a piece of clay some hellish sculptor had molded into a cadaver. The flies had arrived. The bluebottle I shot down in the other room must have been feeding in here. No doubt the corpse had been here yesterday, too, when I bullied my way into his room.

Because Lucy's brothers had seen him two nights ago, he must have died, or at the very least, been totally incapacitated, between that time and eight yesterday morning, when he had been scheduled to drive downtown with Lucy to fetch the wedding license. He might have been here as long as thirty-six hours.

The sun porch held nothing of interest. Dusty and streaked, a row of waist-high windows ran along the wall fronting the alleyway. Several overstuffed chairs were jammed into a corner. Dust-covered cardboard cartons squatted on the floor, bundled with twine.

The front doorbell rang. One of the students answered the door. Then Myrtle shambled out, dish towel in her mitts, and yelped. When she got to the bottom of the staircase she looked up at me.

"That wiring's nothing to be ashamed of," she said, wrenching the dish towel around and around in her gnarled hands. "Nothing at all."

"Your wiring is fine," I said softly, as a pair of policemen clumped into the foyer. "They're here about the dead man I found on your sun porch."

She went down like a lump of lead dumped overboard, just like that, sank into a heap. My first instinct was that she was perpetrating an elaborate hoodwink. One of the older students scooted out of the dining room and knelt beside her.

"Mrs. Sheinwold?" he said. "Mrs. Sheinwold?"

"Upstairs," I said to the two cops.

One was a stern young man with short hair curled tight against his scalp and intense eyes the color of pine bark. His tiny ears lay flat against his head. His partner was a large woman in wire-rimmed glasses and a bulky service coat. I noticed she was taller than he was. Irritably, he noticed that I noticed.

They followed me up the stairs and we all trooped through Lance Tyner's cramped room to the sun porch.

"He's dead, all right," said the male officer, mimicking Jack Webb. He kept glancing at the woman to see how she was taking it.

The woman poked her wire-rimmed glasses several times in succession, jamming them against the bridge of her thin nose, tottered around so that she could see Lance's face right side up. "He's dead, all right."

Every time somebody died in their district a cop had to fill out a report. It was old hat for her.

I told them what I knew, allowed that I had phoned his

fiancée, and suggested they notify the father, who might be able to make a positive ID. I certainly couldn't. The one time I had seen him before, he had had a face full of sand.

Plainclothesmen began arriving and soon the "no parking" area in front of the house was queued up with official cars. I put the seat of my pants on the front porch and gabbed with the female cop in the wire-rims. Her partner stayed inside, quibbling with the resuscitated landlady, who thought I should have been arrested for causing such a ruckus, and thought also this was a plot to gyp her out of Lance's rent.

Her name was Olsen and she'd been on the force almost two years. She loved it. She had never dreamed she would have a life as exhilarating as this one. While we chit-chatted, waiting for the plainclothesmen to emerge from the death room and take my statement, Martin Tyner passed the house in his Mercury, head swiveling back and forth at all the cars with blue bubble gum machines on roof racks.

A minute later he hustled down the sidewalk, accompanied by a younger man in a designer sweat suit. His other son no doubt. They climbed the steps and stared at me. I looked down at Tyner's flushed face, while he caught his breath and peered inside the house, as if whatever he had come to see might be visible from the street. "I'm sorry," I said.

Tyner gulped and said, "You find him?"

"About half an hour ago."

"What happened?"

"Somebody shot him. Near as I can figure it, the night before last."

Turning pale, Tyner seemed about to play a repeat of Myrtle and faint on us, only this was not hokum, as I suspected Myrtle's had been. It was the real deal and his son sensed it too, reaching for his father's shoulders at the same time I grabbed for his jacket. He brushed my hand away tremulously and said in a halting voice, "You look for the will?"

"What will?" I knew about it, but I didn't think he was supposed to. I was shocked that his initial response came not in words of grief, but of greed.

"Lance must have left a will. He was too concerned that

I would get my hands on all that cash. You find it? You look?"

"I tossed the place pretty good before I found the body. I didn't find any will."

"You're a nincompoop," said Martin Tyner, lunging past me and up the stairs to visit his dead son.

"Nincompoop," repeated the man in the designer sweats, putting the bone of his elbow into my spleen. He was bereaved and a cop was standing beside me, so I let it pass.

Two minutes later Martin Tyner stormed down, his son lagging behind, looking squeamish. The old man rushed through the foyer, stomped across the porch and jabbed a forefinger into my chest. "You took it, didn't you? You slimy shithead. You took that will!"

"There was no will," I said, trying to remain calm.

"Of course there was a will. You took it and you hid it. I know you did, shitferbrains. Workin' for that little nigger gal, ain't you? Quite a little butt on her. What'd she promise you? A BJ to C?"

I must have given him a quizzical look because he answered me. "Blow job to completion."

"Button it up, old man, you're making me angry."

"Screw you and the horse you rode in on!"

Olsen jumped between us, facing the old man, and I got the sensation that she could handle herself when the need arose.

"We've had just about enough of this," she said, bracing her nightstick in both hands and shoving it against Martin Tyner's bony chest.

He calmed down immediately. So did she. She stepped out from between us. Before she was even clear the old man made a fist and threw it at my nose. I caught it in my open hand short of its target and swung it down hard, knocking him off balance.

Before Olsen could figure out what this called for, the younger man jumped me. He ran at me, both hands knotted into fists, no visible plan in his wild eyes. I tossed him over my hip and hurled him off the porch. He landed with a series of yelps in a rustling hydrangea bush.

Officer Olsen looked at me in disbelief. "Where did you learn that?"

"It was on the back of a Wheaties package."

Martin Tyner rumbled down the wooden staircase to help his son. But the son had already flopped out of the bush onto the dry lawn, battering the shreds of hydrangea off his clothing. "I'm okay. I'mokay I'mokayI'mokay," he assured his father.

Martin Tyner peered up at me. "You're in cahoots with 'em. I don't know why, but you're in cahoots with 'em."

"Don't get your nose out of joint, old man. I don't know any more about a will than you do. It's all up to the judicial system now."

"I knew it! I knew it!" yodeled Martin Tyner, the veins in his neck noodling out. "Shitferbrains, you're in it with 'em!"

"Go home and soak your head."

"You found the will and you ditched it!" said Martin Tyner. A young man had died and here we were picking over his bones. Grief did funny things to people. At least I chalked it up to grief.

"I didn't find it and I didn't ditch it," I said. "There's no reason why I would do that. Think about it. No reason under the sun."

"Somebody killed my son," said Martin Tyner. "Somebody killed him and somebody pilfered that will. I'm going to find out who it was and when I do, all hell will break loose."

"I know you're distraught," said Officer Olsen, moving down the stairs. "But you're right on the ragged edge now. You've both assaulted this man."

"I'm not pressing charges," I said.

"He ain't pressing charges," taunted Martin Tyner, a minor jubilation ringing in his rusty-motor voice.

"I witnessed it," said Olsen. "I can book you two birds right now if I want."

"Don't get huffy," said Martin Tyner. "He ain't pressin' charges. I don't think you can hold us."

"Want to test it?"

Tyner backed down. His son, the fight drained out of him, had already descended the concrete stairs to the sidewalk. Tyner followed, casting unruly looks up at me.

Tinkering with her nightstick, Olsen pushed her glasses back up onto her nose and said, "Weird."

"There's uh . . . a lot of money involved in this," I said. "A few million anyway."

83

Slipping her polished nightstick back into its loop, Olsen turned and surveyed the derelict house Lance had lived and died in. "You're kidding."

"Nope."

"Damn. You're kidding me."

"A lot of money."

"Why was he living here? He some sort of religious heretic, or something?"

I shrugged.

Chapter Sixteen

Two DOUR-FACED COPS in matching rumpled business suits grilled me for thirty minutes, took a statement, read my card with puzzled looks, then abandoned me to my own devices. I mentioned that the dead man had inherited a good deal of money recently, but, incredibly, neither of them was curious enough to request details. They weren't real thrilled with the case.

It took me twenty minutes to drive to Lucy's house.

A pair of broken-down bicycles lay on their sides on the weedy front lawn as if they had been shot and left for dead. The house was a wreck. It had begged for painting since the late sixties. A board had been ripped off one of the outer walls, leaving a gaping hole, like a child without a tooth.

The front door stood ajar. I could hear a television set, though the denizens of the place were not in sight. I knocked.

I stepped inside and walked down the hallway, sniffing the odor of freshly baked peanut butter cookies. The cookie smell was interlaced with the acrid aroma of old rugs, spilled booze and antiseptic Lysol.

I found them in a small living room under a water-spotted ceiling: two young black boys, identical twins. They appeared to be about nine years old.

Huddled over a chess board, they looked up as one when I entered. Though the day would get hotter and muggier, they wore long corduroy pants, skid tracks fading the knees, and long-sleeved plaid shirts, buttons missing on both. One wore horn-rimmed glasses with Coke-bottle lenses, an arm of which was banded with dirty white adhesive tape. The other twin looked at me as if he needed cheaters of his own.

"Hi," I said. "Lucy around?"

"Lucy who?" said the twin in the glasses.

"Lucille?" asked the other twin.

"Your sister, Lucy," I said.

"Sister? We ain't got no sister. We got a sister, D.W.?"

"No, P.W. We ain't got no sister."

"I don't know of no sister." They both looked at me wooden-faced.

"Lucille Ida Peebles," I said, humoring them. It was apparently a game they were fond of playing. From the positioning of the chess pieces, they were remarkable players, both putting up excellent defensive games. *Idiots savants?* The one in the horn-rims caught me squinting at the chess game and wagged his elbow across the board, toppling every piece on it.

"You're a clod," said his brother.

"You lie," said the one in glasses, rearing back and gently slapping his brother across the face, as if challenging him to a duel.

"My seconds will be calling." It smacked of ritual.

"I'm sorry to be the one to tell you this, but your sister's fiancé was killed," I said, sounding blunter than I wanted. "Or did you already know about it? I need to talk to her."

The boys ceased their foolish sport and gawked at me in tandem. The bespectacled one stood up and said, "We din't know nuthin'. I'll git her." He strode out of the room in a lopsided gait.

The remaining twin rubbernecked at me for a few seconds, sizing me up, reading my clothes and skin to see where I'd been and who I was. Years ago in the police department I had been inside a house several blocks from here. I'd responded to a call and found seven naked bodies stacked up like cordwood in a tiny closet. A boyfriend had gone berserk and strangled his lover, her sister and five children. It had taken me years to forget that incident and just driving into the vicinity invariably whipped up puddles of remembered sadness.

I said, "Are you Austin or Halprin?"

"Where did you hear our names?"

"Your sister told me."

"And you remembered?"

"It wasn't hard. Why do they call you D.W. and P.W.?"

Peeping around the house to see if any of his relatives were within earshot, the boy whispered, "They's initials."

"I figured that. Initials for what?"

"Cain't tell you. Only blood members of our secret club know that."

"How do I get to be a blood member of your secret club?"

"Sorry. Gotta have a quorum to vote on it. We ain't got a quorum. You know why the chicken crossed the road?"

"Yeah, I do."

"You know why the firemens wears red suspenders?"

"Why?"

"To keep their pants up." As he blurted out the answer he sagged backwards over a sofa, clasping his stomach and cackling with laughter. I thought he was never going to quit. Like a snake on ice, he squiggled off the couch and onto the rug, still tittering.

His brother came back into the room, glanced down at him and said to me in a stern deadpan, "He tellin' you jokes?"

"Just a couple."

"P.W., you dope! None of them jokes funny! You know that!"

But even I was laughing by now.

"None of 'em funny, you birdbrain. Get up, blockhead." P.W. was horselaughing, his stomach and chest moving in choppy waves now, the mirth gathering momentum, accelerating.

His brother and I went into the other room to let P.W. run out of steam, which he did immediately, springing up and trailing along behind us in a hobbling, affected gait. Both brothers walked as if they had some sort of congenital defect in their leg bones. They took me into a tall, old-fashioned kitchen where a tray of peanut butter cookies was cooling on the counter. The room was still blistering from the heat of the oven, the door of which had been left open to help it cool faster.

The twins gobbled the snacks one by one, stuffing their cheeks.

"You guys see Lance two nights ago?" I asked.

"Two night?" said the one in glasses, talking around a mouth swollen with cookie crumbs and saliva.

"The night your sister went to choir practice?"

"Oh yeah. He was here." The twins shared looks and something transpired between them, something I would never be a part of. I had known pairs of young twins before, and they usually had ways of imparting information that didn't include words, information that only the other twin would receive. One set of twins I had known created an entire language between themselves before they bothered to learn English.

"He come to see Lucy?"

"He alway come to see Lucille," said the one in glasses. "Seems like that all he *ever* want to see."

"How long did he stay?"

"Which time?"

"Two nights ago."

"Not long."

"He say anything to you?"

"We talk."

"About what?"

He hesitated and they performed their telepathy while I watched. Before he could answer, Lucy Peebles breezed into the kitchen and slammed the oven door.

"Told you not to bake," snapped Lucy. "Mama's afraid you'll burn the house down."

The twins each laid a hand out flat, white palm up, stacked it high with cookies, then scampered out of the room.

Lucy's eyes were puffy with grief. She wore a light cotton dress, fruit-colored flowers imprinted across the pattern of the fabric. Her shoulders were bare. A slanting, cheerless light from the narrow kitchen window shone onto her shoulders and cheeks.

Avoiding my eyes she said, "They're good boys. They just . . . Mama was a junkie when she carried them. They came out with a handicap from day one. They were both addicted when they were born. P.W. is hard of hearing. D.W. has bad eyes. The counselors at school claim they're both retarded as well, but I can't see it. They seem intelligent to me."

"Would you like to go somewhere?" I asked.

She shook her head, but she had dressed to go out. The last thing in the world she wanted was to mope around in the doldrums in this house, in this neighborhood, in this state.

We drove to Volunteer Park and stopped by the reservoir. We strolled through the gardens, finally sitting down on a grassy knoll under a maple. The afternoon was breezeless and portended spotty sunshine, the best we could hope for this summer. Already the clouds had broken several times, dappling the city with bright, unaccustomed light, blinding drivers and wilting house plants.

"Thank you, Mr. Black," she said.

"For what?"

"For bringing me here. Lance used to bring me. And for calling me about him. Somebody else might have let me read it in the paper."

"Nobody would have done that."

"You don't have to protect me. Lance and I already had enough problems to realize what it was going to be like."

"Call me Thomas."

"Thomas." The way she pronounced it, the word became melodic, carried a faintly exotic and foreign ring to it.

I informed her of the details of Lance's death, sparing her the gore and feeding it to her at a pace I thought she could handle. She listened politely, wont to interrupt, but holding herself back. When I stopped to let her speak her piece, she bided her time, selected a blade of grass and began stroking it.

Eventually she filled the silence. "It's funny. I'm a worrywart, I guess. You wouldn't know it to look at me, but I am. I used to make lists of all the problems we were going to encounter, lists and lists. I used to think about the nurses in the hospital when we had our babies, and how they would look at us; I would worry if they would treat our baby less carefully. Maybe they would drop it on the floor and put it back into the crib without telling anybody.

"I used to worry about finding a place to live. About whether the insurance people would try to overcharge us. Where we were going to make our living. About taking Lance to see my grandmother. And then this happens." She snickered bitterly. "All that worrying and I never once worried that he would die."

She laughed mockingly and dug her fingers into the grass, clawing up a chunk of it, flinging it into the air with forced abandon. "Who do you think shot him, Thomas?"

"I don't know," I said. "But there are still several other problems with this case, besides who shot him."

"Such as?"

"His attorney, Jack Thomas, told us he had written two wills and then went home with them, apparently to decide which one he wanted to validate. Where are they?"

Lucy shrugged. Her face looked as if it were carved obsidian and I found it difficult to look away.

"Lance and I wanted to get married, that's all." She sniffled.

"Go ahead," I said, parroting some idiotic movie I'd seen somewhere and remembered too well. My problem was I watched too many damn movies. "Cry if you like. You should cry if you need to."

Shaking her head, Lucy said, "I've been crying ever since you called this morning. I guess I'm about cried empty for a while. I wish I *could* cry now. It felt good when I did it. I don't know why, but it felt good."

"You're a brave girl."

Her lips quivered and her eyes swung around until they were bearing on me. "I'm sorry. What I paid you won't cover anything, and now Lance is gone. I don't know how I'll get the rest to you. But I'll do it. Send me your bill. I'll do it."

"You might be better off than you think."

"How do you mean?"

"I mean Lance's will wasn't up in his room. My guess is that you were an integral part of it. He's got fifteen million dollars and even if he only left you a fraction of what he was worth, it could be quite a bit."

"What if nobody ever finds the will?"

"My guess is it would all revert to his family."

"What if his family finds the will first? And it says it's all for me. What will they do to it?"

"That's a good question."

Hugging her knees, Lucy squeezed tight until the muscles in her thin arms flexed and shone, and said, "It's too bad. I hate to see Lance's dreams die. He had so many important things to do with all that money. You know, he was eaten up with guilt over buying that car."

"Is that why he stayed in the boarding house?"

"Partially, I suppose. That and the fact that he was scared. He was so scared."

"What of?"

"Things. Just things."

I watched her, waiting for her to amplify the thought, but she only hugged her knees and rocked back and forth.

Chapter Seventeen

"WHAT WAS LANCE afraid of?" I asked, watching the slender, almost fragile black woman reposing on the spongy carpet of sod and moss beside me. A fringe of pungent carnations laced the nearby walk.

She spoke slowly, in great deliberation. "He was afraid he would be corrupted."

"Corrupted?"

"Lance was a monomaniac. Day and night, all he thought about was that money."

"He's got at least one trait in common with his father."

"It was a lot to think about. You couldn't really blame him."

Monomaniac, I thought, allowing the syllables to trundle slowly through my thoughts. It had been a long while since I'd heard somebody use that term. Ruthie had applied it to me, years ago when I was still on the police force. Unfortunately, at the time it had been true. It was the chief reason she refused to exchange vows with me and eventually married a Canadian dentist who wore a filter mask in rush-hour traffic, a guy who I thought was a sissy.

"I'll tell you what Lance was afraid of. He was scared all that 'filthy lucre' would contaminate his ideals. With fifteen million dollars, he could buy almost anything he wanted. Real estate. Jewels. Boats. Even people. In fact, one of his sister's supposedly religious friends offered to do anything for a grant to finish college. *Anything*. She was only asking a million for it. We laughed. At that rate he could have fifteen flings and go bust. All sorts of plans buzzed through his head. For a while he wanted to purchase an island and launch an experimental society.

"One day after the court case was over and he knew it

was all his to keep . . . he went into a store to buy a little typewriter—you know, one of those sawed-off jobbies. He wanted to pack up and go to the mountains where he could think and type up proposals, various ideas he had to improve mankind with his windfall. The clerks in the store were worse than rude to him."

"You two get a lot of treatment like that?"

"A few people respond to mixed couples as if it's 1930 and we're in the very bowels of Dixie. But then, he wasn't dressed too snappy either. They thought he was just a bum window-shopping.

"It was one of those downtown office-supply stores, where all the customers wear three-piece suits and the snooty salesgirls snubbed you if you didn't look like you made at least fifty thou a year. It's funny how three-dollar-an-hour clerks take on the fussy prejudices of their clients.

"Lance looked like he made about zip a year. He left the store without being waited on, and, boy, was he hopping mad. To him, snobbery was worse than anything. He swore he was going to buy the place and fire everyone on the spot, making sure that he wore the same ratty clothes when he did it. He stormed off to look up the owner."

"What happened?"

"About six hours later he came to my house all sheepish and kind of depressed. He said he realized the money was taking over. That gobbling up a business so he could sack all the employees wasn't worthy of him. It was the money talking. The money was getting to him. The original idea was to do some good with it, not throw a bunch of people out onto the street, even if they were snobs."

Eyes pooling like melted coal, Lucy bit her lip. A tear rolled down her cheek.

I spoke without a lot of conviction. "Lance sounds like quite a guy."

"He had good intentions, he just struggled putting them into action. I suppose if Lance were one of the seven dwarfs you would have to call him Harmless."

Harmless. Given all that I knew about him, that sounded on target. "I used to be a cop here in town. I've still got a few contacts. Tonight I'll ring a few of them up and see how the investigation is proceeding. Maybe they've already got the killer in the slammer."

"And if they don't?" She had understandable doubts about white justice in the bosom of her mother country.

"I'll work that out when and if they don't. One way or another, I'll unmask the killer."

"You're doing this for me," she averred, gravely, twisting sideways and looking into my eyes. "You don't have to."

She was right. I was doing it for her. And I didn't have to. But there was a gossamer, wounded-bird aspect to her that was pitiful and diabolically bewitching at the same time, and I couldn't quite abandon her—not yet, not until things were settled.

"Let's go some place and eat," I said.

I drove her to a small restaurant on Queen Anne Hill, a tiny undiscovered café perched on the side of the hill with an unparalleled view out over the drowsy Sound. We ate a late and leisurely lunch, sandwiches and beef broth, and chatted about nothing—how the city had evolved in the last few years, how school had treated each of us, about the unusually wet summer. It had been the wettest July on record.

It astonished me to learn how little of Lance's recent history Lucy knew. She had no idea where he resided before he had moved into the boarding house. Or what jobs he had held between the time he was fired from the welfare office a couple of years ago and when she wangled the janitorial job at her church for him. People courted in different ways. What seemed odd to me had probably been perfectly normal for them.

After the meal, I excused myself and went to a pay phone, dropped a quarter into the box and dialed Smithers. This time I caught him, making him promise to get all the dope on the Tyner killing. He said to bop over this evening and he'd give me the scoop. As always, he talked like a disc jockey.

Lucy and I squandered the remainder of the afternoon—sleepwalking through the tourist traps on the waterfront, slurping ice cream cones so big and sweet we had to pitch them into the trash because we couldn't polish them off, watching as ferries glissaded across the water toward Bremerton with cargos of camera-strangled sightseers from Japan and Minnesota and Bay Biscayne.

By late afternoon Lucy was frazzled.

When I drove her back to her mother's house, she hopped out of the truck, thanked me profusely, and tried to shoo me off before trouble ignited.

A heavy-set black woman sat on the porch next to two reedy young men both wearing sleeveless T-shirts and ebony trousers. One man seemed bored, ambivalent toward Lucy and me. The other, taller man eyed her shyly.

But the woman glowered angrily. Muttering to the two dudes beside her, she hunkered in the chair clasping the arms as if steering some sort of wild space-craft—staring at us, staring and staring. She looked to be four or five years older than Lucy.

Lucy angled a look up at the three people in front of the house. "That's Cleata. I better let you get out of here before she starts trouble."

"It's that bad?"

"She doesn't know you. She likes to test people she doesn't know. Once she knows where you stand, it's not so bad."

Cleata's face was angry, and more than a little simian. She was a rough-tough ballbuster and if she was Lucy's sister, I felt sorry for Lucy. I wondered how two such diverse personalities could have emerged from the same womb.

"Thank you for the afternoon, Thomas. It meant a lot to me. You're a nice man."

"My pleasure," I said.

"You made me forget a little."

"I'll be in touch," I said. Lucy smiled her winsome smile.

The woman and two men on the porch glared at me until I was out of sight. In my rear-view mirror, I watched until Lucy picked her way past them into the house. As far as I could tell, no words were exchanged.

I drove up Rainier, down Graham and across to the freeway. I took I-5 through the rush-hour mayhem to the U district and wheeled through the smoggy afternoon to Smithers' place.

Smithers owned a barn of a house in north Seattle, not far from my digs. Ensconced in vulgar baggy swimming trunks that had the inner liner removed, he was reclining in his back yard, availing himself of a sun that had only exposed itself for the past half hour. Smithers never missed a trick, worked on his tan each season, convinced it drove the women wild. He had basted his epidermis with half a bottle of baby oil, was slick and tea-colored in the modest late afternoon heat. As usual, there were no wild women in evidence.

He had a fancy set of earphones hooked up to a wire that snaked around his yard and into his house through a window. My guess was he was plugged in to some hard rock. Whatever the young people listened to, Smithers listened to.

Of medium height, he was chunky and not very fit, carrying a paunch like a sack of sand. Balding in front, he inadvertently exaggerated it by growing his hair long on one side and combing it across. Always, one or two strands got away from him and ruined the effect. We had mustered into the Seattle Police Department together, and that bond still cemented our friendship.

"How you doing, hayseed," I yelled, stripping off my shirt and plunking onto the grass beside his flattened-out lawn chair. "Still trying to learn all about that big city music?"

"Black?" His eyes had been closed, the music holding his senses hostage. Peeling off the earphones, he laid them gently down on the grass, sipped from a bottle of diet soda and looked me over.

"You asshole," he said. "When are you going to get fat?"

"When I get old, I guess."

"Don't give me that crap. You're already old. You still working out all the time?"

"Some. I see you're still listening to that stuff." I gestured toward the earphones.

"Hey, it's that new Sony setup. You oughta see it. I'll show it to you before you leave."

"You find out anything about Lance Tyner's murder?"

Sprawling backwards so that the sun's rays struck him at a more advantageous angle, Smithers cuddled the pop bottle on his paunch, savoring the cold spot on his skin.

"Found out enough. They tell me you discovered the body. What is it with you and stiffs?"

"Lucky, I guess."

"Guy was shot with a pretty powerful piece. The bullet went clean through him. There weren't any traces of it in the place where you found him. Nor in his car. They figure he got it somewhere else and then dragged himself there

96

and died. They had to tear the whole place apart looking for that bullet. I guess the old lady who runs the place like to had a nervous breakdown."

"What'd he die of?"

"Shock. Blood loss, basically. They figure since there wasn't all that much in his car or his room, he must have soaked it up in a rag or something and thrown it away."

"They establish a time of death?"

"Died late Tuesday night."

This was Thursday. The twins had seen him Tuesday night, no doubt shortly before he was shot.

"How about his car?"

"The lab boys are saving it. It doesn't sound like they'll get much. They figured he got shot, got into his car, and drove to the boarding house. Took maybe four or five hours for him to die. No telling for sure what he was shot with. Could have been anything. A .357 most likely. They know it wasn't a shotgun and it probably wasn't a high-powered rifle. They figured because of the amount of powder in the wound, it was at least five, ten feet away. So far they can't find any witnesses. They don't even know what he does for a living."

"Not too much." I picked up the earphones and tried them on. "He inherited fifteen million dollars."

Smithers sat bolt upright, letting out a long, brassy-sounding whistle. "You shittin' me?"

"Nope."

"Going to tie knots in a lot of tails when they find *that* out. You didn't tell them, did you?"

"They didn't ask me."

"You still like to push, don't you?"

"They didn't ask."

"Thomas."

"I had the feeling they were going to stick this in the files and wait for a confession."

"Don't be like that. They're working on it. It's a hard case to figure. All the guys downtown are talking about it. I mean, the guy gets shot and then just goes home and dies? What the hell was he thinking about? Was he scared? Maybe somebody was chasing him and he was hiding out. You know what they thought originally, but you just shot holes in that. Originally they figured he must have committed some crime, got plugged in the act, and crawled

97

home, afraid to show his face at a hospital cause he knew he'd get arrested."

"Ordinarily, that would be a good working premise. But this isn't an ordinary case."

"No." Smithers sipped from his bottle of soda. "None of the cases you get mixed up in are ordinary. How'd you come to find him, anyway?"

"His fiancée had me out looking for him."

"The black broad?"

"That's the one."

"She got any relatives?"

"A few."

"Maybe they were after him. You know they don't like white men messing around with their women."

Even though I had been thinking the same thing, I was mildly embarrassed for Smithers when he spouted the claptrap as if he'd read it in the New Testament, as if it were a universal truth engraved in stone. I thought Smithers was above such thinking. I don't know why. I wasn't above it. But then I remembered ugly, angry Cleata and the two men by her side this afternoon. Maybe Smithers had a point.

"It surely is strange," said Smithers. "A wound like that must have hurt like hell. He sure must have been tangled up in something—to hide the way he did."

"It's beginning to look that way."

Chapter Eighteen

I CALLED MY SERVICE. There was only one abbreviated message. One of the Filipinos wanted to know if I would be there to dribble the basketball tonight. I needed a secretary to handle all this.

Grabbing a burger, rings and a shake at my favorite greasy spoon, I sat in the truck and pigged out. I inhaled the polluted stench of the city and wondered about the dead man, Lance Tyner. No doubt about it, he had been a rube. It was impossible for me to think enough like him to speculate on why he had gone to ground after being shot.

On a whim, I drove north toward Tony Tyner's apartment. It was in Lynnwood, in one of those swinging condominium developments basketball players touted on TV. The joint had it all: cedar-shake roofs, a sauna, cable, swimming pool and the standard assorted bronzed nymphets on the far side of pretty.

Tony Tyner. The brother of the dead man. It sounded like the name of a clown. Or maybe a very short person working the sideshow.

It took me a while to figure out the setup, but a woman was keeping him, an older woman. She was keeping Tony Tyner just like her fuzzy toy poodle. The difference was Tony didn't wear a leash and a tiny azure bell.

A second-floor apartment, their windows overlooked the lighted pool. It was cool enough so that only a few kids were splashing around in the crystal-clear blue chlorine. A pair of young mommies strutted around in last year's bikinis, checking out their spindly reflections in apartment windows.

She answered the door looking as if she had just returned from work and changed. Velma Pearl Dupont, according to the plastic tape I'd seen on their mailbox. She wore an amorphous terry cloth robe and ferried the toy poodle around in her arms as if it were a baby. She had a face like a fallen angel food cake, her cranium topped with a Dolly Parton wig. I had to look twice before I believed it. Only her eyes were alluring, a greenish violet, the lids smeared in emerald eye shadow. She was fifteen years older than Tony, maybe twenty. Hell, she was too old for me, even.

I could tell she thought I was about as thrilling as cold spit on the sidewalk.

"Yes?" she said, swinging the door wide to see if someone more appealing had arrived behind me.

"Anthony Tyner," I said. "I'm looking for Anthony Tyner." I knew I had the right place. The windows were lined in trophies, some of which must have dated all the way back to seventh grade. One or two had been chipped and assiduously glued back together. What sort of yo-yo displayed golfing trophies from way back in junior high school?

Stroking his sparse mustache, he bounced out from the kitchen, rolling on the balls of his feet. He wore another set of sweat clothes, this pair made of gray cotton, a chartreuse headband constricting his forehead. His face was pasty and pallid, his arms formless and without any real muscle tone. He was one of those athletes who was never in very good shape, who maintained his reputation on ball-handling skills and games played years ago.

In his dark brown eyes I could see a slo-mo instant replay of our morning's confrontation. He hesitated four steps from me.

Bored, Velma Pearl Dupont craned around and trod from the room, shunting the poodle out of sight. Tony gave her hootchy-kootchy backside an aggrieved look.

"I need to talk to you," I said. "I'm looking for your brother's killer."

"I don't need to talk to you," he said, suspicion etching his words like drops of acid.

"The sooner this all gets settled," I said, "the sooner the inheritance can be divied up."

Gleaning no apparent rancor in my face, no hint that I was going to cartwheel him off another porch, he said, "Come in," and stepped back, warily keeping his distance.

100

He only half trusted me. To put him at ease, I jammed my hands deep into my pockets and grinned. He edged back another pace. The grin never worked on dogs either.

"I thought the cops were looking for his killer."

"So far they're not having much luck. Thought I'd give them a hand."

The apartment was undoubtedly Velma's. It had been decorated by a woman with a penchant for feathers, stuffed animals, gaudy colors, bamboo and out-of-focus Kodaks of other people's pussycats. One living room wall sported a poster of Burt Reynolds posing in the buff. I tried to conceal my aesthetic ecstasy.

"What do you know about your brother's recent past?"

"Lance was a dope. He could fuck up a wet dream."

Uneasy in my presence, Tony paced without offering me a seat. I had the feeling he never wore anything but athletic togs, that he thumbed through the paper only for the ball scores, and that he wasn't really happy unless he was playing ball. And winning. When he glanced at me, he betrayed a grudging respect for a superior competitor. He was one of those bimbos who might take karate lessons for a month and then tap on my door at midnight.

"Lance lived a real freaky life. He used to be a hobo."

"You mean ride the rails and all that?"

"I don't know if he ever rode the rails, but I know he was bumming it for quite a few years. Couldn't find a job. Couldn't keep a place to stay. He slept here a few nights, but he got into a fight with Velma and she threw him out. Kicked his butt right into the pool out there."

"You remember what started the fight?"

"Some dumbass liberal cause he was always yammering about. Nuclear. It was nuclear. He canoed across the bow of some nuclear frigate and got his ass arrested. Velma thought he was an idiot. He called her some names a gentleman doesn't use and she threw him out. Course he wasn't eating right then, either. I think when he got off his feed his brain started shorting out. Understand? Most the time I'd see him he'd look half starved to death. I gave him some vitamin supplements, but I don't think he took them. That kind of malnutrition affects the brain."

In the other room I heard some electronic voices—a televised game show. Velma was talking to herself, or to the tube, or the poodle. Maybe all three. The poodle yipped.

101

Tony strutted back and forth, puffing up his chest, chawing on a wad of tobacco in his cheek. After a while he sluiced a brown stream into a planter, a trickle stringing down his mouth like fish line. He wiped it off on his sleeve. Yummy.

"You living here?" I asked. It was the address his father had given me three weeks ago.

"Velma's just helping me out until I get on my feet." From the look of things, he had been off his feet several years.

"You were talking about Lance. His girlfriend doesn't seem to know much about his past. Neither do any of the people in his boarding house. A few weeks back when I found him he had been with a couple of characters. You have any idea where I might locate them?"

"Couldn't tell ya."

"Do you know them?"

"I never knew any of his friends. Not even when we were kids in school."

"Know where he was living before the boarding house?"

"Sure. Outside. Somewhere over by the bridge in Georgetown. Somewhere over there by the railroad yards."

"You know the address?"

"Wasn't any address. He lived outside."

"He must have been living somewhere. Even if he was only staying in someone's garage."

"I'm tellin' you, man, he lived outside."

"What'd he do in the winter when the temperature dropped below freezing?"

"Hell if I know."

"He was really on the skids, huh?"

"Went two years without a day of work. Not steady work anyway. He used to push paper in the welfare office downtown but they gave him the boot. The way I understood it, he got too chummy with the trash on welfare and tried to bend too much red tape. Red tape doesn't bend. They fired his ass. He took unemployment for a while and then he just sort of disappeared for a couple of years. I'd see him maybe once every six months. When he came here he was really in a snit.

"Some guard or cop somewhere had rousted him and put a knot on the side of his skull. He was ripe as a polecat. We made him take a bath, threw out his clothes and gave him a pair of sweats. Not a cent to his name. Not one red cent. He walked here from Bellingham, he said. Took him two days, and not a thing to eat the whole trip. Can you beat that?"

"No, I can't," I said, wondering what the fifteen million must have meant to him. It would take a lot more pain and suffering than I had ever gone through to know that.

"He was street people then? Sleeping under bridges, eating out of garbage cans, the whole bit?"

"Yeah, except Lance would never eat out of a garbage can. Maybe that's why he was starving. He had this thing about germs. He'd have to be awful damn hungry before he'd touch anything he thought was dirty."

"You know the names of any of his friends? Even one of them?"

"He went his way and I went mine."

"Why was he so hesitant to give the rest of you a share in the money?"

"Us? He thought we squandered some loot we got a few years ago. One of our aunts from New York died. I paid off some old bills. Hell, I had guys were going to put their thumbs in my eyes. Pop invested his and lost it in some freak deal. And Babs went to Europe to finish her education. Waste? Hell, the only person wasted anything was Lance. He gave his whole stash to some candyass liberal running for Congress. And the guy lost! Some gypsy faggot from the east side."

"You said he was living in Georgetown. You know where?"

"All I know is once I picked him up over there. Seventh and Lucile, he said. It was Babs' wedding, which fell through anyway. The groom kind of went off the deep end right before the ceremony. Got drunk and freaked out. I got there early in my Continental and I found Lance wandering out of the brush next to some warehouse building. He looked like he'd been sleeping in the dirt."

"He have mental problems?"

"What do you mean?"

"He was on the skids for two years. Why? Couldn't he find a job? Was he too wired to work? What?"

"Dippy, maybe. But he was never what you'd call certifiable. Matter of fact, Lance was a real hard worker, when he worked. He just never should have gotten mixed up in that welfare racket. At a regular manual labor job he was a fiend. Sweated his butt off. We worked the same job one summer and on a crew of twenty loaders he was the hardest worker on the dock. He had a good work record, except for that welfare office jumble."

"I don't understand why he was living outside."

Anthony Tyner looked at me. "Man, don't you know nothin'? Down on his luck. We're in a fucking depression. *I* ain't worked in six months. Lance couldn't *find* work. He tried everything there was. Finally, he got so down and dirty and hungry nobody would have taken him anyway. Where you been? I'm talking depression here."

He was right. I'd been secure on my pension so long I had forgotten what was going on in the rest of the world. Once in a while I'd drive past a food bank, or see an article in the paper highlighting the New Poor. But I didn't really understand it, was still shocked to hear somebody I knew was down and out.

"What about your father?"

"They fought. Sometimes they went years without speaking. Anyway, man. I got somebody to see tonight. I'll have to catch you later."

"Sure," I said.

Downstairs by the pool, one of the aging nymphets had been doused by the kids, her hair knotted and straggly. She looked at me and smiled. I tried to smile back but it felt more like frostbite than any smile I remembered.

Chapter Nineteen

I DROVE HOME, fixed a snack, showered and crawled into bed, the elements of the case muddling through my mind as I drifted off. In the morning I remembered only one dream. It was about miniature caskets on the beach, miniature corpses and miniature gravestones. A giant booted foot was crushing all the miniature shrieking pallbearers. I was wearing the boot, and cackling.

Dazed, I got up at 8:40, climbed out of bed drowsy and ashamed of myself. Rarely did I slumber past 7:30. It was Friday and Lance Tyner had been dead three days.

I phoned Smithers. "Anything new?"

"Just talked to Ralph Rasmussen downtown. Nothing. The lab is going over the car today, but we don't think they'll find much. Other than that, nothing. The case is a dud."

"Thanks, Smithers."

Fixing toast, I recalled the pictures I had filched from Lance Tyner's glove box. I pulled them out of my shirt pocket, dug a magnifying glass out of a drawer and sat down under a good strong lamp. For ten minutes I scoured the photos, the bright light playing havoc with my not-quite-awake eyeballs. The pictures didn't tell me anything I didn't already know. Lance was still a rube. Lucy was still inimitable. I was still butting my head up against bricks.

Next door, Horace was sweeping off the public sidewalk, using a thick push broom he had pilfered from the park department. Horace was a retired truck-driver. Each time we crossed paths he strived to say something nervy and snide.

"Hey, Mister Black," he said, when I went out to my truck. "Hey, Smarty? You find that little gal was lookin' for you t'other day?"

"I saw her."

He didn't utter another word, just beamed.

I drove downtown and gave the photographs to one of the detectives who had interrogated me yesterday. He gave me a dirty look and flung them onto his desk.

Overcast, the sky was pasty, fluffy cumulus clouds blotting out most of the blue. A disembodied voice on the radio promised it would burn off by mid-afternoon. My job now was to reconstruct Lance's last day and, failing that, his last week or weeks. The cops weren't going to find his killer. I knew they weren't. Also I had to grill the twins and drag some straight answers out of them.

I drove to Lucy's house. Across the street a ragtag gang of children congregated and gawked at me as I jumped out of the truck. I had the sensation something special had been happening in the neighborhood. Maybe a saucer had glided onto their lawn during the night and the boys from D.C. had arrived in their official coveralls and carted off a tankful of slimy beings from Zeldus 2. The twins, Lucy, even big Cleata, were nowhere in sight.

I should have noticed the hole in the middle of their yard and the charred timbers up alongside the house.

Again, the front door was open. Again, I could hear the insidious, professionally lulling voices from a fuzzy-sounding TV set. I rapped. The twin in patched glasses scurried to the door. His face fell when he saw who I was. "Oh, you," he said.

"Your sister around?"

"Which one?"

"Lucy."

"She here somewhere. Maybe she still in bed."

The other twin popped into the doorway behind his brother, simpered and said, "Hey, man."

"You know how to tell boy sardines from girl sardines?" I said.

His eyes lit up like brown fluorescent bubbles. "How?"

"Watch and see which *can* they come out of."

It took him a few seconds to get it, but when he did he guffawed so hard his knees buckled and he tumbled onto the floor. His brother looked on passively and said, "P.W. You a fool."

"You lie," P.W. managed to burble through his hilarity.

"I need to talk to you two," I said. The laughter ceased. I

106

might as well have cracked a whip, the way they looked at me. "It's nothing like that. I just want to know what Lance Tyner said to you Tuesday night."

On the floor, P.W. rolled over, set his chin on his hands, looked up at me and asked, "Know why the turtle crossed the road?"

"This is serious."

Pouting, the twin with the glasses sat on a broken-down sofa in the vestibule. "Nothing to tell."

His brother scrambled up off the floor and perched beside him, mimicking the incantation, "Nothing to tell." Except for a whitish crescent of a scar running over one of his heavy eyebrows, if the one were to peel off his glasses, I wouldn't be able to tell them apart.

"What time did Lance get here?"

One brother shrugged. The other said, "Musta been 'tween eleven and eleven-thirty 'cause the news was on."

"You boys stay up that late?"

"We gotta see Johnny. He funny."

"What does your mother say?"

"Nobody care 'bout that 'cept Lucy. And she at choir practice."

"Lance usually come over that late?"

"Not usually. Sometime he still be here. He usually come early."

"He usually be here all day," corrected his brother.

"Did he have something important?"

"What you mean?" The twin in the glasses was doing all the talking now.

"I thought he might have had something important to tell Lucy, or you guys. What did he say?"

"Just asked if Lucy was here. Then left."

"That's all?"

The twins shook their heads together, pendulum-fashion, like some sort of daffy comedy act and eyed each other. They were communicating, but they weren't doing it with words.

"Listen," I said. "Somebody killed your sister's boyfriend. The way I understood it, you two liked him. You want whoever shot him to laugh about it for the rest of his life?" It took them several long beats to think it over.

"D.W.?" said the one without glasses.

"No," said D.W. grudgingly. "He come here looking for

107

Lucy. All bent over. Think somebody beat him up. Once when Jerry hit you," he said, turning to his brother, "you walked like that for a while."

"Yeah," said P.W., bygone indignities fluttering through his consciousness. "That Jerry. We never did get him back."

"Show me how he walked."

They got up from the sofa in unison and did a fair imitation of the hunchback of Notre Dame. "That's it," said D.W., calmly.

"D.W. P.W. What do those initials mean?"

Sitting back down simultaneously, they avoided eye contact and the one in glasses said, "D.W. stands for Dimwit, P.W. for Peckerwood."

"You're kidding!"

He shook his head grimly.

"Who gave you those names?"

"Gave 'em to ourselves. It's a joke on everybody. Nobody knows what it means 'cept us. Gave it to ourselves for a joke." The one without glasses began giggling again. His brother elbowed him in the shoulder. "Hold on, man. This serious business. This dude gonna find the sucker what shot Lance."

His brother stopped laughing and said, "We gonna tell him 'bout the cops?"

"What cops?" I asked.

"Last night there was big doin's all 'round this place. Some bad dudes in sheets started a fire on our front lawn. We woke when the fire engines come, but guess we missed it when they slapped Lucy 'round."

Soberly, his brother added, "She din' have no clothes on."

"Who slapped her? Is she all right?"

"Man," said the bespectacled one. "Some guys just came to the front door last night and when Lucy answered it they grabbed her and tore her 'jamas and started boppin' her 'round. She okay. She tough.

"They started a fire out in the yard. Lucy say they's wearin' sheets the whole time. That sound like the KKK to you?" He asked the question the way other little boys asked about the Abominable Snowman, all eyeballs and quivering lips.

"Where'd you guys hear about the KKK?"

"Intolerance, man. Lance took us to see *Intolerance."*

"D.W. Griffith's movie? *Intolerance?"*

"Yeah, that's the one. Took us to the University. Boy, was it long!" I thought about the initials 'D.W.' and their explanation. My guess was they were putting me on.

I recalled some other recent Klan activities in the city. A small resurgent band of racist goons had been toiling in the area. The last episode had involved two eighteen-year-olds in the south end burning a cross on a black family's lawn. They had been arrested and convicted, jailed, and editorialized to death in the local papers, though their indignant parents battled it tooth and nail.

"Did your sister know who they were?"

"Naw. They had masks and hoods."

"They was wearin' sheets, D.W., don't you know nothin'."

"Anything like this ever happen before?"

"Just Cleata's friends runnin' wild. One time we found 'bout four, five brassieres in the front yard. Those weren't Cleata's friends."

"Speak of the devil," said the one in glasses, as Cleata strode through the front door. She looked at me savagely. Several people flocked behind her.

One was a huge lady, arms like wobbly ham-hocks. There were four men: the two that I had seen yesterday; an older man dressed like a minor-league pimp who looked batty, as if he'd just been sprung from the bughouse; and a huge football player type in his early twenties, no doubt out on parole. Cleata looked like the sharpest one of the bunch.

"What you want, honky?" said Cleata, running her words together.

"I'm here to visit Lucy," I said, as they circled me and gawked. The football player wore an old sweat shirt, the arms scissored off, his biceps ballooning. The way he was gaping at me, I suspected somebody told him I had recently deflowered his sister.

"Lucille don't wanna see no fat white ass today," said Cleata.

"Anybody ever tell you, you've got a silver tongue?"

Cleata's woman friend waggled her ham-hock arm at me. "What color your sheets, man? Ya got sheets wid ya now?"

She stubbed closer to me, cornering me against the couch, her drum-tight belly bulging against my crotch. Her cohorts closed in on all sides.

Planting her fists on her wide hips, Ham-hocks gurgled, then spat on my cheek.

"Go get Lucy," I said to the twins, who bounded pell-mell across the back of the sofa, absconding before Cleata could reach out and swat them, though she swung and missed at D.W. He tittered nervously, the sound dribbling back from the other room, growing smaller and smaller behind his receding body.

One of the thinner men moved between Cleata and her girlfriend and shook a piece of charred lumber in my face. "You recognize this, pigfuck?"

I didn't have a gun on me, rarely carried one. Six of them had me backed up against the sofa, my calves touching the cushions.

"Look," I said. "I don't even know what happened here last night. Whatever it was, I didn't have anything to do with it."

"Like hell," said Cleata. "You white, ain't you? You been chasin' a'ter my sister, ain't you? Answer me." The tea party was out of control. The china was going to be broken. I was the china.

"You want to beat up on every white guy you see, be my guest. But you'll never get anywhere that way. You people are as bad as the creeps who came last night, whoever they were."

"You a no-good shiftless bastard," said the woman who had spat on me.

"Yes ma'am," I said, quoting one of my favorite movies. "In my case, an accident of birth. But you . . . you are a self-made woman." It came out slicker when Lee Marvin said it in *The Professionals*.

Cleata said, "He makin' fun a you, Mavis. He makin' fun."

"Maybe we should lay off," said one of the thinner men.

"Lay off, hell," said Mavis, tilting her head from side to side with each word in a unique rhythm. "I wanna know what this genman be doin' in ma frien' Cleata's house."

"I'm here to visit Lucy," I repeated, straining to keep my voice down.

Scrunching up her ropy facial muscles, Cleata shoul-

110

dered forward and shook a fist in my eyes. I noticed she didn't tuck the thumb inside where it would be sprained like most women did. She had slugged people before, and knew how. "Lucy don't need to see no more white ass."

"We don't need to hurt dis dude," said the thin man, sidling away from the troupe and promenading into the living room by himself. From the living room he said, "He weren't here last night. Nobody be dat stupid."

Clenching and unclenching his jaw, the football player type wasn't so certain. Mutely, he stood behind Mavis, her backup, her bodyguard. He looked like he might be her younger brother.

Ham-hocks twisted backwards and swung her fist at me, walloping me across the face. When my head spun around from the blow her cold spittle slid off my cheek and lopped onto my shirt. Without thinking, I backhanded her across the mouth. Crimson squirted from her lip. Great, I thought, a bleeder.

Cleata swung at me but I bobbed out of her way, pushed off on Ham-hocks and rolled on my back onto the sofa, bounding up on the other side of where Cleata had been standing. I sprang up and stepped into a big fist, dodging at the last instant. It grazed my cheek. The bodyguard had anticipated my move and beat me to it.

He swung again and I ducked in front of Cleata. She grasped me by the ears and I formed my fingers into a shovel and gouged her just over the navel.

Letting out an oomph, she released me. I pushed her into the bodyguard and caught another heavy dose of knuckles to the back of my head, behind my right ear. It dropped me to the floor, stunned, but ready to crouch and dash through them to the still-open front door.

"What the hell is going on here?"

It was Lucy, her voice sounding like a cannon shot. I stood up, warily.

Cleata said, "We're gonna get him, Lucy. He hit me."

"Knowing you, you deserved it. Leave him alone. Bart? Jesse? Don't you touch that man! He is *my* guest. He's working for me. Now you get out of here." Her tone left little to the imagination.

The men left, rambling into the living room where somebody turned up the television. Without taking his eyes off me, the minor-league pimp folded up a gleaming seven-inch switchblade and slipped it into his rear pocket. I hadn't seen the weapon during the melee and the sight of the cold steel pumped a spurt of adrenaline through my veins. Perhaps I should begin carrying a gun.

Mavis glared at me, breathing heavily through her flaring nostrils, then left.

Eyes like decay, Cleata stood in front of her sister and ground her molars noisily. Their eyes locked for fifteen long seconds and I saw a part of Lucy she had never wanted me to see—the survivor. Before she left, Cleata said, "You brought this motherfucker in my house. Don' ever do dat again."

"Drop dead," Lucy said, in a voice so flat they could have set speed records on it. Cleata sashayed out of the room in an impudent strut she had had down pat since she was three.

When Lucy turned to me, it took five full seconds before the hardness drained out of her. Inhaling deeply, she looked me over for wounds, and spoke gently. "You shouldn't have gotten physical. Jesse might have killed you. He's bonkers."

I shrugged. "He the one with the knife?"

She nodded.

"I didn't want them to think I was a pantywaist."

With that the tension broke and she burst into laughter. "Let's go outside," she said, walking me through the open door.

In the yard P.W. and D.W. were sprawled in the grass like a pair of dogs after the hunt. They must have fetched Lucy and zipped out the back door and around to the front without breaking stride.

Pulling a handkerchief from my rear pocket, I wiped the remains of Mavis's saliva off my face and shirt, then dug two Anthony dollars out of my jeans and flipped them to the boys, twitching my eyebrows in appreciation. Inexpertly, they twitched back.

"Didn't want them to think you were a pantywaist," chided Lucy. "You're funny."

"Thanks for helping me out of that hoedown."

"Cleata's been drinking with her friends all night."

"I understand you had some visitors."

Lucy walked me down to the sidewalk and we headed up the street, strolling under the observant eyes of the neighborhood children across the street. "Two men came to the door, pretending to be the Klan."

"What do you mean, pretending?"

"I knew them from somewhere. I know I did, but I can't quite recall from where."

"When did it happen?"

"One in the morning. When I opened the door these two men in white sheets pushed their way into the house. Mother was out somewhere and Cleata . . . who knows where she was. She showed up afterwards and antagonized the cops."

"What did they want?" I looked her over, just as she had done me a few minutes earlier, seeing no bruises or scratches.

"It was real hard to tell. They pushed me around a little, pawed me, ripped my nightgown and robe off and tore it all up, then they seemed like they didn't know what to do next. The old one did most of the talking. Kept asking me how I'd like to have Klan members for neighbors, what I thought I was doing dating a white boy. Then he said some real filthy things, some things I don't want to repeat."

I looked at her face. Despite her front, last night's attack had rocked her. "What makes you think it wasn't the Klan?"

"I don't know. Maybe it was. First time I ever met any of them."

Suddenly she halted, huddled against my chest and began sobbing, her elaborate composure splintered. She continued to cry as I walked her back to her house. I signaled the twins who were still on the lawn to stay where they were. I was going to leave her soon, and I wanted someone friendly to keep her company.

Chapter Twenty

SHE WASN'T ABOVE WORKING her wiles on the slack-mouthed detective. I think she knew it gave my ticker a little jump-start to have her tilt against me all soft and smelling of the rich, minty odor of fresh wildflowers.

"They didn't hurt you?"

"Just . . . scared me. They barged into the house as soon as I opened the door, asked who else was home, then pinned me against the wall and began pawing me. The younger one grabbed the front of my nightgown and ripped it off. I think he was younger."

"They touched you?" I asked, various gambits of revenge whirling through my brain.

"Both of them. All over." She shuddered. "The front door was open. I just kept hoping nobody would walk past outside and look in. I would have been so embarrassed. Isn't that stupid?"

"It's fairly normal. What happened after that?"

"They tormented me for a few minutes, asking dumb questions about whether I liked white guys. You know. Then the young one did some things and tried to hurt me. A car came by outside and I guess they got skittish. The old one tried to smack me, but I ducked. Then they went outside. It wasn't till a few minutes later I noticed the flames. They burned a cross in the lawn."

"And you called the police?"

She sighed. Her weeping was finished. I would have handed her my handkerchief, but I was conspicuously aware that it contained a gob of Mavis's spit. Separating awkwardly, her need for me dissipating, she looked across the yard at Austin and Halprin.

"Yes, I called the police. Then Mama came home and

114

went wild. She called Cleata, wherever she was, and she stormed over with a bunch of her friends, mostly the ones you saw this morning. They all tried to start a riot or something. None of us got much sleep."

"How are you feeling?"

"It's losing Lance that really upsets me. I miss him so much. We used to spend the whole day together, practically. In Canada with him it was like a whole different world. It's not like he's dead—except that I know he is. It's more like he was called away suddenly and I saw him off at the bus and he'll be back in another week. That's how I miss him. Only he won't be back in another week. Greyhound can't bring him back."

"I guess that's what funerals are for. They kind of cement your feelings. But it won't be for a while. I doubt if they'll release him for a while."

"Hah. You think I'll be welcome at his funeral?"

I abhorred funerals, hadn't been to one in years. "I'll take you."

"I just feel like I have to reevaluate my whole life. I was thinking one way, had everything planned out with Lance. Now, it's all different."

Two ruddy-faced yahoos in their early teens ogled Lucy with cheeky expressions that I wanted to rub into the oily macadam of the street. Immediately, I felt angst. I couldn't go around smashing people because they had dirty thoughts. I hated to imagine how many times I deserved a thrashing for my thoughts.

"I need to find out more about Lance," I said. "What do you know about his life before you met him six months ago? What did he do? Where did he live?"

Lucy pondered my questions for a few moments. "I really don't know. Do you?"

"Maybe. I think I can find out more. Will you be all right if I leave now?"

"Thomas, you've been so kind," she said, grasping my hand firmly, "you're just like . . ." I winced in anticipation of her word choice. ". . . an uncle to me. You really are. You don't know how much it means to have someone like you here."

"Take care," I said.

She watched me shamble to my truck. I wrenched the steering wheel around and sped across town to the freeway. Traffic was light. I drove straight to the house Martin Tyner was renovating above Poverty Bay.

The Mercury was gone. In its place stood a Ford, a nondescript sedan, one of the rentals I'd seen up in the mountains outside Babs's leased chalet. As I trotted up to the porch, Tyner's dog yipped and tried to seize a chunk out of my ankle. I booted him in the hindquarters and watched him skulk away to cower behind a floppy shrub.

I didn't knock. I just smashed the door with my fist. It popped open. Babs Tyner and three big-eyed girlfriends were standing at the end of the hallway. One of the girlfriends was the dewy-eyed dope smoker I'd talked to at the chalet. Babs was still wearing her black velvet get-up, a chink of bleached flesh showing at her waist.

Plodding into the house uninvited, I said, "Your father around?"

"Not here," Babs answered congenially. She raked my frame with her eyes, and I could see I was fresh meat. The other night at her party there had been too many fish for her to notice. Now, I was fresh meat. The notion numbed me.

"Where is he?" I asked, striding into the small room on the first floor, the room Martin Tyner lived in. I began searching it, tossing clothing and chairs helter-skelter. Babs didn't seem to mind, or even realize what I was doing. I found a gun, a .32 caliber pistol, a police special issued before the police decided their lives depended on how much firepower they could pack. It had been cleaned quite recently, smelled pungently of Hoppe's gun-cleaning fluid.

I did not find Klan sheets anywhere in the house.

"Where is he?" I said.

"Father? I have no idea. Really, I don't. It's just awful about Lance, isn't it? The other night when you came up there, I wasn't even worried, you know. You know?"

"Sure."

"I thought you were on a wild goose chase. Lance wasn't missing. I knew he wasn't. And he was dead all along. Funny."

"The whole thing is getting to be funny," I said. I went upstairs briskly, past her three friends who were admiring the craftsmanship in the one completed room.

I was looking for anything. I was looking for everything.

As usual, in a case like that, I didn't find jack. Babs followed along behind me like a tin can tied behind a newly-wed's car, jangling and spluttering.

The lone finished room in the house caught my attention. The three girls had vacated it and were outside looking at the bay now. Over the mantel hung a Remington painting, a craggy-faced cowboy riding a mean bronc into a dusty culvert during a windstorm.

"That's the real McCoy," said Babs. "Father has four of them. He keeps the others in a vault in town. Rotates them in whatever place he's fixing up at the moment." I stood and drank it in. Directly over the cowboy's hat the painting had been repaired by an amateur. It looked as if it had been punctured recently, then hurriedly patched. Somehow it didn't fit. A bookshelf to the right of the mantel contained several collections of reproductions—Remington, Russell and some others.

"Dad's lived kind of an interesting life. Did you know we're his second family? He had four kids and a wife during the depression. He couldn't make it on the farm in Minnesota so he went out to California looking for work. I guess he got into some sort of trouble out there. Anyway, by the time he got back home with some money, they had all died in a house fire. Real tragic. He blamed himself. He always felt if he had had more money he wouldn't have left them and it wouldn't have happened. I guess he's always been preoccupied with money."

"Where did your brother live before he moved to the U District?"

"Lance? I don't know."

"According to Tony, he lived in the woods, under bridges, et cetera. You know anything about that?"

"Lance? Naw."

"He didn't live in the woods?"

"It sounds like something Lance would do, but I don't think he did it. I really don't."

Outside, the mutt hadn't learned a thing. He took another snap at my leg and this time I caught him in the ribs and sent him flying. He was almost as ornery as my old dog, Booger.

It took fifteen minutes to get to Seventh and South

Lucile. I found nothing but a paint company, a chemical disposal plant that had made headlines in the past few years because of their sloppy housekeeping, some railroad tracks, and a few rebuilt business buildings. I parked the truck, got out and began walking.

Chapter Twenty-one

THE AREA WAS MOSTLY businesses and single-story warehouses, the dusty streets rumbling with heavy trucks and delivery vans.

Sweat-stained and bone-weary, I tramped up and down avenues, circled blocks and skulked through alleys. I even scrambled up the hillside behind the Burlington Northern tracks to a pair of caves under the new Lucile Street Bridge, caves that turned out to have been used only by some errant kids who left behind a trail of shattered pop bottles.

A bird-voiced woman managing a neighborhood grocery told me the bums stayed down the street under the bridge on Fourth, the bridge that crossed over the train yards.

"Golly," she said, flirtatiously, "they wander down here and snitch flowers right out of our front yard. I feel sorry for them or I'd sic the police on them."

"You speak to any of them?"

"One stops in here every once in a while . . . haven't seen him in a few months. Summertime like now's the worst. They'll strip your vegetable garden if you let 'em."

"They're that hungry?"

"Hey, listen to me. Last winter we lost four German shepherds in this neighborhood. Just disappeared." Her eyes slowly and theatrically evolved from ovals into circles.

"Under the bridge?" I asked.

"That's what I've been told. Sometimes when you drive over it you can spot a few gentlemen below."

The bridge was only blocks away. It didn't cross a river or a lake, or even a culvert. It crossed the Burlington

Northern Railroad yards. I checked it out, but nobody was underneath.

Prowling vacant buildings, I searched out cubbyholes, any place where a man might curl up and sleep. Ten years ago on the force I had been called to see a bum who had been inadvertently picked up and mangled in a garbage truck after napping inside a dumpster. It was a desperation most of us had never known, could not dream on a dare.

It took several hours to find it. I must have stumbled past it two or three times in my afternoon roamings.

Tall, dusty Scotch broom ringed the side of the warehouse, planted in a wide slapdash strip of garden between the warehouse and the sidewalk. The sidewalk was seldom used since there was no entrance on this side of the building.

Peering into the Scotch broom at its thinnest point, I spotted a tattered coat dangling from a branch.

I crouched down and shimmied into the brush. The place had been vacated long ago. It was a natural little nest where the thickets grew up against the building.

A hooch. It was a fragile little dry igloo constructed of cardboard boxes scavenged from nearby dumpsters. The cardboard had been wedged into the crotches of shrubs, between branches, until it formed a tiny, three-sided hutch.

It was the type of structure a child would construct, or a drunk with the DTs, or a man down on his luck—far down on his luck.

A fellow could die there and not be found, maybe not for years, at least not until the neighborhood curs began strewing his bones around the block.

Squatting, irrationally fearful of lice, I pawed through the meager belongings: two faded newspapers, an empty pack of Camels, a paper sack from McDonald's jammed with wastepaper, and an empty envelope, time and weather having diminished the addressee. The postmark was indecipherable. By holding it up to the light, I could just make out who it had been mailed to. Bingo! Lance A. Tyner. There was no return address.

Yearning for some sort of understanding of the situation Lance had found himself in, I hunkered listlessly in the brush for a long while, losing track of time, submerging myself in the tawdry ambiance of his gloomy little slipshod wigwam.

He may have taken up smoking to while away the time, the glowing stub of a cigarette a welcome companion in the night. Then, encumbered with civilization again, he had been hooked, had sneaked into Mrs. Sheinwold's back room to suck the smoke into his lungs in private.

I wondered how long he had lived here, what sort of thoughts had buzzed through his brain as he huddled here and peered through the dusty Scotch broom at the world. What had he done for food? For entertainment?

When I emerged I roamed down the street until I came to the Fourth South Bridge again. All afternoon people had been telling me bums slept under there, but I had checked it twice and found nothing but some empty camp-sites.

I crabbed through the hole in the fence, walked under the arch and confronted three drab and dowdy men in work clothes.

They eyed me guardedly. I could see that eviction was never far from their thoughts. Two of the men were young yokels, faces burned by the sun. The third was older, his complexion flushed.

"Evening," I said, approaching the old man. Lids like wafers, his eyes were pinpoints of hopelessness.

One of the younger men grinned a screwy grin and said, "You the sandman?" He should have been in a padded ward somewhere, not living under a bridge like a troll.

The old man rubbed a thumb across his crab apple complexion, smiled tentatively, and said, "Howdy."

"I'm looking for somebody," I said.

"Arnie Ulrich," said the older man, extending a hand.

"Thomas Black," I said, as we shook. "I'm trying to trace a friend."

"Lance?" he said.

"Yeah. Lance Tyner. How did you know?"

"Read in the paper where he got killed. Figured somebody might just be around to ask about him. Real sad. Hobnobbed here once in a blue moon, 'cept his politics rubbed some of the other tenants the wrong way. Nice kid. A little idealistic, but a nice kid. Too bad what happened."

"How long was he here?"

"He never stayed here. Just blew in for a bit of chatter

and then sorta faded away. We figured he must have had a crib nearby. But I never seen it."

"Any of you know somebody named Billy, maybe? Or any friends of Lance's?"

The two hillbilly types looked up, realized I had asked them a question and shook their heads. Arnie Ulrich said, "You a cop?"

"Private. I'm the one who found Lance."

"You think one of his friends might have had something to do with it?"

"I don't know."

"Fella named Billy stops by here in the winter sometimes. Haven't seen him in months. The flour mill over on the river is a good place to scavenge. They leave boxes of contaminated cereal and such in the garbage over there. Billy comes up sometimes when the pickings are scarce downtown. Otherwise he's pretty much a city rat."

"And Billy knew Lance?"

"From what I understand they were pretty thick."

Arnie Ulrich kicked at the dirt, his shoes bursting at the seams, tatters of cardboard poking out alongside a portion of ragged sock. His pants were clean, but his shirt, a plaid hunting shirt, had been through the wringer. Strangely, he was clean shaven, his hair neatly parted and combed. The other two were ragamuffins, down-and-out hobos.

"What's he look like?"

"Billy? I don't know. A pleasant enough chap." A host of trucks thundered past overhead on the bridge, drowning our conversation for a moment. "He's rather slight. Caucasian. Blue eyes. Unkempt. But then, all of us are unkempt."

"Where do you think a guy might go looking for Billy?"

"Might go anywhere. But the guy that finds him is gonna check all around the viaduct."

"The Alaskan Way viaduct?"

"Sure. You know. Underneath. Guys like us have been staying under there for years. Or didn't you know that? There's another place too, under the freeway near Pioneer Square. If neither of those pan out, try some of those abandoned buildings downtown. They're usually loaded with guys at night, not so much in the summer like now, but in the winter you'll find ten or twenty guys in some of 'em."

Arnie Ulrich stopped talking for a moment and stared off into the railroad yards.

He said, "You know, I saw that flick *Midnight Cowboy* when my wife and I were dating. The guys living in the vacant building, scratching for a living. You think a thing like that could never happen to you and then one morning you wake up sleeping under a bridge yourself." Arnie flicked his eyes up at the undergirders of the low traffic bridge.

I held out a ten-dollar bill. He shook his head steadily, his eyes fixed on the two other men fifteen feet away as they hogged down some sandwiches.

"Information is worth money in my business," I said. "You saved me a lot of time." I glanced over at the other two men. Both had stopped chewing, their eyes riveted to the bill.

Speaking under his breath, Arnie said, "Do me a favor and hide it out there by the fence in the grass."

Tucking the bill into my pocket, I said, "That sounds like a deal."

An engine chugged across the freight yards heading east.

"They're not all like that," said Arnie, nodding toward his comrades. "But I don't trust those two. Every once in a while they show up with some used clothing or tools to hock. I think they sleep on the wrong side of the law and I don't trust 'em."

"Take care," I said, standing and stretching. As I sauntered off I took a good look at the two men Arnie Ulrich was afraid would roll him. Still dining, they licked their chops noisily like a pair of dog-eating trolls.

Chapter Twenty-two

I WANTED TO FOLLOW UP on what Arnie Ulrich had told me, but I wanted to go back to Dash Point State Park first. As I drove there, I mentally ticked off the weeks since I had picked Lance Tyner out of the tide pools. I would need the exact date, as well as the number of their campsite. I was hoping the family from Iowa would remember something about the two men who had been camping with Lance.

The campsite number the Iowans had used was 24. Explaining my predicament to the ranger on duty, I found him more than eager to help. He recalled vividly the night Lance Tyner had been hurt. He had packed up Lance's belongings and stowed them.

According to the park register, the family's name was Clark and they hailed from Tipton, Iowa, a mere dot on the map. There was only one Clark family listed in Tipton. Using the phone in the ranger's living quarters, I told the operator to keep track of the charges.

The connection to Iowa took only a few seconds. "They were just a couple of young types," said the husband. "All I remember is that one had long hair and mean eyes and the other looked like he had trouble taking care of himself. That one had blond hair. Neither one of them seemed like they would be able to hack farm work. The police out there never did ask us anything."

"How about names? I know it's a long shot, but do you remember hearing any names?" The family kicked that around between them for a while and miraculously came up with Billy and Leroy. I turned to the ranger, shelled out three dollars and eighty-five cents and pointed the Ford back toward Seattle.

The sun was sliding down behind the Olympics and the

bay reflected a brassy tint. Tourists trotted up and down the sidewalks on Alaskan Way, zigzagging in and out of the shops and restaurants on the piers, inquiring of strangers if summers in the northwest were always this cool. When I got downtown, I parked on a side street off Western. I flung dirt at my jeans in an attempt to look bedraggled, knocked most of it off, and began tramping up the streets. I didn't have far to go.

Arnie Ulrich and his plight had spoiled my thinking. A guy could only swallow so much in one day and my last gulp had me bloated.

The destitute were everywhere—if you bothered to look. On Bell Street I found a rust-worn Dodge Dart bogged down with clothing and people, sagging in one corner from a broken leaf spring, jammed full in the back with boxes and kids. A whining dog was tied to the door handle, his leash neatly plaited from strips of torn cloth. Suckling a baby, a woman slouched in the passenger seat, boxes ricked up between her and her mate behind the wheel. It had been a long while since I had seen people looking more tired. Their corroded license plate said California. We all had our pride, and I tried not to stare as I passed.

The first city within a city I located was under the viaduct three blocks from the Millionair Club, a social service organization that provided food and temporary jobs for the downtrodden. Situated beneath an overpass, the camp was high on a humped embankment that had a flat top. I jogged up the steep hillside to check it out.

The whole shebang overlooked Western Avenue.

It was like a play town some eerie children had set up using castoff furniture. The dismalness of the spot insured privacy. Valhalla for vagrants. Three men, two Mexicans and a bearded WASP who looked as if he should be doing postgraduate work at BYU, lounged in broken-down overstuffed chairs. All three of them were shod in heavy hiking boots.

Comparing my hardy body to their gauntness and feeling too healthy, too brawny, I strode toward them. They eyeballed me. "Evening," I said.

The beard only stared hypnotically out at the Sound. One of the Mexicans folded up his whittling knife with a loud click and palmed it, clenching and unclenching it in his fist. The other Mexican gave me the worst half of a smile, revealing several broken teeth, and spoke in his best urban colloquial twang. "Howdy."

"You gentlemen live here?" I asked.

"No, man. My travel agent set me up with this," snapped the man in the beard, slipping into a pair of nearly opaque plastic sunglasses that had a taped nose piece. He had pulled them out of the trash somewhere. My bet was that some critter in Bermuda shorts from Saskatchewan had dumped them.

"You another social worker?" asked the Mexican. "Come up here, ask a few questions, snap a pic or two, then sashay home to the little wife and kiddies and the four-car garage?"

"I'm not a social worker."

"You're somethin'. People don't pour dirt all over their pants and come sneakin' up here for nothin'. What's a matter? Your old lady kick you out?"

Brusquely, I knocked the dirt off my trousers. "I'm looking for somebody. Did any of you know a guy named Lance Tyner?"

The Mexican shrugged servilely. "Me and my brother-in-law only been in the state a few days. We been mostly lookin' for work in the Yakima valley. Just got here yesterday."

"This is my turf," interjected the man in the beard and sunglasses, refusing to rotate his face from the Sound. "These are *my* chairs and that's *my* digs." He gesticulated toward a hollow in the packed dirt of the hill, a hollow with a small tent pitched in it, a mountaineer's backpack nearby.

"How long have you been here?" I asked.

"Who wants to know?" I handed him one of my cards. He turned it over in his hands, fondling the edges with his fingertips.

"Look, guys," I said. "I'm only trying to help somebody, okay? A guy I knew used to live down here. He got killed a couple of days ago. I'm trying to trace some of his friends. It'd be worth a couple of bucks to me if you knew something."

Handing my card back, the bearded man peered out at the wisps of autumn-colored clouds on the horizon and spoke, his tone somewhat softened. "A detective? This friend of yours have a name?"

"Lance Tyner."

"Doesn't ring a bell."

"How about Billy?"

"Don't ring a bell either. Man, there's a lot of guys living underneath this city. Know what I mean? You got any pictures?"

I showed him a photograph of Lance, one of the Canadian trip photos I had held out from the cops. He whistled. "Pretty lady. But I ain't seen the guy. Maybe. Maybe a long time ago I seen him somewhere. But I don't think so."

"You have any idea where I might look?"

"Sure. I've got a lot of ideas. Under the freeway. Lot of folks been there lately. You can try here, too." He pointed down the hill toward the tracks along the waterfront. "But mostly the gawkers scare them off. Leastways, in the summertime."

"Under the freeway?"

"Start at Yesler and work south. You don't find what you want, start at Yesler and work north. You might try Pioneer Square, or one of the missions. People move fast."

Opening my wallet, I thumbed through my bills. A five and three wrinkled ones. I handed him the five and caught a nostalgic and vaguely tantalizing whiff of lipstick off it. They were still lounging on their dirt veranda when I wheeled past ten minutes later in my truck, lounging and bidding a wistful good night to the city.

I parked on Third Avenue and hiked toward Yesler and the freeway, hoping that I was sufficiently dishabille for the denizens of this part of town. What I found was nowhere near what I had expected.

Within earshot of the white-water sound of rushing cars and tooting horns, I located a subculture, a shantytown constructed of cardboard and tents. It was visible only from the freeway, and then, only for a split second, like some sort of subliminal advertisement for our future.

Fifteen to twenty separate campsites dotted the packed-dirt hillside under the freeway. A quagmire of unrealized dreams. Clothing was hung on jury-rigged lines to dry. Two men at the base of the hill strained to hear a portable battery-powered TV against the strident hissing of the freeway. Farther up the hillside a man was mesmerized by a small transistor radio pressed against his ear.

The eight or ten other men I saw all were fixated on the

freeway, watching the unsuspecting faces of Seattle blur past. These denizens did not look as hopeless as one would expect. Just blank.

Seattle was the rock and they were the bugs, clinging to life on the underside of the rock.

Toward the top of the hill where the overpass abutted the dirt hillside, I spotted a man in a business suit. He looked like me, like another tourist; so, I proceeded toward the familiar, headed up the hillside to his lair. We were both just tourists in other people's lives.

His name was Rutherford and he wore a three-piece suit, sported a neatly clipped beard and told me he had been to five job interviews today. He wasn't another tourist. I was the only tourist on the hill. He lived under the freeway. Had been here for six weeks.

"I'm looking for a couple of men," I said. "They both live down here somewhere. Or at least they've been around from time to time. All I know is first names. Leroy and Billy."

Rutherford scratched his beard, using a perfectly manicured index finger, and glanced around at the camp town. "There's an old man around here somewhere. He was set up directly below me, but I see he's moved. Name is Beanie. They tell me he's been around longer than just about anybody. He's not one of us new ones. Been on the bum his whole life. Guess he knows about everybody in town. Uses a piece of yellow plastic for a lean-to. He might be farther up, under the next overpass."

"Thanks. Any luck looking for a job?"

"I'll know tomorrow. I'm a mechanical engineer, if you can't guess. Got fourteen years experience. Have enough in the bank to stay in a hotel for a while, but I figure this is safer. Who knows how long it's gonna take? When that money runs low, that's it."

"Break a leg."

"Thanks."

The camp town was separated from the next one up the line by a concrete barrier that stretched from the top of the hill almost to the freeway lanes. I spotted the yellow lean-to immediately, situated at the top of the knoll, butting up against the overpass. My guess was the top of the hill was a choice spot: less noise, more of a windbreak. An old man in a baggy turtleneck sweater and a navy watch cap huddled over a small propane burner, warming his hands against the heat from a pot of soup. Beanie.

This campsite had fewer people. One of them was a hard-eyed woman crouched next to a slipshod pup tent. She was the only single woman I had seen in this situation all night.

"Evening," I said, approaching Beanie's campsite warily. His corrugated face looked like a fisherman's, old and wise and lined with experience. From the cunning twinkle in his look, I almost expected to step into some sort of booby trap, to end up dangling by my heels.

I handed him one of my cards. He glanced up from his soup but said nothing. Down the hillside, a young man watched the transaction keenly.

"You a detective, eh?" said Beanie, his voice raspy and choked.

"That's right. Tryin' to locate a fellow named Leroy. A guy named Billy would do, too."

"Any last names?"

"Nope."

"Have some soup?"

"No, thanks," I said, though it smelled grand. Bean soup. Was that why they called him Beanie?

"Sure? Could be I could help ya with yer search. It'd cost you a bit. I'm livin' too close to the bone to give charity away."

I splayed my wallet open and revealed my last three dollars. He nodded, shot a meaningful look down the hill, and said, "That'd do."

He continued to stare down the hillside. I fed him the three limp ones and traced what he was looking at, the young man seventy yards away at the base of the hill, the man who had been observing us so keenly. When the young man saw me looking, he bolted, dashing helter-skelter through the campground toward the narrow bottleneck next to the roadway. He had a satchel in his hand.

"That there's a gentleman named Billy. Don't know if he's the Billy you're looking for, but . . ." I didn't catch the rest of the old man's monologue. I hurtled over a boulder wedged into the dirt and sprinted.

Casting a panicked look over his bobbing shoulder, Billy saw that I was giving chase and began moving even faster, as if he were on a piece of film that had been speeded up. It had been a while since I'd seen anything move like that, not since I'd last watched my dog flush out a spooked rabbit and run it down.

I picked out as many points of identification on him as I could—jeans, gray down vest, red punk-rock tennis shoes like the P-F Flyers I used to own. He was short, had curly blond hair cut close to the scalp.

He disappeared past the concrete barrier. Picking up a head of steam that was almost too much for my legs to handle, I stumbled down the hillside.

The hard-eyed woman at the base of the hill had been watching it all and decided to intervene, stepping sideways and purposely placing her body in my path. I didn't know what she was to Billy. After all, they hadn't been camping near each other. Perhaps just another kindred soul. Just doing a neighbor a favor? One grand, madcap gesture?

"Move out!" I yelled, not sure if I could stop in time, even if I wanted to. "Move!"

She did move. As I tried to veer away, she moved sideways into my path. We collided. I tried to put my hands out to make the collision as soft as possible, but even as we crashed she struggled to get as close to the center of the impact as she could, using her legs like a basketball player guarding an opponent. Somehow she insinuated her thigh between my legs.

It knocked the wind out of me, but I didn't go down. I stumbled, twisting and thrashing, but I caught myself just short of a one-point landing on my face. She wasn't so lucky. The wind exploded out of her like a burst balloon and she rolled down the slope ass over tea kettle.

When I got around the concrete barrier, the men of the first camp were all sitting at attention, watching Billy dart across six lanes of freeway, the first three northbound, the last three southbound. In the last lane of the southbound stack, a Chinese man in a Mitsubishi narrowly missed slamming into Billy. Instead, he momentarily lost control of his vehicle and grazed a concrete pillar, generating a horrendous screeching noise.

I got a run at it and launched myself at the chain link fence just as Billy, on the other side of the freeway, vaulted a low traffic barrier and disappeared around the corner of a brick church. He didn't bother to look back. He did not see me pounce on the fence, didn't realize I was in hot pursuit. Who would be foolish enough to follow across a freeway?

Chapter Twenty-three

TRAFFIC WAS NOT STUPENDOUS, but it is never light on I-5.

Billy had traversed the freeway by dodging and darting, dancing cunningly between lanes like a nervous prize-fighter until the next lane cleared, leapfrogging into it, then repeating the procedure.

My technique was to look for a reasonable gap, sprint all three lanes at once, then climb over the low meridian, and repeat the maneuver.

It took me two minutes, and even then I almost got pulped by a Mack truck.

I hopped over a low barrier on the exit and followed the route Billy had taken. Soon, I found myself on Sixth Avenue, the humming freeway long behind, my prey nowhere in evidence.

Like a true hunter I headed downhill. When somebody wants to move quickly, nine times out of ten they take the course of least resistence and follow gravity. Two blocks below me the traffic light changed so that it was green to cross Sixth Avenue.

Billy emerged from behind the pillar of a building and stepped warily into the street. I headed for a nearby doorway, hoping he wouldn't spot me. I wanted to stalk him, see where he ended up. He flicked his eyes both directions in the street like a chary bird at a new feeder. When he spotted me he began running full tilt. I broke into a run, crossing Sixth against an orange, raised-hand glyph. A taxi driver going fifteen over the limit nearly hit me, then tooted. Without thinking, I flipped him the bird. He copied my gesture and so did his passenger. Life in the big city.

Billy dove into a brick-lined alley. I had sprinted and was only a portion of a block behind him now. When I ran into the mouth of the alley, careful not to slip on the smooth bricks, he was frantically scrabbling at doors, trying to find a hidey-hole, a hare going to ground. The other end of the alley was thronged with people queued up for one of the downtown theatres.

Fruitlessly, he scratched at two separate doors, then disappeared out of sight. When I got to the spot, he was around a corner on a loading dock, prying ineffectually at a pair of tall, sliding steel doors. They didn't budge. At the other end of the alley a mother and teenaged daughter along with several couples lined up for the theatre, avidly watched my sport. It was beat-up-a-bum night. Tickets—two dollars at the door.

Billy ran to the end of the loading dock. He leaped over my head onto the brick alleyway, collapsed with a grunting sound, sprang to his feet and tried to worm out of my grasp. I was surprised he could still move. I thought he had broken his ankle in the fall. I had him firmly by the scruff of the neck.

Snaggletoothed, brushy blond eyebrows, pale blue eyes and a burnt-toast complexion marred by weeks of grit, dust and bad living, he wasn't much to cast your eyes on. He weighed fifty or sixty pounds less than I did. He looked hungry. Even worse, he looked as if he always looked hungry.

I twisted him and pinned him face-first against the building, frisked him for weapons, then spun him around and threw him against the dilapidated wall. Bits of crumbling mortar rubbed off the wall and dropped into his curly, close-cropped hair. He had a distinctive and rather fetid aroma.

"Your name Billy?" I asked.

"Call me Snake."

"Damn it, you are Billy."

"You the fuzz? You the cops? I didn't do nuthin'."

"That's why you ran like a scalded dog when you saw me."

"People pick on me."

Even as he spoke, he looked catatonic. He appeared incapable of forming complete sentences, as if he were tagging along three steps behind the rest of us on the evolutionary scale.

"You knew Lance, didn't you?"

Without thinking, he shook his head and tried to squirm out of my grip. Pinning him more securely against the building, I stood carefully so that he could not knee my groin. "Don't know nobody. Don't know a soul in hell."

"Sheeit," I said, loosening my grasp, but not enough for him to flee. "It's written all over your face. Of course you knew him."

"I didn't kill him."

"Got any ID on you?"

He fished around in his pockets and finally produced a hand-tooled billfold engraved to a Frederick Hemstead. I noticed the satchel he had been carrying was wedged into the pocket of his down vest. It wasn't a satchel at all but a woman's purse, all the buckles and straps scissored off.

Jerking the wallet out of his hands, I flipped it open and dug out his social security card, an old dog-eared union card from an Arizona builder's union, an out-of-date library card from Phoenix, and a Washington State ID card. Everything was made out to William F. Greenlee.

"You from Arizona?"

"Yeah," he said. He looked at me unblinkingly with the pale, albinal eyes of a mutant.

"Why'd you come up here?"

"Why does anyone come anywhere? I was looking for a place where things are better."

"How do you like it so far?"

"I ain't seen the sun in two years. You people up here ain't kiddin' when you talk about havin' webbed feet."

Reassembling the papers, he shimmed them all back into his jeans pocket. "Nice wallet," I said.

He grumbled.

"I wonder if Fred Hemstead knows it's in your back pocket?"

Pale eyes fixed on my skull, Billy shook his head and whined, "Maaaaan."

"Don't give me any shit, Billy."

"Snake. Folks call me Snake."

"Do they?"

"Hell. I tell 'em to. It never seems to take."

"I could turn you over to the cops right now if I wanted."

"Jesus, that's all I need."

"You knew Lance, didn't you?"

"Yeah, I knew Lance. Satisfied?"

134

"Why did you run?"

"Ah, what the hell. You wouldn't believe me, anyway."

"Give it a shot."

"I ran . . ." He inhaled deeply and mopped his face with his bare hands. His palms made a sticky, clicking sound in the slick sweat of his face. "I ran because I just know somebody's gonna try and nail me for it. That's why. I just know somebody is."

"Nail you for what?"

"The murder."

"What makes you say that?"

"I know it. I just know it. I smell trouble."

"What's in the purse?"

He clutched it tighter, a hectic look in his eyes. "It's mine."

"Sure, it's yours. Everybody should carry a purse. This Mrs. Hemstead's?" When I pulled on it, he clutched it tighter. "Fork it over."

As if his world were irrevocably doomed, he removed it from his vest pocket and handed it to me. I felt like the sixth grade bully extorting baseball cards from a third grader. At the head of the alley several of the theatre patrons were taking acute interest in our one-sided negotiations. I would not be surprised if one of them had already done his civic duty, pressed some coins into a telephone slot, and sicked Seattle's finest on me.

Rummaging in the maroon purse, I found nothing except a paper sack wrapped tightly with dozens of crisscrossing rubber bands. When I finally unraveled the jumble, it turned out to contain over two thousand bucks in new bills, stiff, almost chalky to the touch. To show my goodwill, I bundled it back up, tucked it into the purse and jammed it into Billy's arms. So anxious about the safety of his cache that he quaked, he held his breath for a few moments, then sighed, as if it were a palpable sexual experience. The bricks at our feet were carpeted with colored rubber bands.

"I ain't spent a penny," he blurted. "I ain't spent a goddamned penny."

"Where did you get it?"

"I didn't steal it. I never stole it."

"I didn't say you did. Where did it come from?"

"You won't believe me."

135

"Lance give that to you?"

"A month ago. Me and Leroy both. He gave us both twenty-five hundred. He was gonna fix us up with jobs, too. But he never did. He was so dadblamed busy with all them lawyers we could hardly git to him anymore."

"Why haven't you spent any of it?"

"I wanted to. But goddamnit, I couldn't. It's been so long since I've had anything like this. Don't you see?" He bared his jumbled teeth and hissed at me. "I couldn't bring myself to touch it. And I been hidin' out from Leroy. He knows I got this and I'm 'fraid he's comin' for it. Lance dead, I don't dare spend a red cent. People'll figure I robbed and kilt him." He shivered.

"Did you?"

Billy raised his unfocused pale orbs and went almost completely catatonic on me, quivering, his eyes turning into marbles, teeth chattering. When he began to slump to the street, I grabbed him.

"You sick?"

He muttered, "Ain't sick."

"What then?" He continued to shiver. His lungs rumbled with phlegm. "Hungry?"

His eyes tried to realign themselves against reality.

"Let's get you some food. Come on."

"Four bits." He staggered as I pulled him along. "Four bits is all I need, for a candy bar. A Snickers'll keep me going almost forever."

I looked at him, walleyed, emaciated, skin the color of ditchwater, his thinking corroded by poor nutrition and countless nights out in the rain. He had twenty-five hundred smackers and he was starving to death.

Brushing through the theatre queue, I escorted him to a hole-in-the-wall restaurant I'd never seen before where the bedraggled waitress flirted ceaselessly with a party of businessmen. When she wambled over to us, she goggled at Billy and me as if we were in a line-up. Billy sat on the purse and hunched over the table, clasping his twittering hands as he thought about the food he was about to horse down. It was pitiful.

"Tell me about Leroy," I said.

"Leroy?"

"Listen, I'm springing for this meal, but there's no reason why you can't spend some of that money. Open up a bank account tomorrow morning. That way you won't have to tote it around with you. You won't have to worry about getting clubbed in some alley."

He tittered like a young girl and I began to wonder if his ladder reached all the way to the attic. "That's an idea. Never thought of that. I *could* probably put it in the bank now, huh?"

"I don't see what's stopping you."

"But which bank?"

"They're all about the same, Billy."

"You sure?"

"There's one across the street. I used to have an account with them. I'm sure they'd take jim-dandy care of your greenbacks."

"Think so?"

"I know they will."

When the food arrived, he swilled it down so fast and so noisily I was embarrassed. Most of the dinner crowd had left long ago. Our bedraggled waitress was the last one working the joint. Having bade a flirty farewell to the businessmen, she loitered in a doorway and watched Billy shovel down food. Encouraged by me, he gobbled down a full meat loaf dinner, three desserts—two ice creams and a slice of lifeless-looking apple pie. He was like an anaconda who engorged himself every two months.

Afterwards, he wiped his face with a paper napkin and cleared his nostrils into it. Then he slumped back in his seat and tried to let his swollen belly settle. He squinted at me, as if seeing me for the first time. "Who did you say you were?"

"Thomas Black."

"You a copper?"

"I'm working for Lance's girlfriend. I'm an investigator."

"Yeah, he used to talk about her."

"Tell me about Leroy."

Billy unearthed a toothpick from somewhere and began plying his molars with it. "Leroy. He's a bad one. Lance never knew how bad. The three of us used to hang out together. Don't ask me how that got started. And Leroy would always be in these foul moods. Lance would bring him out of it. He was like a fucking nurse. To me, too, sometimes. Lance was a good kid. I worried about him."

Whipping out my notebook, I asked, "What's Leroy's full name?"

"Couldn't tell you for sure. Leroy was in a peck of trouble when he first came out here. Used to call hisself Leroy Scroggs, but I think Scroggs was really the name of his married sister. Fact is, I'm sure of it. 'Cause I seen letters from her."

"How long did you know him?"

"I guess 'bout two years. Met him around the same time I met Lance."

"Where'd you meet Lance?"

"Down here. In the Square."

"Leroy too?"

"Yeah. Same month, I think. Met Leroy first. We was kind of hittin' it off, doin' a little grab and run down at the Market. We wasn't eatin' too bad when we was goin' good. Then Lance came along. Lance's only problem was he was a little naive. Plus he wanted everybody around to be as straight-and-narrow as he was."

"You said Leroy was in trouble. What sort of trouble?"

"Not really sure. He came here from somewhere in the midwest, Illinois or some hick place like that. Did some time back there. Lance thought he broke probation, but I guess it was worse than that. Leroy got drunk one time, I mean badass drunk, and he started mouthing off about doing something to some little person. I couldn't tell if he was talking about a woman or a kid. I mean, it sounded like maybe he hurt somebody real bad. Maybe even killed 'em. He was always sweatin' getting nabbed by the cops. He didn't want his name on no teletype."

"What else do you know about him?"

"Just his sister. She lives out here. That's why he came out. He told us he did a few armed robberies back where he came from. Once in a while he'd show up with a coupla hundred in cash, so I speculate he was pullin' one off around here every now and then."

"When was the last time you saw Lance?"

"Weeks ago. Geez, it was weeks."

"You went to Dash Point State Park with him?"

Billy shifted uneasily in his seat. "Maybe."

"Don't fool with me, Billy. I know you were there. Tell me what happened."

The toothpick bobbled between his uneven, discolored teeth. "How you know I was down there?"

"I'm the one who found Lance on the beach. In fact, he was about two minutes from drowning when we got there. The people in the campground gave a pretty fair description of his two companions. Sounded like you and Leroy to me."

"I didn't want to leave him out there, man. I even apologized to him later. Leroy's the one who crowned him. Leroy was pissed off 'cause he knew Lance had all this money and all he give us was twenty-five hundred apiece. Lance kept tellin' us he was gonna get us jobs, that money would run out, but if he got us jobs we'd be set up for life. I guess in a way he was right. But it was hard not to be mad at him. I mean—fifteen million? Leroy and I were expecting maybe about a hundred grand each. Know what I mean? When he didn't get it, Leroy blew his stack. He swore he'd get some of it somehow."

"Why the beach? Why did you go there?"

"It was Lance. He had the car. He didn't want to dicker with Leroy downtown. He figured, I guess, if he could get Leroy out in nature and all that, Leroy would see what he was talkin' about. Lance was always on his high horse 'bout somethin'. Nature was one of his favorites. But I didn't mean to hurt him. I didn't have nothin' to do with that. It was all Leroy. We went down to screw around on the beach and Leroy slugged him with a piece of pipe he kept taped to his leg. I don't know what he was thinkin' about. He grabbed Lance's wallet but then a boat came by real close and he got scared and ran. I put the wallet back."

"And you ran too?"

"What did you want me to do?"

"You didn't try to stop Leroy?"

"Get serious. Look at me. Leroy was afraid of me like he was afraid of wild worms. I ain't stopping nobody from doin' nothin'."

"What was Leroy's plan exactly? I mean, you don't slug a guy and pull a million dollars out of his jeans. What did he expect to gain?"

"Leroy? Who knows? He goes off his nut every once in a while. He just kept thinking about all that money and wantin' some of it. I didn't know he was going to do it, I swear. Tell the truth, I bet he didn't know he was going to

139

do it either. I seen him down in the Square one time smash a bottle in some guy's face. Didn't even know the guy. Did it out of spite. Leroy is like that. Goes off his nut."

"Do you know where he might be right now?"

"Leroy? Hell, no. I ain't seen him since that day at the beach. Hey, man, I wouldn'ta left Lance there if I'd known about the tide. After the boat passed by, I tried to wake him up, but it was no dice. I didn't know what to do, so I hightailed it. I just figured it was safer for little Billy if he got his ass back to Seattle pronto. Savvy?"

"What about this sister of Leroy's? Ever see her?"

"Sure, I seen her. Even been out to their place in Holly Park. We hitched out there a couple a times and had a few brews."

"You think Leroy might be staying there with her?"

"You goin' after Leroy?"

"I want to talk to him."

"He might be stayin' with her. I don' know."

"Got any pictures of Leroy?"

"Me? Are you kiddin'? What? You think I'm a fag or something? Leroy didn't let nobody have pictures of him. That's one of the reasons I think he's in so much trouble back east. He didn't let nobody have no pictures of him. Even took a razor to the family album at his sister's place. Whoee, was she mad! Cut the whole album up, takin' his face out of every picture."

"What's he look like?"

Billy shrugged. "I don't know. A regular guy. He's got this sort of mean look in his eyes sometimes, though. You'll know it when you see it."

"But what does he look like?"

"Mean."

"Great." I could see I wasn't going to get much more than that. I tried two or three different avenues, but none worked.

"You don't think I did it?"

I looked him over. He wasn't a taker. Billy F. Greenlee was a victim. Petty theft, swiping Hershey bars and snatching purses would be the very height of his criminal bent, the apex of his career.

"No, Billy, I don't think you did it."

"You think Leroy did?" He screwed his face up and his lower lip flexed in spasms.

140

"You apparently think Leroy did, don't you?" I said.

"Me?" said Billy, peering around the restaurant to see if anybody was observing. "Damn right I think he did it. Leroy is one bad dude."

"You got an address for his sister?"

"Naw. I don't recall exactly which house they lived in. But the last time we was there she was talkin' about movin' anyway. Her guy is up in the prison at Monroe."

"Great," I said.

"Hey, guy," said Billy.

"Yeah?"

"Don't underestimate Leroy, huh? That was Lance's trouble. He didn't believe Leroy was as bad as he was. Just don't underestimate him, huh? I don't think they make 'em any badder than Leroy."

Chapter Twenty-four

DOLING OUT ONE OF MY CARDS to Billy, I made him promise to keep in touch. A curiously vacant look veiled his pale blue eyes as he perfunctorily stuffed the card into his pocket.

I got coy, paid for his meal with a piece of plastic, and tailed him. Old habits.

Billy was no longer running scared and I let him wander blocks ahead. I stalked him for an hour.

He toured Pioneer Square, managed to cadge money off two jittery women waiting for the bus on First Avenue, then tried to bum a drink from an Indian napping on a bench and nestling a bottle of Chablis. When that didn't produce refreshment, Billy vanished into a tavern. I dawdled outside, window-shopped, and turned down a fat, one-eyed hooker soliciting from a paint-chipped Chevy.

Fifteen minutes later he emerged from the tavern, walking unsteadily, tottering down brick-lined alleyways, unwary. This part of town was an interesting amalgam of the refurbished and the rundown. I had to be circumspect, as there weren't any other people in the alleys to confuse my quarry should he turn around and spot me. Indeed, in the last hour the number of people in the area had thinned considerably.

In an alley a couple of blocks from the main business corridor, he stopped at an old wreck of a building, bent himself almost double and wormed out of sight into the side of the building.

Allowing him a modest head start, I proceeded to the spot. He had gone into an opening behind a loose board, wriggled into a vacant four-story building. Cocking an ear to the hole, I could hear somebody far away, scrabbling through darkness and rubble. The opening smelled of plaster, dust, mold, and fresh human shit. I left him to it, confident that the next time I needed to locate him I would be one jump ahead. That was me. Thomas Black, always looking for an edge. Well and good. It was the only edge I had in the case. The only scrap of knowledge that was even close to an edge.

The past couple of years I had been leasing a downtown office in the Piscule Building, a cozy, view suite on the tenth floor. I shared it with a religious advisor, a kindly, blue-haired lady in her eighties who had the vigor and looks of someone thirty years her junior. She used the office Mondays, Wednesdays and Fridays, and I availed myself of it Tuesdays and Thursdays, when it suited me, and once in a while on weekends. I didn't really need or want an office, but some clients felt uneasy if they couldn't meet you in one. The Piscule Building was about six blocks from where I stood, so I walked toward it, mulling over the case, and watching a patrol of low clouds drift in over the Sound.

Except for a few low-life taverns and some soiled doves accepting car rides with strangers, except for down-and-outers rooting around for a place to sleep and a trio of empty buses and their lonely, red-eyed drivers, the city was a shell.

Lance had been beat up by his own brother.

Lance had been mauled by Leroy, alias Leroy Scroggs.

Then Lance had been killed by a person or persons unknown.

As far as I was concerned, there were several prime candidates for a murder rap. Though I could be wrong, I couldn't envision Billy hurting anyone. Besides, if he didn't feel he could spend money on food, how could he ever spend it on a gun? And why would Lance keep quiet if Billy had done it? It didn't seem like Billy would inspire fear in anyone.

I was discounting the possibility that Lance's own father had been so infuriated over Lance's penny-pinching that he had gone hooly-gooly and fired a bullet into his son. That was possible, but doubtful. As long as the lawyers were still dickering, Martin Tyner would bide his time.

Cleata and her friends were something I would have to investigate further before I scratched them from my list. I didn't really have a feel yet for the delicate seesawing relationship that Lucille intimated had existed between Lance and her sister. Could Lance have gone to see Lucy, found her absent, then gotten into a donnybrook with Cleata on his way out? Could she have drilled him with a pistol? But then, why would he keep mum about it? It seems like almost anybody would be happy to put the finger on Cleata. I was swimming in a sargasso. I needed to find Leroy, then I needed to find the weapon.

On the tenth floor of the Piscule Building I checked my answer phone for messages. There was only one. Some pipsqueak had dialed my number and played a filthy recording into it. I telephoned Smithers at home, but there was no answer. I dialed his precinct and got him. "Just leaving for a tour," he said. "What's up?"

"You're late." His tour began at eight. It was half past eleven.

"I had some paperwork to clean up."

"Anything new on the Tyner killing?"

"Why don't you talk directly to the guys downtown? They'll talk to you."

"This way is better for me. If you don't mind. They weren't overjoyed the last time I saw them."

"Spoke to one of them when I came on shift. Not a thing. It looks like it might be one of those cases they keep open forever."

"How about the gun? Anything new?"

"Like what?"

"Have they found it?"

"Naw. Nothing new at all."

"Do me a favor, Smitty?"

"Sure."

"Keep up on this?"

"Sure thing. But I still think you should call the boys yourself."

I tramped downstairs and walked to my truck. The long hike provided me plenty of time to think. There was only one point in this case I was certain of. Sooner or later, Leroy would return to bully the money from Billy. Billy was certain of it, and so was I. If nothing else panned out, I could stake out Billy, use him like the sacrificial goat. The Billy goat.

Before I reached my truck, I ran across the family in the broken-down Dodge Dart again. They had moved, but were still parked on the street, the children in the back asleep against stacks of clothing, the mother in front fussing with her baby. The man in the painter's cap behind the steering wheel had a practiced look of unconcern that slipped expertly past my eyes.

I stopped, looked them over, then knuckled the window. Eyeing me with sudden belligerence, he cracked the door open. No doubt the window was broken. "Yeah," he said, gruffly. Life was hard. The only thing to do was get hard right back.

"You people looking for a place to stay tonight?"

The man cocked around and glanced at his wife, who gave him a mournful look and avoided my eyes. Her stringy hair had not been shampooed in a week or more. "Supposin' we are. What's it to ya?"

I spiraled a key off my ring and handed it to him, scribbling my address on a page from my notebook, along with directions on how to find my place. It was all over for Thomas Black. He had turned into Mr. Soft Touch.

"This is my house," I said, handing him the key and the directions. "It's yours until tomorrow night. If you can't come up with something else by then, there's an apartment in the basement I can let you have for a month or so."

"No thanks," muttered the man, speaking low so the children would not awaken.

"There's a ton of food in the fridge," I said. "I expect it all to be gone when I get back. Just straighten things up before you leave, hear?"

"Who told you about us?"

"Nobody." He searched my face, deciding whether to believe me. "I just saw you here. I'm not going to be home for awhile, so take it. I live alone. Nobody will bother you."

"We don't need it."

"For the baby," I said.

"I got laid off, man. It wasn't my fault. The whole damn town got laid off. My father. Both brothers . . ."

I held up my hand. I didn't want to hear the rest of his shopworn yarn. I didn't want to know about them. I just wanted out of there. And besides that, my police brain couldn't help wondering if they were going to rob me blind.

I got my truck, parked it in an all-night lot and went back to the Piscule Building and made up a bed on the couch in the waiting room. It wasn't the first time I had slept there. I had to be careful to scram before the old lady came in the next morning. She was an early bird and tomorrow was one of her arranged Saturdays. If she saw me sleeping on the couch like a common tramp, she would have a shit fit.

Tossing and turning, I slumbered like a log in the October surf. Half asleep and half awake, my brain churned over the details of my day, ruminating, chewing the events into flashes and kaleidoscopic perceptions.

At half past six I got up, stumbled into the tiny bathroom and took a quick shower. It was the only office on that floor with a shower stall and it was one of the reasons I had selected it when the old lady advertised for somebody to share the rent. Since I had neglected to bring in towels, I let myself air dry, then put on the fresh set of duds I kept stashed in the closet behind the old lady's umbrella collection.

I had just finished running a comb through my sopping hair when someone knocked at the frosted glass door. "Are you in there, Thomas?"

It was Kathy Birchfield. I wished she hadn't come.

She greeted me with a peck on the cheek, breezed in past me and plunked onto the sofa. She wore a white blazer, white skirt and large circular earrings. A bracelet matched the earrings. Her hair was sculpted into a chignon. She hadn't worn it that way in a while. It seemed to pull her face tight and make her look chic and scandalously rich.

"You look like hell," she said.

"Thanks." I went to the mirror and switched on my battered Remington shaver, the one that nipped me relentlessly.

"No. You really look like hell. What have you been doing?"

"Working on the case."

"It's not going to be one of *those*, is it?"

I shrugged.

"You got anything yet?"

"Hard to tell."

"You sleep here?"

"On the couch."

"I figured as much. I stopped by your place this morning on the way to work. There were some people staying there.

They said they didn't know where you were. They didn't even know *who* you were. Said you gave them the key . . ."

She was apparently waiting for me to explain myself.

"They needed a place."

"That's not like you, Thomas. You don't even give to UGN."

"I know it's not like me."

"You don't have to snap."

"I wasn't snapping."

"You could have slept over with me."

"What about your *cat?*"

"Cat? Oh. That was nothing. You should have called."

"Next time," I said, without conviction.

"What's the matter, Thomas?"

"Nothing." I deflected her. "Just this case. Night before last two men put on sheets and played a little KKK with Lucille. Pushed her around, started a barbecue in her front yard. It wasn't nice. Then I began tracking Lance's last couple of years. That's not very nice either. Last night I traced one of his old friends. Lance gave him twenty-five hundred bucks cash, but he carries it around in a purse, scared to spend a cent. You know those ancient brick buildings down by the viaduct, the vacant ones? He sleeps in one of them. Either there, or down underneath the freeway. There's a regular camp town under the freeway. Reaganville, one guy called it."

"You've been busy." She leaned back on the sofa, threw her arm up across the back, crossed her legs and observed me. "You should have called. I've got plenty of room at my place."

"I wanted to," I said. "But I was afraid I might step in some kitty litter."

Miffed, she shot back, "Thomas, you're insufferable. I thought we were friends. I thought we could talk about anything. I thought my moving wasn't going to change any of that."

Pinching the bridge of my nose, I rubbed the remainder of my fitful night out of my eyes. "Give me a break. I've got things on my mind."

Lower lip jutting, Kathy gave me a hurt look, a parody of a young child. We exchanged glances, then broke into laughter, the signal for a temporary truce. The laughter died off and we kept looking at one another.

147

"You know anything about Lance Tyner's will?" I asked.

"Everything there is to know about it. Martin Tyner and his son were parked in our office most of yesterday morning. I'm sure they'll be there when we open up today. I guess he spent the afternoon at Northgate with his regular attorney, Jack Thomas, trying to pump him for information. What a pain in the arse. The guy is indefatigable. I think he's going to flip out if he doesn't find that will soon."

"You're saying Jack Thomas wouldn't give anybody a clue?"

"Professional ethics and all that. He wants Lance's wills to be found before he gives out any information. As you know, Lance had two wills. It was apparently a toss-up as to which one he was going to endorse. And I'm sure, whichever one it is, it will be challenged. We were hoping you would come up with something."

"Not yet."

"What did Martin Tyner want the other day when you went down there?"

"Wanted to hire me away from Lucy."

"To find Lance's killer?"

"That was the stated offer. I think finding the will would have sufficed."

"I'm sure it would," said Kathy.

A set of keys clinked against the lock on the office door and the old lady—dressed to the nines—trotted in. "Oh," she wheezed, spotting us. Kathy rose and I introduced them. They chatted for a few moments and then Kathy and I left.

"How old do you think she is?" I asked. We were in the corridor.

Kathy shrugged.

"Take a guess."

"Fifty-eight?"

"Eighty something."

"You're kidding."

Downstairs on the street, Kathy waved her hand in front of my face until I noticed it. "You with us, Thomas?"

"Just working on the case," I said. "What is it?"

"I want to know about it. I want you to call me."

"I will."

"When are you going back home?"

"Tonight. Maybe."

"My door is always open."

"Sure," I said. I watched her move down the sidewalk and turn the corner. So did several other male pedestrians. Kathy had always been a crowd pleaser.

I went to a bank machine and got two hundred dollars in cash. Then I went to the Municipal Building and bribed a clerk for the name and address of a low-income subsidy housing renter in Holly Park—one Colette Scroggs.

The addresses in Holly Park confused me, so it took a while to find out that Scroggs had moved. Cupping my hands to the front windows, I could see nothing in the apartment, nothing except litter and discarded Pampers.

"You a bill collector?" I turned around. A Junoesque woman in a babushka and amber coat speckled with cat hairs stood behind me, a heavy shopping bag dragging down each of her arms. She wore glasses and had no teeth, constantly rubbing her gums with her lips folded inwards. Her accent sounded Middle European. She looked of an age to have fought the Nazis. My guess was she had butted them to death using her skull.

"Bill collector?" I said. "No. I'm looking for Colette Scroggs."

"Ain't here," she said, looking like the cat who ate the canary. I could see we were going to be swapping gossip any minute.

"Know where they went?"

Her gummy grin was wet and well drilled. "No. They left owing most of the neighbors money. She owes me three cups of sugar and ten eggs."

"Is there anybody around who might know where they went?"

"I live next door and I don't know. People like that is always in a hurry. Packed everything into a car a couple of weeks ago. Think it was her folks. The license wasn't from around here."

"Out of state?"

Breaking into a slimy grin, she said, "Could have been from anywhere."

Chapter Twenty-five

I HEADED FOR THE CENTRAL post office. Uncle Sam knew where everybody lived. Everybody. It was Uncle's job to keep tabs.

Parking in a two-dollar lot, I trudged to the post office, waited in line ten minutes, handed the clerk a buck and asked her for the address of a Colette Scroggs. It was a simple procedure. Anybody could work it.

A few minutes later the clerk bustled back and handed me a slip of paper upon which she had scribbled the address in Holly Park, the address I had been at an hour ago. She moved to assist the person in line behind me.

"No, no," I interrupted. "I *have* this address. Apparently it was changed. This isn't good any more."

Perturbed, the clerk scratched her nose with a pencil, sized up the growing line and scurried out of sight. People wanted to skip town, wanted to hide out from all sorts of horrors, from creditors, landlords, from spouses. It seemed they wanted to hide from everything but the mailman. We wouldn't want our annual Sears catalogue to be delivered to a stranger. We wouldn't want those nasty credit bureau letters to be shredded by someone else. It would be a shame if the cable television people couldn't badger us.

This time she gave me an address in Monroe, Washington.

A small town at the base of the foothills to the Cascade range, Monroe was a haven for the state prison. It was approximately an hour north of Seattle. A year ago I had practically camped out under its walls, hacking away on a case for an inmate. His teenaged daughter had run away from home, from his wife and his wife's new boyfriend. It turned out the milksop boyfriend had been putting the make on the daughter. We got it all straightened out, in a roundabout, if slightly perverted and ultimately distasteful, manner.

The daughter now resided in the home of her grandparents in Tukwila. The milksop boyfriend had fled and was licking his wounds in parts unknown.

I reached Monroe by mid-morning. At a blighted two-pump service station, an avuncular man in a skewed baseball cap, his mind noticeably uncluttered, pointed me in the right direction. Colette Scroggs had moved to the outskirts of town and was holed up in a shabby, unpainted rental.

All of Monroe was flat and rural. At this end the houses were sparse, the lots large and sprawling, uncared for. A junker Chevy that hadn't seen action in years lay in the front yard. When I got out of the truck, a light mist peppered my hair as I traipsed through the tall, damp weeds. A red-winged blackbird chortled in a nearby bush, sounding like a bottle whistle. A flock of titmice twittered from shrub to shrub. The block was alive. I noticed a rainbow running at a cockeyed tangent to the distant walls of the prison.

Scanning the house and yard, I looked around for signs of Leroy Scroggs. Leroy was nowhere within miles of this place.

A squalling baby riding her hip, she greeted me at the door, dull-eyed and not surprised at my visit.

Colette was trash. It is not right to call people trash; garbage is trash, sewage is trash, kitchen scraps frosted in blue mold are trash, but Colette—much as one felt sick saying it—was trash too.

Bent and smoldering, a brown cigarette sagged off her jutting lower lip. Colette Scroggs's tawny face was made up as if she were about to take a ride in a hearse. Large, and almost as tall as me, she wore a man's sleeveless T-shirt, no brassiere underneath. Her tiny, formless breasts hung like the wet of broken eggs.

"Eh?" she said, as if the effort required to burble actual words was too much for her.

I peered into her eyes, brown blobs, and then looked past her into the house. Ramshackle furniture, a tricycle, two or three pairs of children's shoes scattered on the floor, a ragged hole punched in one wall, possibly hammered out

151

by fist or foot or both. Brother Leroy was nowhere to be seen.

From somewhere in the rear of the house a child and an animal of some sort squawked in terrified unison. At least one of them was terrified. Honking at the top of her lungs, Colette shouted, "Gilbert! You leave that goddamned cat alone! Hear me? You little fucker!"

It almost blew me off the porch.

"Who are you?" she asked in a sandpaper, honky-tonk voice.

"Cousteau," I said. "I'm looking for your brother. He told me I might be able to reach him through you."

"My brother . . ." She brushed a hand through her wispy peroxide mop, tucking miscellaneous strands behind her ear. "Leroy?"

"Yeah. How many brothers you got?"

"Just Leroy." The baby on her hip looked at me as if she expected me to clown. "He ain't here."

"Yeah." I scratched my head. Being around her was beginning to get me jumpy. "You know where I could get hold of him?" The cacophonous squawks in the rear of the house had continued unabated. Now they crescendoed in an undeniable din.

"Just a minute," said Colette icily, swinging around and marching through the house. She tottered, her cheap plastic shoes drumming a staccato beat. I was afraid one of the heels would snap and she would topple onto the baby, who was looking backwards, watching me making faces. I wondered how many babies she had already crushed under her sloppy bulk. She screeched, "Gilbert! You little bastard!"

I mugged one last time at the baby before they swung out of sight. I stepped into the house and closed the front door. The room smelled of sour milk and cheap perfume. I had the feeling somebody was watching me. I scanned the room and finally saw a little person peeking out from behind a water-spotted curtain at the living room window.

"Hi," I said.

The curtains rustled. The little person disappeared.

On the floor near the wall, the wall with the hole in it, rested a fresh diaper, a diaper smothered in feces. That corner of the room suffocated in the humid reek. It had been there a couple of hours, at least. Colette stomped back from

152

her sortie, not the least bit surprised that I had invited my-self in. She lived in a world where men did as they pleased.

"Have a beer?" she said, tracing her tongue all around her lips. I was ice-bound in her conniving eyes.

The little person behind the curtain peeked out again. I waved. The curtains swished and the moppet disappeared. Colette sat heavily on a threadbare sofa and let the tyke roll off her hip. The girl, about a year and a half old, miraculously tumbled to her hands and knees on the davenport and stared at me, wide-eyed.

"Sit down. I got some beer. Sure you don't want any?" I was a teetotaler, but I sensed this was not something Colette would take kindly to. She had the complexion and vigor of someone who subsisted solely upon beer and ciga-rettes. Her idea of a balanced meal would be switching brands for dessert.

The house, the woman, the children looked like some-thing out of the *Helen Keller Joke Book*—interesting, but definitely offensive.

"I really have to find your brother. I've got something for him."

"Like to help you," she said, belching. "But see . . . Leroy's got standin' orders not to tell anyone where he is. When somebody wants him, I take their name and phone number, see, and Leroy gets back to 'em. See?"

"He's quite a guy."

"Leroy? He's my brother." Her tone gave me no clues whatsoever.

"It's kind of important. One of his friends just died . . ."

"I'm sure Leroy didn't have nuthin' whatsoever to do with that. Leroy's a good old boy." Her tone belied her words.

"I'm sure he didn't either," I said, wondering how she knew the death I was talking about involved accusations. When you mentioned somebody dying, the initial reaction was to ask how they had died, not to deny complicity. "The deal is, this guy who croaked was a good friend of Leroy's . . ."

"Leroy didn't have nuthin' to do with that. I told you."

"The guy just inherited fifteen million bucks. I'm trying to find Leroy. He might be in the will."

"Say that again?"

"Fifteen million bucks."

Without further ado, she stood up, her knees cracking, and clopped off toward the kitchen. A piebald cat raced through the house as if it were on fire. Colette clopped back, two beers in hand. She popped the top on hers and tossed mine across the space between us. She did not have much. She was being generous. She took a hearty swig.

She was put together by some god with a penchant for pranks. Knock-kneed, eyes the undistinguished color of dirt, hipless, flabby arms, she was a caricature of the spent woman.

Sipping, she fired up a cigarette. The child at her side watched in awe. Colette spoke around the smoking butt. "How much did you say?"

"Millions."

"Think Leroy might be in the will?"

"I wouldn't be surprised."

"God, I wish I knew where he was." She looked around the room hastily, then drank from the aluminum can, draining it in one swoop. "You wanta stick around for a while? My boyfriend is in California lookin' for work."

"I've got to find Leroy," I said.

"I can put the kids in bed at six." The child beside her grabbed at the beer can. Colette cocked her hand back and slapped the child across the side of the head. Accustomed to such treatment, the tot rolled over like a stunt man, got up and trotted out of the room. I resisted an impulse to throttle Colette.

Chapter Twenty-six

"Sorry," I said. "I have to be south by tonight."

She took a drag on her cigarette. "You change your mind, I'll be here."

"You and Leroy from back east, somewhere?"

"Missouri." It wasn't until she said it that I placed her accent, a weak twang that had been diluted by twenty years of *Howdy Doody* and *Happy Days*. "I came out first cause Carl wanted to work at Boeing. Then Boeing wouldn't take him and he got in trouble at the union hall down on the waterfront. Gawd, the people in this state are so damned immature. Everywhere we go, one of us gets into a fight with someone. We have to keep movin'. Jesus H. Keriste. You'd think people could act a little civilized. When do they turn into adults, anyways?"

"Your folks grew up back in the midwest?"

"They came out two weeks ago. Moved out when Pop retired. He lives in a trailer out by Sequim. You know it never rains out there. It's some sort of freak of nature. It's just like Las Vegas or someplace. That's why they moved there."

"Sure wish I could find Leroy."

"You stay here for a minute?" Colette asked. "Make sure the house doesn't burn down?" She said it as if she had had houses burn under her before. "Maybe I can use the neighbor's phone again. Might be able to find Leroy."

"Sure thing."

She got up and cantered out the front door, leaving it ajar. I followed her and snicked it closed, watching her through the window as she picked her way through the yard to the house next door. The little person behind the curtains peeked out, then dove back into hiding. I went into the kitchen and picked up the baby, who didn't seem to mind. Strangers probably picked her up all the time.

Dandling the dough-faced baby in my arms, I located Colette's sacklike purse on the stove, planted atop a cold burner. One-handed, I pawed through it. Her driver's license was made out to Irma H. Scroggs. Her Penney's credit card was made out to Carl Scroggs. Her welfare papers were made out to Irma Scroggs. In fact, I couldn't find Colette anywhere in the purse, except on a prescription—a plastic vial of tiny white pills prescribed for 'nerves'. The photograph on her driver's license showed her hair as tangerine-red.

Most of their meager belongings were thrown into battered cardboard boxes. I sorted through seven boxes in the kitchen, then went into the hallway. A tyke in one of the empty bedrooms looked up from a fresco he was daubing on the wall in scarlet lipstick.

"Nice picture," I said. He beamed, his diapers drooping at half mast. His little sister in my arms began blowing bubbles, noisy bubbles that sounded like a tiny outboard motor. Spit dribbled off her stubby chin onto my sleeve.

Kneeling, I quickly fumbled through five more cardboard boxes in the hallway. Nobody had bothered to pack any of them. The belongings were just tossed helter-skelter into boxes. The jackpot was in a corner of the living room. I made a quick check of the front window. Colette was still next door.

Gently, I grabbed and squeezed the tiny head behind the curtains, said, "Hi, guy," and pulled a picture album out of one of the boxes.

The baby still on one arm, I crouched and split the album open over one knee. It was half empty, a pathetic offering to time. I found several photos that must have been taken in Missouri. I also found three grade school composites. Irma Scroggs was not hard to pick out in any of them, though as a youth her hair had been rust-colored, not tangerine or peroxide blonde. I ran my finger across the legend and traced her maiden name. Irma Hutchcroft. Voila! Leroy's last name was Hutchcroft. The computer was bound to get a fix on him now.

In the contemporary photos I gleaned nothing. Colette (Irma) had apparently posed for a photo with every man she had ever met. She had five kids. Not one of the three I had seen so far looked as if he had been sired by the same father. I could only guess how many men she had been with. My conservative estimate was: every man in Missouri.

At the back of the photo album, I discovered four pictures of brother Leroy. In each picture somebody had taken a knife and sliced out his face. In two of the pictures the crude knife work had effaced most of the picture, ruining it. Except for Colette in a corner plopped in the lap of a gentleman who looked like he'd flunked Remedial Reading IV, she probably would have thrown them out.

In one photo the knife work had only taken the head off Leroy Scroggs. From the neck down I could plainly see what he looked like. Lean. Thin, yet muscular. He wore a sleeveless black T-shirt. On his right shoulder I noticed something. I had seen this man before. In the last few days, in fact. A butterfly tattoo lay on his right shoulder like a stain, or more like a large thumbprint.

Colette barged through the kitchen door. I removed the photo from the album and slid it inside my jacket. I folded up the album and dropped it back into its cardboard nook. She didn't notice. She was all burned up.

"Some people have all the nerve," she said, picking up my beer from the floor and gulping from it. "That old battle-ax really burns me. If she wasn't so old, I'd smack her right across the chops. I almost did anyway. What a bitch."

"What happened?" I set the child down and patted her head. She looked up at me, her brittle blue eyes unsmiling.

"My neighbors. She seen little Dewitt last night bumming cigarettes and had the nerve to tell me he shouldn't oughta be up that late. Twelve-thirty? You kidding me? I was the one who woke him up. I needed cigarettes. I'm stuck here all day. I ain't got no car. So I sent the kid out for ciggies. What's the big deal? You see anything wrong with that?"

"How old is Dewitt?"

"Eight."

I shrugged. I did not like getting into it with clients, or with sources. It didn't pay to muddy the waters.

"No, really. You see anything wrong with that?"

"Yeah. I'd say you're out of line sending him out to beg a

smoke off one of the neighbors in the middle of the night. I'd definitely say you're out of line."

"Well, fuck you!" Her face took three seconds to turn livid. Her ears went bright scarlet. She gulped from the Olympia can again, as if to douse the internal fires, then said, "Get the fuck out of my house!"

I left.

Following me, she harangued until I was out of the front yard. "What's your first name anyway, Mr. Cousteau?" She was getting ugly now, her face contorting as if spitting, her lips forming the funnel of a pale trumpet. Squabbling was a pastime she had honed with practice.

"Me? Jacques."

"A goddamned Frenchman, huh?"

The tot behind the curtains was visible from outside. Jam on his cheeks, he watched me intently. I formed an imaginary gun of my thumb and fingers, pointed it at him, and shot. I smiled. His sullen expression did not change, though his tongue moved into one cheek in an effort to stave off something that might have been the beginning of a smile.

"Jacques Cousteau. I'll remember that name, you asshole! I'm going to report you to the sheriff! Come in here, drink my beer, tell me I don't know how to raise my own kids, make a pass at me . . ."

"A pass?"

"Yeah, a pass. You want into my pants something fierce."

"Good luck with the sheriff, honey."

Chapter Twenty-seven

CATTY-CORNERED FROM A GAS STATION where I tanked up on the way out of town, I located a phone booth. I wedged myself into it, broke open the dog-eared book and looked up the local CPS chapter, a county unit.

The lady at Children's Protective Service took careful notes. I gave her Scroggs's address in Seattle too. I didn't have high hopes they would correct the situation; CPS was so swamped it had to be a pretty severe case before they tackled it. Sending your kid next door at midnight for cigarettes or swatting a toddler across the face was small potatoes compared to some of the downright gruesome child-rearing practices they routinely ran up against.

Highway 203 took me down through the valley, through Duvall, past Carnation, through farming land dotted with ramshackle barns, broken-down barbed wire fences and a smattering of complacent Holsteins. Though the sky was layered in gray, it was warming up now, growing muggy. The air felt like the air in a cramped, unventilated bathroom five minutes after someone had drawn a hot tub. I drove past Fall City and into the foothills, cranking the wing window wide, letting the highway air bombard my face.

I had no idea whether or not Babs was still running her fandango, but I knew of nowhere else to look. The last time I saw him, the man with the butterfly tattoo was living off her largess. If the party was still humming along, I figured the chances were good that Leroy Hutchcroft, alias Leroy Scroggs, would still be there, humming right along with it.

It took me a while to locate the summer cabin. At this elevation, the sky was striated with an azure blue. Snow capped a nearby peak. The sun shone through in patches.

Rumbling through the walls of the building, the din was louder than it had been the other night.

I parked my truck next to Martin Tyner's Mercury, pocketed the keys and, like a simpleton, without plot or constructive thought, trotted up the steps to the chalet. On the porch the floorboards vibrated under the load of the house.

I waded into the party, neck-deep in dancing young men and women. We were all smothered in decibels. The first floor was a combination of wild dancers and game-playing zombies, buglike video eyes riveted to consoles. I felt like an amoeba on a platter.

Waves of body heat emanated from the congregation. Sweat dribbled out of my hair and down my cheeks. I didn't recognize a soul on the first floor. Twice as many people were packed into the chalet as the other night. I left the front door open but a minute later a suction from the heat of the bodies slammed it shut.

Leroy mingled on the second level, half a flight up from the abbreviated first floor. He disappeared into the herd before I could see who he was with. Sauntering, gabbing, laughing, he had appeared to be in no hurry. I would flush him out.

I picked my way up to the second level, stepping over a prone couple pawing one another and swapping spit.

The room was dominated by a huge picnic table laden with food. Video games lined the walls, all hot with use. Beer was being dispensed from a keg. Soft drinks were impregnated in a mountain of chipped ice in a cooler. The pungent odor of burning hashish assailed my nostrils. I heard somebody nearby say "Things go better with coke." He wasn't talking about the cola.

These types were easy to peg. In my short college career I had been surrounded by similar minds. It's fashionable, so why not do it? A little weed. A little snort. It won't hurt. In a year they would quit. In five they would forget it had ever happened. In ten, should anyone ask, they would deny it.

Sidling into the crush, I elbowed my way through the jitterbugging figures and across the floor. Women pressed into me. A man accidentally kicked my shin. Another young man brayed like a stir-crazed donkey in a pen. Before I could get to Leroy, Martin Tyner barked at me.

"Black! Black!" He sounded like a quacking duck. He still had not calmed down, and probably wouldn't until he had spent a good portion of the money.

I twisted in the melee of dancers, waiting for him to pounce, ready for either theatrics or fisticuffs. "Black! You find out anything?"

"Mr. Tyner. How nice to see you again." I was surprised he was not swinging his knobby fists, surprised and mildly disappointed.

"Goddamn it, what'd you find out?"

"What are you doing here?" I asked.

"Came to visit Barbara. But I can't take this commotion anymore. What have you found out?"

"You can speak to the police, or you can speak to my client. I won't divulge a thing."

"The nigger? She'd probably charge me an arm and a leg if I asked her something."

"That's a tack I doubt she's thought of," I said. "I'll be certain to suggest it."

"Listen, Black . . ." He grasped my arm and pushed on it, attempting to steer me off into a corner. I spotted his preening son on the balcony chatting with a brunette in patch-pocket hiking shorts and a purple leotard top. I did not budge when Martin Tyner yanked my elbow. After the second yank he stopped trying. His breath smelled of beer and something worse, offal. His yellow teeth were speckled with bits of food. No doubt he had been too busy the last few days to say his prayers and floss.

"Listen, Black. The lawyers tell me you're a man of integrity. They tell me . . . I suppose I was wrong about you. Ethics. They say you've got ethics. What do you say? Tell me where that will is?"

As he spoke, one record ended and another began. When the relative calm of the record change had subsided into uproar again, I looked at him. "Why don't you go home and pound nails or kick your dog?"

"You came up here? For why?" He was so agitated he barely made sense. I noted, too, that there was no residue of our former disagreeable encounters on him. Not in his voice. Not in his eyes. Not in the way he seized my arm and leaned into me to speak above the roar. No. Something bigger than petty bickering had swallowed his psyche. "You

161

came to see Babs? I'll get her for you. What? Does she have the wills? Does she know where they are?"

"The killer knows where they are," I said.

It stopped him in his tracks. "The killer?"

"Yeah. Whoever killed your son."

Tyner looked like a man trying to stuff ten pounds of shit into a five-pound bag.

"Your son? The one who was shot? He probably had the wills with him at the time. Since they're gone now, I can only guess that the person or persons who shot him has them. Either that or Lance ditched them somewhere near the scene of the crime."

My thinking was far too serpentine for him to follow in his present state. To Martin Tyner, it was all gobbledygook.

I brushed him off, left him gasping for breath among the dancers and went looking for Leroy.

Chitchat with Martin Tyner had sharpened my thinking. I was not afraid of Leroy. Perhaps I was being stupid, but I was larger than he, and, when it came right down to it, despite his reputation, I was probably meaner. But I did not carry a gun and sometimes I wished I did. It was a rare day when I needed one, but then, this might be that day.

Not since the night I put a bullet into a teenaged boy's eye had I been dependable with a gun. It had happened years ago, when I was still on the police force. The boy had hot-wired and swiped a Volvo. Then he had cornered me on foot in one of the narrow downtown alleyways and tried his best to crush me against a wall. I had been a dead shot. I aimed, squeezed and put a bullet into his face. Right through the windshield of the car. I had been justified. Assuredly, I had been. My partner testified in my behalf. Two civilian witnesses even testified for me. But he was dead. To his mother and father and sisters he was only a dead boy.

And that did not help me sleep any better.

I was never able to use a gun again, at least not reliably. Now, if I snatched up a pistol in anger, it only trembled in my fist. I had come to the conclusion that I was better off without one. The only hitch: Leroy Hutchcroft Scroggs was known to carry a length of pipe taped to his calf. Indeed, if he had killed Lance, he probably had a pistol on him as well.

I would have to take him by surprise.

But first, I had another chore.

In a room off the kitchen, I found a telephone. I called Seattle, billing it to my home phone. Smithers had been off-shift for several hours, enough time to be sound asleep. I dialed anyway. He lifted the receiver on the third ring.

"Smitty?"

"No, Thomas. Don't tell me it's you. Every time you get on a case you do this to me."

"Disconnect your phone if you need sleep. You answer it, I figure you're up."

"Dammit, Thomas."

"Okay, I owe you. I'll take you out to dinner. I'll introduce you to someone."

"Who? What's her name?" Since his wife had run off with her Spanish professor, Smithers was invariably hard up for a date. "What's her name, Thomas?"

"Babs."

"Babs?"

"You'll love her. She's just your type."

"What's she look like?"

My words were mellow and misleading. "Last time I saw her she was wearing black velvet. Nothing but black velvet."

"Hot dog!"

"Leroy Hutchcroft. Can you get me something on that name? It's an emergency. He's from Missouri. I'm up here with him right now and I need to know."

"Sounds like a party?"

"This is Babs's place. There's always a party here. Until the money runs out."

"Hot dog! Spell that last name for me, Thomas." I spelled. Then I gave him my number and hung up. I didn't know how Smithers took it so well, my breaking into his naps. To me it was noon. To him, this was one in the morning. He worked the eight P.M. to four A.M. shift. He had probably been asleep three or four hours.

Chirps and squawks issued from the party rooms, overflowing from time to time into the kitchen, past the small telephone room I had commandeered.

Through the crowd I caught fleeting glimpses of Leroy. Six or seven gold chains dangling from his neck, he wore a silk shirt the color of overripe strawberries and skin-tight

163

black leather pants. His straggly hair flowing, he cut rather a dashing, if not villainous figure. Something hard and malevolent glinted in his eyes.

Babs followed him around the gathering like a puppy.

It made sense that a weasel like Leroy Hutchcroft, sensing Lance's generosity had been plumbed to its depths, would seek out another well to plumb. No doubt Lance had innocently groused about his sister's spendthrift ways, about her naivete, not realizing Leroy was filing it all away for future reference.

Waiting, jittery with anticipation, I ogled the jiggling dancers. It had been quite a while since I had been around a bunch of young people. Not since the last time Kathy had dragged me off to a school party.

Though drugs were being dispensed, I sensed that a lot of these kids were not taking them, were only bent on having an old-fashioned Good Time. When the phone rang, I snapped out of my daze.

"Yeah?"

"Thomas? You really got a fellow named Leroy Hutchcroft up there, you better call for help. A and D."

I peeked out at the crowd. He was gone. Without thinking, I said, "A and D?"

"Armed and dangerous. He served time in Illinois for armed robbery. Then he jumped parole after beating up his girlfriend. She's in a wheelchair now. He's also wanted in connection with a cop killing in Chicago. He's got a sheet that goes back farther than you wanta know. Just call the cops and stand clear. There's a warrant on him from Missouri for parole violation and one from Illinois for bail jumping and armed robbery. The FBI is looking for him."

"How about distinguishing marks?" A pulse was jumping in my neck. Things were finally going my way.

"I wrote it all down. Let me check." I could hear paper rustling. "A scar running down his neck toward the left shoulder, the result of an altercation while he was serving time in Joliet. Brown and brown. Five-ten. One fifty-two. Not that big, but they say he's nasty. Oh yeah, a tattoo on his left buttock that says 'If you're reading this—I love you' and one on his right shoulder."

"What's the one on his shoulder?"

"A butterfly."

"That's all I needed to hear."

164

"He's known to use a gun, a knife, brass knuckles, you name it. He beat up his girlfriend with a lawn mower handle. Where are you, Thomas? Maybe you better call somebody up there to help."

"Up near Snoqualmie. I'll call the State Patrol as soon as I hang up."

"And I wanta meet this Babs gal pronto. Okay? You owe me."

"As soon as I can arrange it."

Chapter Twenty-eight

I DIALED THE OPERATOR and asked for the State Patrol. I explained the situation to somebody named Brookshire. He told me he would start units on the way, but that there had been an accident on the other side of the pass and he could not guarantee how long they would take. Traffic was tied up for ten miles on the other side of North Bend.

What a deal.

A young man popped into the doorway, scratched his unruly mop of russet hair and pleaded for the phone. I surrendered the instrument.

Easing into the main room on the second level, I tried to remain unobtrusive waiting for the troopers.

My eyes collided with Anthony Tyner's.

Standing on a low balcony, he sagged against the railing and fixed upon me. He was like a boxer psyching up before round one. I was the opponent. He obviously wanted me to try something. Unless he'd taken a crash course in self-defense, he had some sort of weapon on him. You could bet on it. I broke the connection, glanced around the room and looked back. He was still staring at me.

Behind him, Leroy Hutchcroft smiled, hugging Babs Tyner in one arm, another woman in the other. A black leather coat that matched his trousers was draped over Babs Tyner's shoulder, clutched in Leroy's grip. He had not had the jacket when I'd seen him earlier. He was leaving.

I plowed through the dancers and eaters and video bugs and inserted myself in the path I knew Leroy would have to take.

They took their time, Leroy and the two women, moseying along, jabbering with anyone who wanted to jabber.

I felt alone. I did not have anything here. Just an ominous feeling Leroy was best friends with everyone in the building. The haze of cigarette and marijuana smoke was making my eyes water.

I stood in the middle of the assembly and waited for Leroy, Babs and the other woman to reach me. When they did, Babs gave me a goofy look, her eyes glazed, unfocused. From the balcony, Anthony Tyner continued to glare at me.

Leroy Hutchcroft stopped smiling when he spotted me in his path. He moved to the right and so did I. We did an identical jig to the left. He was not used to having people get in his way. "Whatthefuck?" he said, yelling to be heard over the tumult. "Whatthefuck you want?"

Babs craned her neck and yelled something at him. He did not need to hear it twice. He grabbed a young man in front of himself, pulled him roughly out of the way and began bulling through the crush, making a run for it. Babs must have mentioned I was a detective working on her brother's murder. What a deal.

Using the rowdy techniques of a lineman on a football team, Hutchcroft battered his way through the crowd. I picked my way through the assemblage, moving sideways, snatching unsuspecting dancers out of my path. One ruffled young man in rimless spectacles waited until I had passed and then punched my shoulder lightly.

Leroy Hutchcroft made good time. I made better.

He shielded something, a bundle tied up inside his jacket. It made it difficult for him to slip through the crowd. Cradling it in his arms like a watermelon, he had to punch through the crush, while I nimbly sideslipped a lot of it. We were not heading for the stairs to the first-level exit, but for one wall, a wall that had a great wide table heaped with food abutting it.

He would have to go through me to reach the exit.

Several of the dancing couples we had just bruised quit twitching to watch the fracas.

When we reached the table there was only one obstacle separating us, a voluptuous woman gnawing a cold turkey leg, her luxurious hair the color of melted chocolate. Reaching out and bracing her, keeping her body between us, he feinted and dodged left, then right. Her hair flapped like a flag. I matched him feint for feint. He was not going

167

anywhere. The woman had eyes that quickly froze into marbles. Our roughhousing had stupefied her. She smiled widely, flashing beautiful teeth, a rictus.

Leroy twisted the woman around until she was facing me. Putting his back into it, he shoved her against me. She stumbled forward and squealed.

Spinning, she plummeted into my arms and I caught her halfway to the floor. I lifted her and she scampered over to the crowd, weeping and whickering like a terrified heifer that had fallen out of a truck.

Leroy tried to rush between me and the table. I lifted my left foot up, caught his torso squarely and kicked him backwards. He crashed to the tabletop and skittered across it on his rump. Silverware and glasses clattered onto the floor.

My actions produced a ragged sigh of disapproval from the growing crowd. I did not feel good about these people.

A platter of Jell-O flopped off the table behind Leroy and shattered on the floor, making a loud crack like a faraway pistol. More dancers and even a few video freaks stopped to watch our sport.

Leroy climbed to his feet amidst the emerald globs of gelatin, his boots crunching shards of broken glass. He reared back as if in a slingshot and tried to run past me one more time.

"Motherfucker! Don't mess with me, motherfucker!"

He ran squarely into my arms. I caught him, lifted him off his feet and pitched him back onto the table where he skidded backwards and swept the tablecloth and the rest of the contents off the far end. Bowls and platters thumped the floor in sequence.

As he flew backwards helplessly, his jacket whirled out of his hands and parachuted open, a bundle of bills raining upon the party. He must have had ten thousand dollars in that coat. The money exploded into the air as if his coat had been a giant firecracker and the bills the paper packing.

That tore it.

When Leroy got up, a fourteen-inch piece of pipe was clutched in one knuckly fist. I had visions of him clunking me with it, knocking me unconscious and then pulping my skull into jelly. Looking into Leroy's eyes, I could tell he had the same visions.

The girl he had shoved slunk away through the crowd. Most everybody had ceased dancing now. Somebody jerked the jukebox cord out of the wall. Several of the closest onlookers shushed the crowd. Even the folks on the first level were still, all heads turned our way, listening for the rosary of violence.

A lone voice issued from the kitchen at the back of the house. That would cease, too, when they realized how much fun we were all having in the mezzanine.

Chapter Twenty-nine

LEROY APPROACHED ME like a dangerous single-clawed lobster, his arms out, the pipe bobbing agitatedly in his right fist, legs spread, his eyes ugly with menace.

Maintaining perfect balance, he shifted expertly from side to side, ready to strike out in any direction. This was not his first fight using a hunk of pipe as a weapon. Not even his second. I knew I could not fend it off with a forearm. A tap from that pipe would crush bones. I collapsed a folding metal chair and raised it, part shield and part spear.

He drew jagged half-swastikas in the air with the pipe. All of the swastikas were centered on my eyes. He said, "You're making a big mistake, cracker."

"Leroy Hutchcroft," I said.

His reptilian eyes widened in surprise, but he did not take them off me. He had the angry, stunned look of a man who had just been bitten by a dog and now wanted revenge. "Who you talking about?"

"You. Bozo."

"I dunno what you're saying."

"Sure you do. Leroy Hutchcroft. You're under arrest." I spoke loudly, clearly. "I'm making a citizen's arrest. This man is wanted for parole violation in Missouri. He's also wanted for questioning in connection with the murder of Lance Tyner."

The crowd let out a collective gasp and backed away, giving us more than enough room. A young man beside Leroy Hutchcroft stooped and tentatively fondled one of the bills without picking it up, a hundred.

"Boy, you wanna keep 'em, you get your cotton-pickin'

fingers off that money!" The young man retreated, hang-dog, and melted into the rear echelon of the watchers.

"What's going on?" Babs Tyner squeezed her way through the crowd, bumping her friends aside. "Lee?"

"It's a frame."

Preparing to come at me, Leroy Hutchcroft slipped on some food and did a queer balancing quickstep in his clunking boots, but did not go down. The loss of face was something he would take out on me. I could see it in his ever-hardening eyes, like ones on a pair of dice. Here was a man who would happily kill over a point of pride.

I took a step forward so that he would have to launch himself out of the scraps, while I kept to the dry floor. Using the chair, I might be able to ward him off, keep him at bay until Smokey arrived.

"Where'd you get that money, Leroy?" I asked.

"I gave it to him." Babs stepped forward.

"Stay back." She kept coming, teetering on rickety strapless heels too tall for her to control. She wore another velvet pantsuit, this one cinnamon-colored. This was going to queer the blind date with Smithers.

"Leroy is the one who beaned your brother down on the beach three weeks ago."

Disbelief contorting her voice, Babs said, "No."

"He used a piece of pipe just like the one in his hand. Keeps it taped to his leg. We found one like it in the tide next to Lance."

Babs Tyner turned to Leroy.

"Don't believe him, baby. This guy is nuts. I found this pipe on the floor. Pick up the money for me, would you?"

"How much did you give him?" I asked Babs.

"Four hundred dollars."

"Take a look. There's eight or ten thousand there." Babs peered down. Hundred-dollar bills dappled the floor like a carpet. The partygoers also peered down on my cue. I noted that except for Martin Tyner, who was buried in the crowd somewhere, Leroy and I were the oldest in the chalet. And Leroy looked to be a couple of years younger than me. Grampa Black.

"Pick it up, babe," said Leroy, clenching his teeth and wagging the pipe at me. Anger rippled through the ropy

171

muscles in his face. He was a man used to losing control. Right now he was on the jagged edge, on the verge of losing all his buttons. I was the only one who saw it.

"Come on, man," said a voice from the crowd. "Leave him alone."

Leroy's eyes became like steel pinpricks. "Yeah, lemme alone! It was a bum rap!"

"Hey, buddy. Citizen's arrest? What a laugh!"

"Let him go."

"You a cop or something?"

I said, "You people just keep out of this."

"Let him go. Have a little heart, buddy."

Somebody else mimicked, "Have a little hard-on, buddy."

Guffaws rolled through the crowd like distant thunder. A chorus of voices concurred. They were young. They could have a hootenanny and roast me on a spit. They were accustomed to rallying behind sudden antiestablishment causes. They wanted me to let him flee. The big bad detective was harassing the cool dude in black leather pants. Though nobody looked as if he wanted to interfere physically, I was surrounded by a roomful of scowls.

"The State Patrol is on the way," I said, soothingly.

Babs Tyner crouched down and began scooping up the money, depositing it into a paper sack she had produced out of nowhere. Leroy swayed, showed me his teeth and stroked the air with his weapon. He feinted once, but could not sucker me. The only exit was behind me and he was cornered between the table and the wall of partygoers.

He stepped forward and slashed at my cheek with the pipe. I fended it off against the metal folding chair in my hands. A clang rang out. We sounded like two clashing swordsmen. The room was dead silent. Even Babs stopped scrabbling on the floor. A Mexican standoff.

Something went beep. Leroy peered around the room. Another Lilliputian beep answered it. Another tiny beep. Beep. I flicked my eyes up at the huge Swiss clock on the wall. It was twelve o'clock. Several of the digital watches in the room were going off.

"Police radio," I whispered to the still room. "They're here."

172

It rattled him just enough to enable me to cock the chair back and stab the rubber-tipped legs into his stomach. He made a grotesque noise and doubled over. When his head was low enough I swung the chair upwards and caught him under the chin. The pipe clattered to the floor. I booted it out of sight in a sea of legs.

Some kid in the crowd gasped, "Dirty move."

Before Leroy could collect himself, I pinioned his left wrist and twisted it behind his back, crossing my own left forearm across his throat and effectively choking off any fight. The ends of his greasy hair pattered against my face as he struggled, momentarily rendering me blind.

When I could see again, Babs Tyner was coming at me wildly, the paper sack in her hands lumpy with greenbacks. I turned Leroy around and used him as a shield. She battled and slapboxed, trying to reach around him. I circled, outmaneuvering her. I couldn't fight her off and hold onto my prisoner at the same time.

Then the young man who had earlier punched me in the shoulder separated from the congregation, came around behind me and tried to loop a half nelson over my head. His beer breath fell hot and humid on my ear.

"Man, lay off. We're just tryin' to have a good time. You cops are always on our backs."

"Quit hasslin', buddy."

A consenting chorus of hoots and jeers emanated from the crowd. Someone in the back yelled. "Let him go, Twink!"

People laughed. I was losing control. Where was the cavalry when you needed it?

The young man behind me twice tried to fit me into a wrestling hold. Before he could execute it, I stomped my heel down hard on his instep. He screamed, flopped onto the floor and retched. I was fairly certain I had broken his foot.

"Anybody else?" I said, mimicking a hundred tough-guy movies. I had handled near-riots before. You had to get tough with them. Nothing to it. "Anybody else?"

Three guys came at me simultaneously. One man reached past Leroy and put his fist into my nose. My eyes

173

watered. Blinking hard, I couldn't see what was happening, but I did not let go. Staunch to the last.

Somebody slugged me in the back, over my left lung. If that was all they had, they were in trouble. They slugged me again, harder. My back sounded off like a drum. The muscles of my left shoulder spasmed. I twisted around, using Leroy. I was going to lose him; I knew it. Somebody snared my ankle and we all went down in a heap, floundering in the slop.

Catching me harried and unaware, Leroy slammed his head backwards and nailed me in the lip. I let go and clasped my face in both hands, thinking that at least one of my teeth was buried in his skull, the whole front of my mouth numb.

"He's an armed robber," I said with a lisp, struggling, trying to keep a grip on at least some part of his body. "What's wrong with you people?"

I grappled with him, caught him by the ankles and pinned them together as he tried to squirm away. Halfway to his feet, he went down hard, sprawling across the screaming young man I had downed.

Leroy kicked his feet, thrashed, and lurched; but I held him fast, my mouth numb, my teary eyes beginning to clear. His struggles were hauling me on my stomach through the goop.

I hadn't been in this kind of a screwy deal in a hell of a long time.

Suddenly somebody had hold of my left ear, and was slowly ripping it off my head. In the confusion Leroy had twisted around and decided my ear would make a splendid cuff link. It was the sort of dirty infighting they taught in the pen.

I sank my teeth into his forearm as deeply as I could. Even that didn't release his grip, not immediately. Finally, slowly, he eased off. He reluctantly freed my ear.

Babs was shouting, "Pig! Pig! Pig!"

"Okay, okay," Leroy said, simpering in agony. "You let go. I let go." I grunted in assent. He let go completely.

I let go of his feet, released his forearm from my bite and we began wrestling. It did not take long to see that I was stronger and would soon have him pinned.

174

Suddenly Leroy stopped moving. I stopped. I gently released Leroy Hutchcroft. He shook his forearm and rubbed the spot where my teeth had dug into him. The people in the room all backed off another five feet.

Four inches from my temple Anthony Tyner held a .357 Magnum. I was too close to it to see whether or not it was cocked.

Chapter Thirty

MARTIN TYNER STEPPED FORWARD, an identical pistol in his hands, a nickel-plated Colt .357 Magnum with a six-inch barrel. Leroy slowly rose and spanked some of the crud off his leather pants.

Anthony Tyner said, "Real tough guy. Let's see how tough you are now."

"You been watching too many cartoons, Bozo. All you're going to get is a prison sentence."

"What for? For breaking up a fight? You think they'll put me in jail for that?" It was a rhetorical question. He had no worries.

The old man looked at Leroy Hutchcroft almost greedily, the key to a Byzantine puzzle.

"If you'll care to come with us," he said, gentility and duplicity infusing his words, "we'll give you a lift back to town."

Accepting the sack from Babs, along with a peck on the cheek, Leroy collected his jacket, and followed Martin Tyner to the front door. Anthony Tyner stayed behind, tightening the drawstring on his jogging sweats, training the barrel of his pistol on my right eyeball, gloating.

Shaking his head as if lecturing a schoolboy, he said, "You don't mess with me. You know what I'm talking about? Nobody messes with Anthony T. Tyner and gets away with it."

Still on the floor, I didn't want to make a dive for his legs. It was a toss-up whether or not he was going to pull the trigger. I don't think even he knew. I decided not to precipitate anything. It was a lot harder for somebody to initiate violence than it was to react to it. I needed to make it as difficult as possible for him to use the gun. My guess was he had never shot anyone before, probably had never even fired a gun, was being propelled by circumstances bigger than any he had ever been involved in.

"You fire that gun and you'll never spend a red cent of your brother's inheritance."

He ground his teeth together and stabbed looks around the crowd. The mass kept a respectful distance, unsure of exactly what was transpiring.

After thinking it over, he turned and jog-trotted out of the chalet. He reminded me of a professional ballplayer jogging lazily out onto the field after being introduced over the loudspeakers, a chaw tucked snugly into one cheek.

For a long while I sat on the floor, a houseful of revelers standing around in various states of amusement.

I was the geek.

What a story this would make. Boy, would they drum the dorm up into riotous laughter with this one. Nobody said much for a while. I sat covered in vomit, emerald Jell-O and blood—my own, I presumed. My left ear felt as if it had been ripped partially off. I touched it. It seemed to be intact, though perhaps a mite longer than my right one. Face flushed, Babs Tyner stood over me, hands on her meaty hips, mildly reproving, but with a twinge of something else in her eyes, too. Curiosity? Lust? No. Lust? Had she enjoyed our tussle that much?

"Hate to be a party pooper." I scrambled to my feet. The young man with the broken foot writhed on the floor eight feet away. "Better get a doctor for him."

Nobody spoke. Everybody watched me. If I had had my balls with me I would have juggled.

I strode through the mob, looking for the bathroom. My nose was bruised and my two front teeth and lip felt as if they had been Novocained. In the mirror, my upper lip looked puffy. I compared my ears but they seemed to be the same length. By the time I had cleaned myself up, scrubbed my face and found a comb to curry small particles of glass and glop out of my hair, the party had heated up again. The jukebox roared, couples twitched and video consoles were being battered by excited players.

Slipping into the back room, I phoned the State Patrol and gave them a thumbnail description of Martin Tyner's car, along with the license number. Brookshire couldn't promise anything. He said the traffic tie-up from the accident on the east side of North Bend had worsened, that a tractor trailer rig had gone off a cliff.

When I walked through the dancers to the front door, I caused a minor stir.

Babs Tyner breathlessly handed me a cowboy hat. "Yours," she said. I had never seen it before. It was feathered and white and I took it and plunked it on my head to show her it wasn't mine. It dropped down around my ears. The fit did not faze her. "Do you think he really clonked Lance down on the beach?"

"Yes, I do."

"I don't believe it."

"Then why ask?"

"I just don't believe it."

"I have a friend who wants a blind date with you," I said.

"Is he cute?"

"The cutest."

"Tell him to give me a ring."

From the porch I could see that Martin Tyner, Anthony Tyner and Leroy Hutchcroft were long gone. Not that I would have chased them. I was unarmed and they weren't, besides which, they were as skittish as colts under new saddles. Custody of Leroy wasn't worth getting plugged for.

The State Patrol would have him cuffed and booked within the hour. No doubt about it. There were not that many roads to Seattle and the State Patrol was good. Cuffed and booked. No doubt about it. If I hustled and kept my eyes open, I might eyewitness the arrest along the roadside.

Chapter Thirty-one

I TILTED MY HAT, wheeled the Ford pickup onto the highway, and headed toward Seattle, nattering to myself.

I-90 would take me through Issaquah, across Mercer Island and over the floating bridge directly into Seattle, thirty-five minutes tops. Traffic was sparse. Sunlight was patchy. I was battered.

Issaquah was a valley town. The entire valley lay sprawled out before the highway as I wended down the mountain. To the north of the freeway someone had mapped out a small airfield, a popular spot for nervous parachutists along with their ground-bound spouses.

I almost missed it.

Somebody had flung a pair of peach-colored sweat pants high into the branches of a young birch alongside the highway. I wouldn't have thought anything of it, except Anthony Tyner had been wearing sweat pants that color.

Swerving onto the parking strip, I skidded to a stop and checked it out in my rear-view mirror. I flicked on the hazard blinkers and backed up the hundred or so yards to the birch. A yellow stripe running down the side, they did indeed look like Anthony Tyner's. Snared in the uppermost limbs, they bowed the thin branches under their weight. The bases of the trees were situated below the level of the road, planted in an enormous ditch, which placed the top branches only about ten feet above the road level.

Farther down in the same tree, I spotted another pair of trousers, a baggy puce pair flapping in the breeze. Then I saw a jogging shoe tangled by its laces in the V where two branches joined the trunk.

I shut off the motor and climbed out of the truck, walking around to the upper lip of the culvert. It was all there.

The remainder of their clothing was strewn in the birches, article by article. An old man's dingy underwear, shorts and sleeveless undershirt. A scuffed brogan. The top portion of the peach-colored sweat suit. And last but not least, a jockstrap, fluttering in the breeze like some fisherman's stupendous lure cast too enthusiastically, tangled and lost.

Presumably the dirty deed had been done from a point not far from where I stood. The sandy bank was dimpled with footprints.

Then I saw one of the birds, a flash of white skin and a rustle of panicky movement below in the brambles. Martin Tyner, naked as a jaybird, was below me, picking his way through the gravel of the culvert on tiptoe, hopping from bush to bush like a frightened desert lizard.

"Hallo!" I shouted.

Anthony Tyner's head popped up from behind a shrub, a startled jack-in-the-box. The look on his face was a curious mixture of animosity and cockamamie chagrin.

"You?" he said.

"You boys having a picnic?"

The white flashes that had been darting from bush to bush stopped, and Martin Tyner, two hands cupping his genitals, stopped in an open spot and squinted up the embankment at me. His skeleton poked at his chalky skin everywhere except his lower belly, which protruded like a small, slack bowl. "Black? Get us out of here. Get them danged clothes down here to us."

I glanced over at their clothes distributed in the flimsy branches, kissed by the slight breeze stirred up by the eighteen-wheelers and the other traffic on the highway.

"Wish I could."

We might have been able to tackle a couple of the younger trees, if all three of us worked together.

"Fetch 'em, Black. Dang it. We need our clothes. You think we're going to town buck naked, boy?"

"Don't be preposterous," I said, calmly. "Clothes are merely a social convention."

The veins in his neck bulged and his head began to turn lavender, his eyes bubbling like a flounder. "Get 'em before I blow my cork!"

"You're hung up on looks, old man. In reality, looks mean nothing."

Anthony Tyner tiptoed across a swatch of gravel and

180

cowered behind his hunched father who, rather than cupping his genitals, was now clutching them. I gestured. "You boys planning to follow this ditch all the way to Seattle?"

"Black, quit playing around and go get our clothes."

I sat down in the sunburnt grass and tugged out the tall thin stalk of a weed, crunching the sweet end between my teeth. "That would be too much work. Way too much work."

Peeping over his father's bony shoulder, Anthony Tyner queried, "You're not going to get them?"

I mulled the proposition over. "Nope."

"You're an asshole!" said the younger Tyner.

"You look like a pair of Mongolian wild asses yourselves."

"Be a pal. Get 'em."

"Get 'em yourself."

"Asshole!"

"Want a ride into town?" They were two zoo animals inspecting the tourist through the bars. "You apologize?"

"Apologize for what?"

"You called me something my Sunday school teacher told me never to say."

Without waiting, the old man poked his son in the ribs and murmured advice. "Yeah," said Anthony Tyner, in a voice that was a mere echo of its former self. "Yeah, I apologize."

"Okay. But you boys be nice. Otherwise you're going to hurt my feelings."

They scrambled up the hillside, looking like Christmas turkeys climbing a snow bank. When they got to road level, they ducked down, only their heads showing from the freeway, waiting for a propitious moment to dash to the truck. Though traffic was light, the intervals were hardly long enough for a safe dash. The truck keys safely in my pocket, I lounged in the grass and watched their flight.

"Now!" said Anthony, urging his father on. Picking themselves up, they bobbed and weaved across the littered parking strip to my truck, pulled on the door handle, then turned around and screamed at me. It was locked. The amused driver of a passing Plymouth laid on his horn when he saw the two men, leaning on it until he was a

181

quarter of a mile down the road. The Doppler effect was interesting. I shambled over to the driver's door, got in, and unlocked the passenger side. The two men sprang into the cab.

"Goddamn it, Black! You scoundrel!" The old man sat next to me. His son, sitting by the door, could only huddle and cover his lap with both forearms.

Finally, the younger Tyner turned and said, "Where the hell did you get that hat?"

"You like?"

"It looks like shit."

They exchanged glances, reviewing their story no doubt, and the old man spoke in a subdued voice. For a minute, I thought he had actually grown humble. "Maybe you have a blanket or something we could cover ourselves with?"

I motioned for them to lean forward, tilted the seat forward and dug a monstrous wool blanket out from between the seat and the gas tank. Hastily they draped it across themselves, tucking it meticulously down around their legs and pulling it up to their necks. I noted that for all his athletic togs and his swaggering bluster, Anthony Tyner was built like a nonathlete, had a layer of fat on his body that made him look girlish.

"Thug," said Martin Tyner, as I pulled out into traffic. "You're no better than that thug who just robbed us."

I tipped the cowboy hat back on my head. "Hey now, pardner. Don't be thataway."

"He stole my goddamned car," said the old man.

"Don't worry about it. Smokey is looking for it right now. Which way was he headed?"

"Same way we are."

"That's where they're looking. Unless he stops and switches vehicles, they ought to nab him."

"I could have taken him," said the younger Tyner.

"Shit!" said the old man. "He had that Mexican knife shoved halfway up your nose. You were sniveling like an old woman."

"If he didn't pull the knife, I could have taken him."

"But he did pull the knife."

"If he didn't, I could have taken him."

"Sure you could have. You had a .357 stuck in his face."

"What happened?" I asked.

The old man cast a furtive glance my way. "We got in

182

the car. All we wanted to do was ask some questions. I drove and Tony rode in the front. He got in the back with that sack of money. Hell, I knew he had that bar, but we never saw no knife. Not till he shoved it up Tony's nose."

"He meant business," said the younger Tyner, rubbing one nostril carefully, probing it with his thumb. "I thought he was going to slice me open."

"Must have seen *Chinatown*," I said.

"No. It was just Issaquah." He continued to caress his nostril. "And we didn't see nothing. We was just drivin' along peaceable and all of a sudden he pulls out this knife and sticks it in my nose."

"Not exactly peaceable," admitted the old man, grudgingly. "We had your gun on him the whole while." His voice got gruffer. "And why not? He killed Lance."

"What makes you say that?"

"You were after him, weren't you? You said he was a wanted man. He must have killed Lance, or he wouldn't have run like that. You should have seen the buzzard. He was like a wild man. He brandished that knife like he wanted to chop us both to pieces. Must have been ten inches long. A big old Mexican thing with an eagle's head on the handle. I never did see where it came from."

"Probably taped to his other leg," I said. "A guy like that isn't likely to walk around without an insurance policy. He's spent time in the jug. Wanted in Chicago for a cop-killing. You birds were lucky to escape with your lives."

"I'm gonna blow his fucking head off when I find him," said the younger Tyner, sounding as if he had already given it a lot of thought.

"First," the old man advised, "you better make sure he doesn't have a knife on him."

Chapter Thirty-two

"WHAT DID HE SAY to you?" I asked.

"Not a dang thing," said the old man bitterly. "We did all the talking. We were trying to find out where the wills are. We thought we might drive him up on one of these here side roads and *make* him talk."

"Good thing you didn't."

"Why?"

"For one thing, I never would have found you. For another, he just might have done you both in and dumped you into the proverbial shallow graves."

The old man pondered that.

"He tell you what he was planning to do next?"

Tony replied, "Said something about a long vacation. That's all. Said he was going to get himself some women. Some real wild women."

"He hurt Babs, I'll kill him," grumbled the old man.

"Peninsula women," added Tony, planning his own future vacations. "Are they wild over there? I never heard. Them farm girls might be."

I said, "Did you ask him if he killed your son?"

"Course we asked him. That's the first thing, after he wouldn't tell us where he put the wills. Even offered to cut him in on a slice of it. Bullheaded is what he was. He could have been rich. Damn piece of paper ain't going to do him no good."

"I'm gonna fuckin' kill him when I find him," said Tony Tyner.

"If you two birds had just stayed out of it, the State Patrol would be questioning him right now. And maybe we'd know who killed Lance. We might even have found out where the wills are."

Sulking, Anthony Tyner stared ahead, hypnotized or nearing total exhaustion. He sulked for the remainder of the trip, immobile, foul-tempered.

"Why were you after him?" asked the old man.

"Because I knew he was the one who beaned Lance down on the beach. They had a history of violence together. I was after him for a lot of other reasons, too. Your son didn't have a hell of a lot of friends. I needed to find out who some of them were. I needed to talk to this guy in the worst way."

I debated whether or not to turn these two over to the cops. Frankly, I doubted whether either of them would spend a minute in a cell. Tony had pulled a gun on me back at the chalet. That was their only real crime. And my guess was that witnesses from the party would not be eager to testify in my behalf.

Leroy Scroggs Hutchcroft's escape wasn't as bad as it could have been. I now knew several places to look for him. He might hide out at his sister's, or at one of the hobo camps, or go to the building I had spotted Billy F. Greenlee crawling into. And I had the added bonus now of knowing what he looked like.

We crossed Lake Washington on the floating bridge, past the spot where Eve Tiffany had spent two years on the bottom of the lake.

"A rather tragic thing happened the other night," I said. Anthony Tyner appraised me and then turned back to the road. "Some folks dressed up in white robes like they belonged to the Ku Klux Klan and went over to Lance's girlfriend's house. They tried to get tough with her. It's not so bad her fiancé just died, but somebody has to play games with her. You have any idea who that might have been?"

Neither of the men said a word. Five minutes passed like that.

I drove them to a cab company on Capitol Hill. "You can get out here. A cabbie will give you a ride home. I'm sick of you."

"Here?" asked Martin Tyner in a falsetto. "Not here!"

"I ain't gettin' out," said Anthony. "You make me get out."

"First," I said, tipping back the huge cowboy hat, "I want you birds to know that the next time you go after Lucy, I'm going to round up that whole neighborhood of

185

hers and give them your names and addresses." Martin Tyner's eyes blazed at me.

"We didn't go after nobody. Don't even know what you're talking about."

"Yeah, you may be innocent. You may be."

"You ain't gonna tell them we did it when you don't know."

"I might."

"That's just what we need is a bunch of porch monkeys chasing all around town after us."

"Get out."

Chapter Thirty-three

I SLIPPED THE TRUCK INTO GEAR and left them, a couple of freshly plucked fryers. Ten blocks away I stopped at a booth, double-parked and dialed Smithers. No answer. I dialed a downtown number and got a cop I had known while I was on the force, now a sergeant in homicide.

"Max? Thomas Black here. I'm working on the Lance Tyner murder case and I'm trying to trace down a fellow named Leroy Hutchcroft. He was pals with Tyner and I think he might know something about Tyner's death. He stole a car from Tyner's father about an hour ago on I-90. Last seen heading for town. In case you're interested, he's got two nickel-plated .357 Magnums on him."

"What makes you think he knows something about Tyner's death?"

"He slugged Tyner a few weeks back, put him in the hospital. He's a rough customer and he knew Tyner had money."

"What do you have?"

I gave him the particulars, including the Mercury's license number and the address of Hutchcroft's sister in Monroe. Some people would have saved the dope from the cops and gone after Leroy themselves, but I couldn't see any percentage in that. For one thing, it was a quick way to become a two-line blurb on the last page of the *Times*, right under the escort service ads. For another, I didn't have the apparatus to track a stolen auto across the state. Especially if, as I suspected, he had stopped somewhere and rifled fresh plates off someone else's bumper. Nor did I have time to hop from county to county looking for him. The cops could do that just fine.

I drove to my place off Roosevelt.

The case was like an exploding cigar—just when you feel you're going to relish it, something blows up. The couple I had given my house key to were gone. They had taken my advice and cleaned out the fridge. They had done something more too. They had walked off with my Sony.

"Oh Lordy," I said, quickly inventorying my other possessions. I was most worried about the guns in my hideaway in the closet. But they were intact. The television seemed to be the only item they had bothered to take. Too bad. During the drive from Monroe to Snoqualmie I had remembered a friend who might be able to give the painter some steady work. And I had vowed to lend them the apartment in the basement until they got on their feet. In the end, the Sony would cost them a lot more than what they could sell it for at a flea market. There was no point in reporting it.

Bushed, I flopped down on the couch and tried to take a catnap. I hadn't slept soundly since this thing started.

After five minutes of tossing and turning, I got up, took a leak, and phoned Lucy to tell her how the case was shaping up. P.W. answered in a fruity voice. "Peebles residence. P.W. Peebles at your service."

"Hey, guy. This is Black. Lucy there?"

"Lucy ain't here, man."

"Know where she is?"

"She's out wid some guy. He taken her to buy some tapes."

"What kind of weed doesn't grow in the garden?" I asked.

"Dunno. What kind?"

"Seaweed."

The line was silent for a split second and then P.W.'s raucous laughter burbled into my earpiece. "That's good, man. That's real good." He laughed again.

"You know why Willie Nelson got hit by a truck?"

"No. Why?"

"He was playing 'On the Road Again.' "

Again the raucous laughter.

"Man, you funny."

"Yeah," I said. "Thanks. What's going on over there?"

"Same ol' jive. Cleata runnin' 'round wid her friends tryin' to stir up trouble. She found out about all dis money Lance 'posed to have and she think she should be gittin'

188

some." He spoke derogatorily. "Since she and he be such *fine* friends and all."

"What's she doing?"

"Dunno. She been gone all aft'noon."

I suited up and went over to the school and shot baskets for two hours. Sometimes it takes something like that to recuperate. I ran and dodged and bobbed and weaved and jumped as if I were in the wildest pickup game of my life, charging around the court until sweat slid off me every time I blinked. When I got out of the shower the phone was ringing.

"Hey, long time no see, guy. What's going on?" Kathy's voice sounded sweet and somehow nubile.

We had been together only that morning, but it seemed like ages. "What's going on, sister?"

"You know, Thomas, you're the only guy I've ever known who called me sister."

"What's up?"

"I'm having my housewarming tonight. Can you come?"

"Probably. I can't stay long."

"The case?"

"Yeah."

"How's it going?"

"Badly."

"We'll talk about it tonight."

"Sure."

Perched on the side of Queen Anne Hill, her apartment had an open balcony overlooking the summertime sailboats and float planes buzzing around on Lake Union. I had to admit, it was much plusher than my basement, and she had begun to furnish it in her inimitable style.

Kathy always threw strange parties, blending people from the most diverse walks of life, mixing and matching. I was one of her favorites. The private detective. She knew more people than any friend I had. Her network of schoolmates, ex-boyfriends, business colleagues and casual acquaintances was mind-boggling.

Wearing pressed slacks, a sport coat and an open-necked shirt, I found myself underdressed. Conservative three-piece suits and coiffed ladies in evening dresses were the norm. The chatter was light, urbane and surprisingly literate. I don't know why I was surprised. Kathy's parties were always successes. I suppose it was the mental juxta-

189

position with Babs's bawdy ongoing bash in the chalet that put me off.

"Thomas, you look even worse than you did this morning. What happened to your lip?"

"Kissed a horse," I said.

"You just fooling around, or are you going steady?"

I shrugged. As usual, she was startlingly beautiful. Looping fingers into one of my buttonholes, Kathy walked me over to a corner near the window as if I were a dog on a leash. We stood very close, like lovers, something we had never been.

"How's the case going?"

"I found the culprit who beaned Lance three weeks ago on the beach. That's about all. I almost had him this afternoon, except the Tyners broke into it and helped him get away. It's a long story."

"Have you found out any more about Lance's past?"

"Lots. But not really enough. It's pathetic, if you want to know."

During my monologue she kept her fingers riveted to my buttonhole, pulling me close when I threatened to lean back. Twice, guests meandered over but she managed to wave them off each time without offending anybody.

Tonight she wore a low-cut black evening gown, two thin straps running up over her firm shoulders. It reminded me of what someone had said about a dress Norma Shearer once wore: It's not a dress; it's an invitation.

She had the rapt attention of at least two eligible-looking men across the room. I hadn't met him, but I surmised that the one in horn-rimmed glasses was Peyton, the younger Bemis from her law firm.

He was tall and broad, good-looking in an Ivy League way. He flicked intermittent jealous glances at the way she kept her fingers snagged in my coat, the way she tapped her long coral nails against a button, the way she listened dutifully to my speech.

When I had finished Lance's saga, Kathy tidied my shirt collar, a cat stroking her kitten. "So what are you going to do?"

"I've got a couple of leads. There's just one thing that doesn't compute though."

"What's that?"

"D.W. and P.W. told me that when Lance came over

Tuesday night they thought he had been beaten up. That just doesn't compute. The autopsy didn't mention anything about that. First he gets beaten up, then later on he gets shot. How much trouble can one guy get himself into in an evening."

"I don't know, Thomas. When did he die?"

"The boys saw him between eleven and eleven-thirty Tuesday evening."

"I still don't understand why he went back to his boarding house."

"Lucy thinks he was afraid of something. So do I, though what, I have no idea."

"Maybe one of his hobo friends tried to put the bite on him? They got into a struggle. One of them produced a gun. It went off."

"Yeah, fine. Except why would Lance hide after a thing like that? I'm still ruminating over the possibility that his own brother shot him. He blackened Lance's eye a month ago. Anthony once had guys who were going to put their thumbs into his brain. A gambler. Desperate. Could be he sniffed all this money, thought it was in the bag, and began betting heavier than usual, got into debt, then asked Lance for an advance. Wouldn't it be natural for him to anticipate the inheritance—run up some debts—and then maybe get a little crazy trying to scrounge up the loot when things didn't pan out?"

"Maybe, Thomas. I wish I felt something on this one. Something that might help." She was referring to her prescience, or ESP, as some people labeled it. More than once she had been invaluable on cases. "Maybe Lance just went up to his room to think things over and got too weak to move."

"I'm going to go over to his brother's and see if I can determine where Tony was Tuesday night. Mind if I use your phone?"

"It's in the kitchen."

Dragging the volume of white pages out, I looked up Velma Dupont's number in Lynnwood. She answered on the third ring. Tony was out bowling, she said. Reluctantly, she agreed that I could come over and speak to her for a while. I could have asked her on the phone, but then I wouldn't have seen her face when she answered. I needed that.

Kathy slunk across the living room and headed me off at the front door. I noticed the guy in the horn-rims didn't seem to be able to take his eyes off her.

"Be careful, Thomas."

"Sure thing, sister."

"And Thomas?"

"Yes."

"Would you like to go out with me next Saturday . . . that is . . . if you're off this case?"

"Out? What do you mean?"

"Don't be dense." She grabbed my face and bussed the tip of my nose. "You know what I mean. Out. Dinner? A movie? There's a great show at The Egyptian."

I glanced around the room, suspicious that perhaps this was some sort of practical joke that everyone was in on but me. "A date, you mean?"

"Yeah."

The guy across the room in the horn-rims had spilled a drink on his wrist. He was looking at me the way a man with a screwdriver looked at an oyster. "You're asking me for a date?"

"Yes, I'm asking you for a date. And don't make it so difficult. I'm not used to asking guys out."

"A boy-girl date?"

"Yes."

"Popcorn?"

"Yes."

"Necking by the beach?"

She raised her bare shoulders a notch and spoke as noncommittally as I had ever heard her speak. "Whatever."

I touched her bare arm and said, "Saturday. Sure. I'm looking forward to it."

Chapter Thirty-four

"VELMA?"

She wore a damp bathrobe. Though she looked as if she had just stepped out of the shower, her face was made up and the wig was stacked on top of her head like an old rag pile.

"Come in. I ain't got all night." Our meeting was nothing but annoyance for her.

The poodle yipped and leaped happily up at my knees three times before Velma stooped over and picked it up. The little boy in me peeking down her bathrobe, I could see she wore a full lacy corset. Remarkable.

"Tony's not here?"

"I told you. Bowling four times a week. Maybe gonna turn pro next year." She spoke mulishly. Judging by her tone, my guess was it was a bone of contention between them, but to me, a stranger, she would brag it up.

"Pro, huh? Marvelous. Was he bowling Tuesday night?"

"I think he was. Tuesday? What is this? That's the night his brother got it. You think Tone had something to do with that? Come on. Gimme a break. He went bowling and what's more, I saw him there." She was getting vociferous now. "So did about a hundred other people. He got drunk and I had to practically carry him home on my back. He was celebrating 'cause he thought we were rich—finally. Puked all over the carpet there where you're standing."

I stared at her painted toenails, wondering how much of this I could believe. She was a decade older than Tony and not what I would have expected him to choose in a mate.

"We already got a house picked. At the north end of Lake Washington. Big old mansion. Four thousand square feet. A sauna room. It's got a little forty-foot dock for the boat we're getting and everything. You'll have to come and see it when we get settled." The invitation was only manners, or bragging. We both knew it by the quick, careless way she spit her words out. "They wanted to do the paperwork today, but things had to wait. Good thing I didn't quit down at the big zit. I almost did too."

"The big zit?"

"I work for Confederates Oil in Ballard. Fuel oil? We call it the big zit. Cute, huh?"

They hadn't received a cent, his brother had died two days ago, and they were signing papers.

I noted a Mexican serape hanging on one wall over a row of dusty baseball trophies. The serape was squared up beside a flashy black velvet oil painting of a bullfighter.

"You like? We picked that up in Tijuana last spring. Tony took me down there." Even though it was her money, probably her car, *Tony* took *her.* The man would always be on top in her family, no matter what.

Sitting decorously on the sofa, Velma arranged the poodle in her lap and picked up a bottle of nail polish, slowly brushing the vermilion onto the dog's nails.

"Keeps them hard," she explained, when she saw me looking. Her voice slipped into childishness. "And sooooo pretty."

"When was the last time you saw Lance?"

"Lance? Gosh, that's too bad about what happened to him, isn't it? I mean, it's just terrible."

"When did you see him last?"

"In court a couple weeks ago."

"Did Lance and Tony get along?"

"Tony? Tone gets along with everyone."

"That's not what I heard."

Suspicion burgeoning under her chalky facial powder, she looked up from the dog's nails. Her eyes had turned into marbles. Her voice was like a motor somebody had poured sand into. "What did you hear?"

"I heard old Tone liked to slap his brother around. In fact, when I saw Lance three weeks ago, he had the remains of a shiner somebody told me old Tone gave him."

She spoke glibly, as if I hadn't scored a point. "Poppycock." The way she pronounced it, it came out 'puppycock'. "I don't think Tone has an enemy in the world. He'd give you the shirt off your back." She did not catch her malapropism.

When I left, I began rapping on doors in the apartment complex. Nobody answered below.

Across the court on the other side of the shimmering night-lit pool, two roommates inspected my ID and took my business card through the chink in their chained door before cautiously letting me in. Even then, they insisted on leaving the front door wide, a cool summer draft playing about my ankles as we spoke.

They sat on opposite ends of the rented davenport, both wearing signature jeans, rumpled socks and T-shirts.

One was a redhead in spectacles and the other was a brunette, her teeth jailed in braces. They worked for an insurance company, processing forms. This was obviously the first time away from home for both of them and the newness of the experience still sent ripples of excitement through their conversation.

"Whooooo," said the redhead, touching her glasses, rubbing a droopy eyelid. "I'm glad you showed us that detective thing right away. You scared the soup out of us."

"There's been a lot of attacks in the area lately," added the brunette.

"Tell me about Tony and Velma."

"She the one with the wigs?" the redhead asked excitedly. To many people, having a detective knock at the door and ask about the neighbors was a fantasy come true.

"She's the one with the wigs." I took a seat opposite them. "He runs around in jogging clothes."

Tony and Velma, it turned out, were a major source of amusement in the complex.

"Oh, they're weird. She works all day and he doesn't get up until around one or two in the afternoon. I had a vacation last month, that's how I know. Didn't have anywhere to go, so I kicked around here for two weeks."

"When she comes home at night they fight and fight. He never does anything around the place. I mean, he's a drone."

"A drone?"

"You know. A male bee? Good for nothing? Does no work? Fertilizes the queen and dies? A drone."

"You ever see his brother over there?"

I described Lance Tyner and produced the small, square photo his father had given to me so many weeks ago. They both shook their heads solemnly. If they had seen his photo in the paper and knew about the murder, they gave no indication of it.

"Was Tony here Tuesday night?"

"Tuesday? What's on Tuesday?" The redhead looked at her roommate. The brunette spoke rapid-fire, listing several television shows, none of which I was familiar with.

"Yeah, I think he was gone."

"You know how long?"

"Till late. We go to bed a little past eleven. He wasn't back then. He never is."

"How about Velma?"

"Wig?" They looked at each other and giggled, sharing a long-held secret. "Whenever the guy goes out Wig has friends up there." Their tittering lapsed into irreverent cacophony for a few wild moments. Then the redhead controlled herself and said, "Wig's got this thing about young guys. I bet she's slept with every guy in this complex under twenty-five."

"Twenty-two," corrected her roommate.

"Yeah, maybe twenty-two. With all the people moving in and out around here, she's busier than a puppy in a fire hydrant factory. She's just got this thing about *young* guys."

"You're saying she had somebody with her Tuesday night?"

"Sure, she did. Jimmy from down in 202. It's so funny. He's only about seventeen. He lives there with his folks. And the laugh is, his old man is always hitting on Wig. You can tell he thinks he's going to get something off her if he keeps at it."

When I walked out to my truck they were still giggling.

So, Velma had lied. She hadn't been bowling with Tony. She had been playing games with Jimmy from 202. Whether she lied because she knew something or merely because she did not like me, I had no way of knowing. Maybe she didn't want me to dig up her infidelities. Hell, maybe he *had* been bowling.

All the trophies in their apartment had been inscribed Paramount Lanes. His bowling-ball bag had been inscribed Paramount Lanes.

I drove to Highway 99 and asked a harried female attendant at a Gulf station where the Paramount Lanes were. At the lanes I spoke to three different people. They all knew Anthony Tyner. Two agreed that he had been there Tuesday evening, but only one of them had any idea when he had left.

She was a hardbitten little woman with razor-thin lips and desiccated tea bags under her eyes. She probably smiled once a year at Christmas. "Near as I can recall, it was a little after 10:30. He was in a real snit. He wasn't playing well. I guess he bet some money with his pals and lost. Quite a bundle, from what I gathered."

Ten-thirty gave him plenty of time.

I drove to downtown Seattle, parked on Alaskan Way under the viaduct and got out a powerful hand lantern from behind the seat. The building I had seen Billy Greenlee disappear into last night was about two blocks away, at the edge of the renovated section.

Bit by bit, the city fathers had been restoring the Pioneer Square area, replete with old-fashioned street lamps and brick-lined alleyways. Even the cops paraded around in bowlers, swinging vintage nightsticks and wearing authentic uniforms from ninety years ago.

The building stood on the fringes of the renovated area. I skimmed the night faces for anyone I recognized, then ducked into the alley. It took me a while to find the crawl hole Billy had vanished into yesterday.

The last person to come out had stamped the boards so that several loose nails were embedded in the wall. I could see the prints of a sneaker or athletic shoe. It couldn't have been done from inside. That meant that either nobody was inside, or that there were other entrances and exits.

Prying the boards off and hinging them aside, I carefully put my head into the cavernous building and shined the lantern around in great sweeping arcs.

The first room was littered with broken wallboard, old smashed office furniture and several assorted plumbing fixtures lying like dinosaur bones.

I snaked into the orifice, located a path with the yellow beam and picked my way through the flotsam. To the left and around a corner, I discovered several other rooms and a sturdy but slanting staircase leading up into the heart of the building. The stairs had a path worn on them. The other rooms were drenched in a thick layer of dust and soot.

Climbing, I stopped periodically to flash the lantern's

beam around, making certain I wasn't going to fall through a hole and that nobody was about to clobber me with a two-by-four.

Billy F. Greenlee's lair was on the second floor, in an abandoned office that once belonged to a man who collected hunting trophies.

Two stuffed bears snarled mutely at me from the darkness. Several smaller trophies had been piled into a corner and battered or stomped to form a makeshift mattress. A boarded-up window looked out onto the alley over the back windows of a busy restaurant. The clanging of pots and pans and the moist smells of good living perfused his nest. Billy had constructed a little bookshelf out of salvaged bricks. It was jammed with tattered Louis L'Amour paperbacks.

Pawing through his personal effects, I found a handwritten resumé, a crib sheet he no doubt used when applying for jobs. It had the address of his high school in Tulsa, the addresses of two former employers as job references. On the back of the crumpled sheet he had jotted down a list of about thirty local companies, each X-ed off in dark pencil. He had made the rounds and come up empty. What a deal.

I began to search the rest of the labyrinthine building.

It didn't take me long to find him.

Billy was in the room next door, sprawled under a pinup calendar advertising Bagshaw Bearings. The model gracing the calendar looked almost prudish compared to recent trends in gynecological pinup photography. The year on the calendar was 1957.

Somebody had been at Billy with a knife, somebody with a much stronger stomach than mine. The deed had occurred so recently that tendrils of steam rose up from his exposed innards in the sword-beam of my lantern. The colors were bright, straight out of a medical text.

I stood very still, listening, wondering whether I was alone in the room, in the building. I regretted all the noise I had made breaking in.

Chapter Thirty-five

"THIS IS A LOT WORSE than a simple murder. It ain't pretty."

"No," I said. "It rarely is."

I was chatting with Bill Crum, a downtown detective with the SPD. "This is the second murder you've been involved in in two years, Black. That I know of. Or have you been involved in more that you're not telling?"

"You know me, Bill."

"That's just the trouble. What happened to your lip?"

"Kissed a horse."

"You kissed the wrong end." The corners of Crum's mouth curled upwards into a brief smile, then flattened as if some invisible artist had laid a steel ruler across his mouth and etched a straight line. "Now what's going on here? Who is this guy? I've got the feeling he's not just some de-horn you came up here to swill Thunderbird with."

Somebody had set up a generator and plugged in a string of portable lights. Several men were combing the room under the harsh, uneven glare of the bulbs while a ruddy-faced gentleman snapped flash pictures from every conceivable angle.

Bill Crum had buttonholed me and guided me to the wall where, through a slit in the boarded-up window, we could observe the kitchen activities in the restaurant across the alley. It was a tad better than watching a bunch of professionals fiddle with a split-open cadaver.

I said, "The guy's name is Billy F. Greenlee. There's no ID on him. I checked before I called you."

"You checked?" Bill Crum grimaced. "You touched him?"

"You might find something in the other room. And there

should be twenty-five hundred bucks cash around here somewhere. He had it on him last night. I tried to talk him into depositing it in a bank, but I don't think he fell for it."

"Where did a guy like this get twenty-five hundred bucks?"

"Lance Tyner gave it to him."

We both turned to Greenlee's body, crumpled in a corner of the bare room, a dirty and wrinkled shirt knotted around his face as a gag, hands wired behind his back with a steel coat hanger. His eyes resembled two pollywogs. Dead men's eyes didn't ordinarily look that odd, especially so soon after death. I had to assume someone had tampered with them, either before or after he expired, had poleaxed them with the same instrument they had used to slice him up.

"Lance Tyner? The guy they found shot in the U District Wednesday morning? These two guys are connected?"

"They were friends."

"Oh, shit."

A small, tidy man going bald, Bill Crum kept his hair cropped close to the skull, kept his nails immaculate and brushed his teeth after meals, even at work. If one gave him a chance, he would discourse indefinitely on the dangers of gum disease. His eyes were a jet-stream blue, piercing and frequently watery. Tonight they had been watery since the moment he had seen Greenlee. He was a gentle, soft-spoken man and his job was affecting his health in almost the same way it had affected mine.

"The Tyner killing? You messed up with that?"

"I'm investigating it for Tyner's fiancée."

"That little black gal?"

"Word spreads fast, doesn't it?"

"You know how it is when the city gets an interesting case. They didn't think it was much, at first. But he's engaged to this black woman. I understand she's quite pretty. And the guy's worth . . ."

"Fifteen million bucks."

"I guess you know that already. So how does this all hook up, Black?"

"All I know is the dead man and a gentleman named Leroy Hutchcroft were bosom buddies. Been calling himself Leroy Scroggs out here. Turns out, that's his sister's married name: Scroggs. And they both knew Tyner when

200

Tyner was bumming. I guess the Tyner kid had some hard times. Hutchcroft is wanted in Illinois for a number of offenses. Parole violation. Something to do with a cop killing. I had my hands on him this afternoon, but a couple of NRA-type crackers broke it up. Tyner's father and brother, the whole clan in fact. His sister even got a shot in."

"Sounds like you've been doing a lot of legwork."

"Some."

"Ralph doesn't know about it, if you have. Ralph's handling the Tyner case for the department."

"I try to stay out of the obvious places. I figure you guys are going to cover those pretty good."

"Why work at all? Why not just let the department handle it?"

"You know as well as I do that once a case gets cold it's twice as hard to follow a trail. I figure if we get in each other's way, we'll let each other know. If we don't, having me work on the case only doubles the chances we'll solve it."

"What you mean is, you don't think Ralph is going to put his heart and soul into it the way you will."

I shrugged.

"Well, you've got a good record. So you think Hutchcroft came after this guy?"

"When I talked to Greenlee last night, all he knew was that he had twenty-five hundred bucks and he was afraid Hutchcroft would take it."

"This man's been tortured," said Bill Crum, his voice lowering until I could barely hear it.

I almost said, "no shit?" Crum dry-washed his face in both palms. I watched an Oriental chef stick his head out the restaurant window below, hawk and spit, ignorant of the drama above him. "I know."

"Have any idea why a body would do that?"

"I'm afraid my imagination is played out."

"In the circles this poor slob traveled in, twenty-five hundred bucks cash was a lot of money. He probably had more than one acquaintance who might do this to him. You should see some of the things these de-horns do. Last summer a guy strung up his buddy, then poured lighter fluid all over his pants and set him ablaze. The poor bastard lived through it. He's still up at Harborview on the burn floor."

201

One of the men in rumpled suits carried a bone-handled knife over to Bill Crum. He held it delicately with a piece of Saran Wrap, using two fingers to lift it by the tips of the hilt. Crum said, "You ever see that before?"

The knife blade was powdered with dried blood, a quarter inch of the tip broken off, probably buried inside Billy Greenlee somewhere for the medical examiner to find. Stringy ribbons of flesh and other, unidentifiable matter girdled the base of the blade.

"It was laying under the body," said the dour man in the crumpled suit, the death technician.

About fourteen inches long, the knife looked cheap, made of poor, discolored steel, and had an eagle carved into the handle. The initials scratched on the side of the eagle read, 'LH.'

"I saw it, but only when I looked for his wallet."

Crum said, "What do you think 'LH' stands for? Leroy Hutchcroft?"

"That or Lemonade Herkyweather." Crum gave me a look. "Just a joke."

He nodded solemnly. This was not joke time.

I gave him the address of Leroy's sister in Monroe. Then I told him about the dusty footprint on the boards across the entrance to the building. When the cops arrived, they broke in the front door, so Bill Crum hadn't been through the crawl space. I took him downstairs and showed it to him. He ran over my story several times, then had one of the lab men take pictures and secure the boards as evidence.

Taking me back upstairs to view Greenlee, Bill Crum and another detective stood at Billy's feet and tried to reconstruct the murder while one of the death technicians cavalierly paged through the pinups in the 1957 calendar. Life went on. What a deal. It was dispiriting, all us detached professionals coldly poring over the crime scene while Billy slumped in the corner trying to watch it all through his flat pollywog eyes, the gag still in his mouth, his wrists still wired, his scrawny shoulders posed in a shrug of frozen agony. He had been tortured and eviscerated. Whoever had dispatched Billy had spent a good deal of time at it. So much time, in fact, that when the police arrived, they had cordoned the block off and searched the

202

building thoroughly, hoping the killer might still be nearby.

All they found to roust were three bearded de-horns sleeping in the basement. I had been keeping an eye on the building, too, since I'd arrived, and had seen nothing. My guess was I had missed the slayer by something under thirty minutes. I didn't know whether to be grateful or flustered.

By the time I got home it was almost two o'clock. I took a hot shower, scrubbing and shampooing myself diligently three or four times over. I needed to wash off the stink of death. I flopped into bed, hair still damp. This time, despite what I had just seen, I had no trouble sleeping. If I dreamed, in the morning I had no memories of it.

At 7:30 Saturday morning, I rolled out of bed and spent a few minutes with a wet comb trying to plaster my hair back down. I dressed in faded jeans, a striped shirt and a corduroy sport coat. I stashed a tie in my inside pocket.

The phone rang before I left the house. "Thomas?"

"How you doin', sister? How was the party last night?"

"Thomas. Martin Tyner just phoned me at home. He said you were involved last night in a murder downtown."

"How did Martin Tyner find out about that?"

"I told you he spends half the day hanging around our office. I guess he spends the other half pestering the police."

"Yeah, there was a little trouble last night."

"What happened?"

I explained briefly.

"Thomas, be careful."

"Sure."

"No, I mean it. It's too late to get another date for Saturday night."

I drove downtown and spoke to a man with a greasy face in the homicide/assault unit. He wasn't impressed that I had been a Seattle patrolman for ten years. Nor was he impressed with my private investigator's license. Glum, taciturn and just a bit conceited, he would only tell me that Leroy Hutchcroft had not been apprehended, and that nobody had been detained in last night's case.

At my local bank machine I punched my card into the machine and relieved it of two hundred bucks. It might be a long day.

The drive to Monroe gave me plenty of time to think, but

of course, thinking doesn't do you a bit of good unless you come up with something, and I didn't—only rehashed the case. Once in Monroe, I went straight to the house Colette Scroggs rented, tensely scanning the street and yard for a purple Mercury wearing stolen plates. The only car in her yard was the junker Chevrolet, and it had not moved an inch.

I decided a chat with the "battle-ax" next door might be in order before I went barging in to see if Leroy was hiding in a closet, a pair of cocked, nickel-plated .357s in his fists.

The white-haired widow who answered the door was in her eighties, perhaps early nineties, but was as nimble-witted as they come. She peered at me through a pair of bifocals, her fading hazel eyes taking me in.

"You were here yesterday," she announced, her voice quavery with age.

"Indeed I was."

"What happened to your lip?"

"Kissed a horse."

She cackled at that. "You wanted a kiss, old Loretta ain't been kissed in twenty years."

I laughed, too.

"At least you weren't on a toot. My old Henry used to go on a toot every once in a while and fall on his face. Come in, come in. Don't let me stand here and warm up the whole town." Even though the temperature outdoors was in the low seventies, I could feel the heat blasting out of her home. A lot of old people tried to hold the Fahrenheit number even with their age.

"I'm in a hurry," I said. "Is the lady next door home?"

Her eyes grew wary and frightened. "Haven't seen hide nor hair of her since last night just before dusk. Some whippersnapper drove up in a motorcar and picked up her and all the young'uns."

"Do you know what kind of car it was?"

She shook her head. "The guy who picked her up was a strange one, though. He wore long hair and had on shiny black pants. I think they must have been made out of leather. Can you imagine that? I thought leather was for handbags. And he had on a red shirt that was all torn to pieces, like maybe he was trying to get through a barbed wire fence in it. I guess I don't get out enough to keep up with things."

"A purple Mercury?"

"I don't know if it was a Mercury. I never did learn to drive so I don't pay much attention to motorcars. Every time I brought up the subject of driving I got in Dutch with Henry. Henry wouldn't hear of it. But now that you mention it, it does seem like it was purple. You're the third person to come and ask. The sheriff stopped by late last night. Then right after I got up, about five-thirty, a couple of fellers from Seattle came asking after him. You from Seattle, too?"

"Yeah, I'm afraid so. What'd those other fellas do when you told them they were gone?"

"Same thing you're gonna do, I 'spose. Went over and knocked one more time, then left."

I nodded. "Say?" She touched an arthritic hand to her face. "I hope you don't think I'm an old busybody, but those other fellas kept pretty mum about it. Why is everyone looking for her? She in trouble?"

"They're looking for the guy in the leather pants. He's her brother. He's a convict."

While she chewed that over, I went next door. Nobody answered. No tiny heads popped up behind the curtains. I walked around to the back, peering into each window as I passed, listening to the walls of the house.

I popped the back door without making too much noise, shouldering it and merely pushing until the lock popped. I didn't even break the jamb. I had popped more doors than I cared to recall and more often than not nothing broke, they just sprang open.

The kitchen had that hollow sound vacant houses all give off. It also had a queer smell I couldn't identify, not until I spotted the squashed diaper in the kitchen sink under a stack of cruddy dishes.

They had carted off some of the cardboard boxes, but not enough. I found the carton with family photos and other memorabilia in the living room. I hauled it into the kitchen and sorted through it at the table. I discovered one dog-eared envelope mailed from Sequim, Washington—pronounced skwim—the rainless capital of Western Washington.

The letters had originated from the Lone Vaquero Trailer Park and had come from Fritz and Irma McDougal. The last name did not jibe, but I could guess that Irma was

205

the grandmother of the children I had seen in this house yesterday. No doubt she had remarried. Probably several times. My guess was her first husband's name had been Lee Hutchcroft, Senior.

I drove to Mukilteo, waited an hour and took the ferry to Whidbey Island, then drove halfway up the island and got there just in the nick of time for the Port Townsend ferry run. The sun was shining on Whidbey Island, but by the time we steamed into Port Townsend it was drizzling. I took Highway 20 down to 101, then proceeded west.

It was a few minutes before one when I got to Sequim. Sure enough, the sun was out. Cumulus clouds banked up back in the foothills.

An efficient, smiling grease monkey told me how to find the Lone Vaquero Trailer Park. Before I drove out there, I stopped at a pay phone and dialed the county sheriff's office.

The dispatcher let me talk to a young-sounding deputy named Bradbury. Bradbury thought I was some sort of meddler. "You got *who* out in that trailer park?"

"A parole violator," I repeated. "His name is Leroy Hutchcroft and you can check with Seattle. He's wanted in Illinois and now he's wanted in Seattle in connection with a murder. He's armed and dangerous."

"And just what is it you want us to do?" Bradbury was either dense or he thought I was.

"I would like you to come out here and arrest him."

"Well sir, when we get confirmation of this information from the authorities in Seattle, *if* we get confirmation, we'll be happy to act. But until then, I'm afraid you'll just have to sit tight."

I was on the corner, half a block off 101 in a phone booth, watching traffic plod past. It was an interesting conglomeration of farm vehicles, pickup trucks, flatbeds and teenagers in hotrods. Small town life. What a deal.

A peroxide blonde riding in the passenger seat of a mud-spattered four-wheel drive gave me a look, twisting her head around, her eyes blazing with recognition.

It wasn't often Jacques Cousteau appeared on the streets of Sequim.

It was Colette Scroggs, alias Irma Hutchcroft. An old man in a battered derby was driving her and I could see at least two towheads sitting between them. The old man must have been Fritz McDougal. Half a block away, the truck burned rubber. The jig was up.

"Uh, Bradbury. I can't sit tight. I'm talking from a public phone booth in Sequim and I've just been spotted by one of Hutchcroft's relatives. I'm going out there to see if I can stop him."

"You just stay right where you are," Bradbury admonished. "Where are you?"

Hastily I gave him the address of the Lone Vaquero Trailer Park and hung up. I could only guess if they would hustle out there in time to save my butt.

Chapter Thirty-six

SEQUIM IS A SMALL TOWN overlooking the strait on the north point of the Olympic Peninsula, sheltered to the south by hundreds of miles of the rugged Olympic Mountains.

Meteorologists were fond of bragging that the wind currents off the Pacific dumped all their moisture on the mountains and were wrung dry by the time they hit Sequim. The hamlet received about seventeen inches per year.

Because of its rainless reputation and its moderate winter climate, Sequim had long been a favored retirement zone in the state. The hills and furrowed farmlands surrounding Sequim were choked with trailer parks and slapdash A-frame vacation housing on oversized, uncared-for plots.

It wasn't until I had gotten thoroughly lost that I knew Hutchcroft was going to have the jump on me.

On a country road I hailed a pretty girl astraddle a trotting horse.

"Lone Vaquero Trailer Park?"

"Sure," she said. "You're about five miles off, is all."

Following her convoluted directions, I found myself wending along a road overlooking the Strait of Juan de Fuca. Out in the strait several distant fishing boats chugged toward the Pacific and a tug towed a raft of logs east, inland to the mills. In Seattle, people paid through their noses for a sliver of this view. Here, it was all farmland, unused farmland, weeds and scrub pine.

Housing four hundred or so mobile homes, the Lone Vaquero Trailer Park was situated atop the bluff, but had sprawled out slowly since its inception. Outside No. 114, in the gravel and log-partitioned parking lot, I found three vehicles: a four-wheel drive truck, a tiny bashed-in Japanese coupe and a purple Mercury I was sure was registered to Martin Tyner, even though the plates were not his. The four-wheel drive was the same one I had seen on the street in Sequim.

Beyond the trailer, near the bluff, I could hear the windblown squeals of children.

Killing the engine, I left my Ford parked squarely behind all three vehicles so that none of them could get out. Then I took a handy-dandy ten-inch section of crowbar and sheathed it up my left sleeve, holding it in place with my curled fingers.

Colette Scroggs met me at the door. Her peroxide hair was in disarray. There were bags under her eyes.

"So what happened to your lip?" she asked.

"Spider bite. Your brother in?"

"Ain't seen him." She was lying. She had spoken too quickly and without thought. She had been rehearsing the lie for twenty minutes.

A gnome of a woman inserted herself between Colette and the door frame, fixing her muddy gray eyes on me. Her salt-and-pepper hair clung to her skull like scribbles. Cigarette smoke spiraled up from a stub in her knotted fist. I could see that her credo was "A man in the nest is worth two on the stoop."

"Don't just gawk at him, Irmy. Invite your gentleman friend in." She took a deep drag on the butt and eyed me with what I could only surmise was astute appreciation.

Colette gave her mother a look no daughter should bestow. Obviously momma did not understand all the implications of my arrival. Smiling gamely, she pulled her daughter roughly out of the way. I stepped inside the trailer and wondered what was next.

It was a double-wide, and I imagined it had two or three bedrooms hidden away in the back. The living room was larger than mine. The furniture was a bit shoddy, but everything was clean, except for an open disposable diaper on the end of the couch. Colette had already made her mark. Her pixie mother, almost a foot shorter than Colette, sat opposite me on the sofa and offered me an overstuffed easy chair. With some misgivings, I sat down, my back to the wall. What the hell.

"You a friend of Irmy's?"

"No, Mrs. McDougal. Actually, I'm looking for your . . . I assume he's your son. Leroy Hutchcroft?"

"Leroy! Of course, he's my son. Leroy come out here! Leeeeeroy?" She yodeled the name like some people yodeled hogs out of a wallow, her irritating voice an open invitation to mayhem.

He stumbled out, wearing his leather pants and a checkered wool shirt. His hair was lank and greasy and a lump blossomed over his right eye, presumably a memento of yesterday's scuffle. He carried a nickel-plated Colt in his right fist, dangling it down at his side so that neither of the women was aware of it. His knuckles were yellowish on the butt of the revolver.

The old man who had been driving the truck came out behind him, bleary-eyed, stammering something at Leroy, who paid no attention. I think he was timidly asking about the gun. The ramrod of this household was sitting across from me making squinty goo-goo eyes and sucking a hard glow into her stubby Chesterfield.

"Afternoon, Leroy."

"You shouldn't have come here, you scab."

Staring at the gun in his fist, I said, "You're right. I shouldn't have come. I wish I hadn't."

"So why did you? Damn it all to hell! If you just let things rest I would have been okay. Don't you see nuthin'? I ain't never going back to the jug. And you nor no one else is ever gonna make me." He began to lift the Colt, then thought better of it and let it pendulum at the end of his arm, ticking off the time for one of us. "It was a bum rap. Everything they ever got me on was a bum rap."

"You a policeman?" the old woman asked, her eyes growing wide as the cigarette smoke boiled around her face.

"He's a detective, Mama." Colette Scroggs went over and sat on the sofa next to her dissipated mother. Doing so gave Leroy a clean shot, should he choose to run up his tally.

"How'd you find this place?" Leroy combed his free hand through his hair, flopping the strands back over his ear. They did not stay. The gun arm, as if it were asleep, remained limply at his side. "Irmy saw you in town. How'd you find this place?"

"I'm a detective."

"Big shot. You and Lance's father. Both a couple of big shots."

"Why'd you kill him?"

"Lance's father's dead?"

"Lance."

"What are you talking about?" asked his mother. "Leroy?"

"Stay out of this, Ma. This is important stuff. Man stuff."

"Why'd you kill him, Leroy?"

"You're on the same damn kick those Tyners were on. I never touched Lance. Well, I touched him. I slugged him once, put him down for the count. But he pulled out of that like an angel."

"Yeah, he pulled out of it because we dragged him out of the surf. If we hadn't found him, he would have drowned. He'd have been dead weeks ago and you'd be in the clink."

The old man, bowlegged and leery of his gun-toting stepson, moved around and started to speak. "Maybe we should all . . ."

"Oh, come over here and sit down, you old fool," said his wife.

He plodded over and plunked down on the sofa beside Colette. The three of them sat wordlessly and watched our play, Colette firing up two cigarettes and handing one to her stepfather.

"What do you mean, he would have drowned?"

I explained briefly. Leroy looked startled when he discovered how close he had come to murder three weeks ago. It was hard to know why he cared. That was just water under the bridge compared to Billy F. Greenlee, or the actual murder of Lance. "So? I didn't *shoot* him. Hell, I never even carry a gun. It just ain't my style."

"Till now?"

"What did you want me to do? Those two were going to take me out where nobody could hear me screaming and bushwhack me. I don't think they were sure they could go through with it, but that was what they were planning. Sure, I swapped that old knife o' mine in for a couple of pistols. No big deal. I ain't plannin' to do nothin' with 'em."

"You should have come peaceably with me yesterday."

Leroy's lip curled into a sneer of contempt. "You've never spent any time in the slammer, have you? Course you ain't, or you wouldn't be talkin' like a greenhorn. You think I'm going to let some jughead like you take me back? Think again."

I let the cold crowbar slip down into my grip, then pulled my jacket open using both hands. "I don't have a gun on me, Leroy. I don't carry one."

"That's your tough luck, ain't it?"

"Leroy," his mother cautioned. "Now don't you be doin' somethin' fool-hardy. Not with your momma and your daddy squattin' right here."

"He ain't my daddy."

"Your stepdaddy. And you watch your tone."

"Yes, ma'am."

"Listen, Leroy," I said. "You've got a stolen car outside. It's got stolen plates on it and you've got a bundle of money that I doubt you can account for. I know where you are. I found you this time and I can find you again. Go ahead, run. You'll be in handcuffs before the sun sets."

"That money is all mine. Lance gave it to me a week ago. It was to get me a lawyer so I could get out of this jam I'm in."

"And that's why you were hanging around Babs Tyner? Trying to get out of your jam?"

I thought I saw a blush creep across his hard features. "Babs don't have nothin' to do with it. I was just . . . I was just havin' a time for myself while there was time left to do it. That's all. I called me a lawyer in Chi. He's only waitin' on my check in the mail to start work."

"You tryin' to tell me you're going back on your own? You're turning yourself in?"

"Maybe. Depends on what this legal eagle can come up with. I ain't settin' myself up for another fall. But I figure maybe he can get a deal for me, you know, now's I got some cash to grease the skids."

"What about that car outside?"

"What about it? You think those two goons are going to prefer charges?"

I wasn't certain I believed any of this. Maybe Leroy was bullshitting, maybe not. I noted that he no longer wore heavy motorcycle boots, but instead was shod in an old pair of jogging shoes. I wondered what kind of prints those soles would make.

"You check it out. I bet they never reported that Merc stolen. Bet they never did."

"Still, the cops want to talk to you about Lance's death."

"I'll get to 'em. I'm gonna call my lawyer today."

"Today's Saturday. You think he works weekends?"

"Monday, I'll call him."

"What about that gun in your hand?"

Leroy looked down at the pistol. "The gun stays. Otherwise you'll try an' break my arm like you did yesterday."

"So what about Billy?" I was on the rim of disaster now. If he had butchered Billy last night, he might explode.

"Billy? What the hell are you talking about?"

"You're good," I said, cradling the crowbar in my left fist, warming it. "You sound almost as if you don't know."

"Know what?"

"Where were you last night around ten, ten thirty?" The cops were going to hate me. They liked to be the first to spring questions like this one.

"Last night? I was . . . Irmy and the kids . . . I picked 'em up yesterday afternoon and then I had some errands to run. I was in town until late. We grabbed the 12:15 ferry."

"You were with him that whole time?" I turned to Irma Scroggs. Before replying, she looked to her brother and got the nod. Had he known why I was asking, he would have been more wary. Or would he? It could be that he was a whole jump and a half ahead of me, playing the innocent to the hilt.

"He dropped us off in Holly Park. Picked us up right before the ferry left."

"So where were you last night between say, nine thirty and eleven?"

Leroy shrugged. "I was around. Like I said, I had some errands to run."

"You have anybody who can testify to that?"

He shook his head. "They was personal errands."

"Billy Greenlee was killed last night about that time. In Seattle."

"Billy?"

"Your old pal, Billy."

"You're lying."

"In that building across the alley from the Chinese restaurant. You ever go up there with him? Maybe not. He was hiding out from you."

"He went back there? Sure, we used it last winter. No place else to go. The missions didn't have room. What do you mean he was hiding out from me?"

"Lance gave you both twenty-five hundred bucks, right? Billy was afraid you were going to come after his share."

"Me? Hell, Lance gave me the twenty-five hundred and then he gave me ten grand for a lawyer. He said he'd get me more if I needed it. There! That's proof. Why would I plug Lance if he was going to give me more money for the lawyer when I needed it? That would be slitting my own throat."

"Anybody but you hear Lance say he would give you more when you needed it?"

Leroy mulled it over. "Lance was a man of his word, even if the rest of us weren't. He said something, you knew he meant it."

"Sure, you knew he meant it, but could you prove he *said* it?"

"What are you gettin' at?"

"You say Lance was going to give you more money when you ran out. You say Lance gave that ten grand to you of his own volition. If you don't have any witnesses to either of those things, do you think the cops are going to believe you? You think a jury will? They're going to think you robbed Lance and then killed him."

"A jury! What the hell is this? This smells like a frame. This smells like another goddamned frame!"

The gun arm rose as he spoke, whether voluntarily or through some subconscious impetus, I could not tell. The weapon wobbled in his fist. I saw the nickel-plated hammer glitter as it flicked back and pounded at the chamber.

A surge of adrenaline raced through my bloodstream.

I kicked myself backwards, toppling the easy chair against a rickety tea table, somersaulting onto my back.

"Shit!" he said at the same time the gun popped.

It didn't roar, it popped. It sounded as if we were all inside a tin can some child had smashed with a stone. My ears rang and I lay still, sprawled behind the tipped chair as if I had been hit, not certain that I had not been.

"Oh, dear God," came the cigarette-mulched voice of his mother.

Footsteps padded across the hollow trailer floor and I could feel the air pressure change as he opened the door.

Chasing him wasn't in the cards. My stubby crowbar was good for mice and the occasional inebriated Girl Scout, but it wasn't going to do much against his .357 Magnum.

"Fritz, check him out. Fritz? Is he dead?"

"I ain't gonna check him out. What if he's . . ."

"Look at him, Fritz! You're the man of the house. Go over there, damnit, and see what happened to him."

I had not moved, was listening to Leroy outside starting the Mercury, listening to the whining engine as it whirred while he tried to maneuver around my pickup. In a minute, he would come back for my keys. I did not move an inch. The crowbar was in my right hand now, my thumb caressing its dull edges.

"Fritz! Get over there, you big sissified laughingstock! See if that man is dead. Lord almighty, my Leroy kilt a man in my own living room and my husband won't go see."

"So what, Momma," said Colette. "He was a dork."

The old man tiptoed over to where I lay face down behind the capsized easy chair, peeped over the chair and announced, "Yep. He's dead all right." He wasn't getting any closer then he had to.

Outside, I heard a clang as metal crunched against metal. Leroy was trying to bull his way out, no doubt ramming my pickup with Tyner's Mercury. Fixing it would take a week of my spare time and a couple of pounds of Bondo.

A car door slammed. The air pressure in the trailer changed again as Leroy burst into the room. His mother greeted him, "You kilt him, Leroy! He's dead as a mackerel."

"Bull! I didn't even aim at him. Get up, you fake!"

I didn't move. "Get up or I'll drill you where you lay, you queer worm!"

"He's dead, Leroy."

"He ain't dead. I didn't aim at him. He can't be dead."

She said, "He ain't moved an inch since you been gone."

Fritz spoke. "Maybe you didn't aim, but you musta hit him, 'cause he's dead. I checked."

"Oh, hell," said Leroy, the tone of his voice sampling despair. I had one ear flat against the trailer floor and it magnified the sounds of their movement. He walked toward me and pulled the chair away, a sound like cannons.

215

Before he could check out my recent death, a child ran into the trailer wailing, "Momma! Momma! Momma!"

I had heard terrified skirls before, and this sounded genuine. "Momma, Sunshine fell off the cliff. Sunshine was playing outside the fence. She fell off the cliff."

Judging by the speed they used evacuating the trailer, Sunshine was not the pet dog, but rather one of the younger children, possibly the toddler in diapers, the one I had carried yesterday.

I looked up. I was alone.

I dropped the crowbar into my back jeans pocket and shambled after the parade.

In the distance, if you listened very carefully against the susurrus of the wind off the strait, you could hear, coming our way, the whimper of a siren.

Chapter Thirty-seven

A WOODEN SPLIT-RAIL FENCE zigzagged along the edge of the bluff, running toward the woods which lay to the south. Judging by the distance to the water, at least from where I was running, the bluff sloped precipitously a couple of hundred feet.

No child could survive that fall.

I trotted after the clot of frantic relatives, who in turn trotted after Leroy Hutchcroft, racing along at the head of the pack, the forgotten pistol still in his hand. When I got there the knot of relatives and concerned neighbors was milling back and forth on the cliff edge, rubbernecking, speechless with grim dismay and foreboding.

The children screeched like birds, "Don't move, Sunshine! Don't move!"

Colette kept muttering, "Why'd you kids let her get so close? Why'd you kids let her get so close?"

Jaws clenched, Leroy was just beginning his descent, oblivious of the crowd and of me. I could not see the pistol. It was not in either hand. He needed both of those to keep his precarious grip on the bluff.

The bluff was some sort of crumbly sandstone and had been wearing away for centuries. Tufts of Scotch broom grew along the edge, not enough to break a fall, but certainly enough, if one were careful and did not tug too hard, to use for handholds.

"Get back. Get back," I said, warning them all off. "You're standing way too close. All we need right now is somebody else to go over."

Kneeling in the sand on the cliff edge, I peered down. Leroy was ten feet below me, chipping stubby stirrups into the cliff face with his feet, digging handholds with the bar-

217

rel of the pistol, which he tucked back into the waistband of his pants.

Below him, clinging to a small Scotch broom shrub, Sunshine was frozen, one bare and scraped leg cocked up over a portion of the crumbly scree, and another dangling over a one-hundred-twenty-foot drop to the log debris on the beach.

She was the child in diapers, the one I had dandled yesterday.

It was a sight nothing would ever erase from my brain. It didn't look real—to see a child's death that close—looked more like a doll someone had flung away, except for the fear moving in her eyes.

I wheeled around and addressed the group. I pointed at a man who had slicked-back, silver hair.

"You!" I shouted. "You're in charge of keeping everybody back from the edge. Has anybody gone to call the fire department?" They stared at me like scared students on the first day of school. "You . . ." I jabbed a finger at a spry-looking man in his late fifties. "Go phone the local fire department and get a unit out here." He turned and galloped away toward the trailers. The silver-haired man was already organizing the crowd, herding them back, assigning people to watch the children in the group.

"Now," I said. "Who's got some rope?"

"I got a ski-tow rope," a woman volunteered.

"How long is it?"

"Fifty feet."

"Get it."

I turned and looked down at Sunshine and her uncle. She had fallen down the sheer drop about fifteen feet, then slid in the loose sand another ten. Her perch now was the last stop before the beach. The bluff sloped steeply to where she held on. It was difficult to see how she had avoided sliding over the edge.

One man going after her was dangerous enough. If I went, too, I might dislodge enough earth to push her off. Leroy was making slow, precarious progress.

Sunshine began losing her grip.

"She's going!" I shouted.

Leroy looked up at me, then down at his niece, whose tiny hands were beginning to open.

Without pausing, Leroy jammed the pistol into his

218

waistband, cocked around in mid-air and leaped like some sort of gigantic flying squirrel.

He seemed to hang in the sky over the beach forever. He landed far down the scree, spurring both heels into the loose sand and pebbles. For a moment I thought he was going over, or that the small landslide he had created was going to wash Sunshine away. But they both held. He grabbed her by her tiny white shirt, then by the rear of the diaper, and finally hugged her around the waist, hugged her so tightly that her face turned bright pink.

"Don't move," I said. "The fire department will get you up." Leroy looked at me, then down at the waves on the beach.

"Not likely," he said, grinning ironically. He began digging his toes in and making his way up the scree.

When he was halfway up, the lady with the ski-tow rope arrived, panting, and we rigged a line, flipping Leroy Hutchcroft an end of it. As he looped the line around Sunshine and knotted it into place, he looked up at me and I saw something in his eyes I hadn't seen there before. Frustration? Despondency? Resignation? I could not tell. He realized I could hoist up the child and leave him marooned.

We hauled Sunshine up, then cast the line down for Leroy. I could have left him stranded, bullying anyone who wanted to help him up, but the slope was bad enough that he might have fallen. I wanted him in custody, not splattered at the base of a hundred-foot cliff. A siren screamed through the trailer park. I guessed it was a sheriff's car, although it might have been the fire department.

When Leroy crawled up over the bluff edge, I said, "The jig is up, fella. That gun you've got is full of sand and the sheriff is here. Why not come in peaceably and call this lawyer of yours in Chicago?"

He shot a look of sudden concern past my shoulder and like a dope I half turned to see what he was looking at. Two big-bellied sheriff's deputies in goofy-looking cowboy hats were traipsing across the end of the trailer park, heading our way.

Before I could turn back to face Leroy squarely, something hard glanced off my skull and the cosmos flashed blue and starry and unbelievably bright in my eyes. Leroy floated over my head and grinned like a circus clown. Trying to recall what I was doing in this world, I sank to one knee.

Leroy sprinted across the field, hoping no doubt to get in amongst the trailers and confuse the cops. By now both the deputies were jogging, and both had their long-barreled pistols drawn.

I got up and chased him, my legs rubbery at first, then gathering strength.

He wasn't much of a runner and he wasn't expecting me to sneak up from behind, had his eyes alternately on the bumpy ground in front of him and the two deputies who called out to him, their words lost in the wind of our running.

As in a dream, giving one final spurt of effort, I caught him low, behind the knees. We went down in a sliding, tumbling muddle and—luck of the draw—something very solid hit me in the mouth, smashing my lip again. I had to shake my head to clear the pinprick stars out of my eyes.

When I could see, Leroy was standing over me, his sand-filled pistol aimed at the deputies.

Chests filling quickly with rapid bursts of air, both of their pistols were trained on Leroy. It was another Mexican standoff.

"Don't do it, Leroy," I whispered. I could have kicked at the pistol in his hands, but I was afraid it would precipitate a shooting.

"Drop that weapon, motherfuck," said one of the cops.

"The gun is full of sand," I said. "It'll blow up if he fires it."

"Drop that weapon, motherfuck." A lot of cops thought they had to use gutter talk when making arrests. They thought it was because they were tough, but I had been a cop, and it was something else, something a little more basic. It was a mouthful of fear.

"I'm telling you," I said. "His gun is spiked. It's filled with sand."

Of course, they could not take my word for it. I might have been in cahoots with him.

"Just let me go," Leroy said, bartering. "Let me get out of here. Damn that Colette. She watched them damn kids, this never would have happened. This always happens to me. Damn, nothing ever goes right."

"You can make this go right," I said. "Drop the gun in the grass, Leroy. That's the only way it'll turn out right."

"You gotta drop it," said the second deputy. "We can't let you go. You must know that."

"Let me go."

"You gotta drop it."

"Put it down, motherfuck."

For almost a full minute all four of us were etched in time, three pairs of eyes focused on Leroy.

Somebody moved.

It happened so quickly I couldn't be sure, from my position, whether it was one of the deputies or Leroy.

Four shots rang out in succession, sounding no more lethal than extra-loud fire crackers. I only saw one of the flashes, and it had leaped from the bucking muzzle of the deputy's gun, the deputy who had been using the harsh language. Leroy crumpled like a rag doll.

Feeling woozy, my lip swelling along with all the soft stuff inside my skull, I rolled to my hands and knees, shook my head only enough to find out that it hurt like hell, and crawled over to Leroy. He lay flat on his back. I picked the nickel-plated Colt out of his hands by the end of the barrel and tossed it aside.

The deputy had pumped all four shots into a close grouping in the center of his chest. I figured he had about two minutes to live, if that. I didn't have the presence of mind to tell the deputies to radio for an ambulance, or for medics, or for whatever they had in this county. Not that it would have made any difference. His left lung was collapsed and his shirt was sopping with bright, scarlet blood.

"Ain't doin' so hot today, am I?" Leroy gasped, his words coming in tiny gulping bits and watery pieces. My guess was his remaining lung was filling with blood.

"You're all right, Leroy," I said. "You saved Sunshine. If you hadn't been there, she would have fallen."

"Yeah, I guess I did, didn't I?"

"You were great."

"Buried the money. It's down by the big log by the beach. Tell the family, will ya?"

"Sure."

"Leroy." Both deputies were bending over us now, pistols still drawn. I looked up at the one who had done the

221

shooting and said, "Hell, you got two more rounds. Let him have it."

He gave me a sickeningly guilty look and I was immediately sorry I had blurted the words. Shooting someone was always difficult. For me it had been so traumatic it resulted in my resigning from the force.

"Leroy," I said. Staring up at the sky, his eyes were glazed, but he was still passing air. "Leroy? Did you kill Lance Tyner?"

"Hell . . ." He gasped for air like a beached bass, speaking as if a great animal were resting on his diaphragm. "I tole you I didn't. Nobody ever believes ol' Leroy. What difference does it make now?"

"Did you?"

"You figure it out."

"What about Billy?"

"Billy?" He seemed to have forgotten Billy Greenlee was dead.

"Do you know who killed Billy?"

"Billy was a homo. He had a lot of rough friends. Hell, he'd blow a guy for two bits."

"They found a knife under Billy's body. It was Mexican, had the initials LH on it. About ten inches long." Leroy focused his eyes on me and they remained focused. "Leroy?"

I pressed an index finger up alongside the carotid artery in his neck, finding nothing. He was no longer breathing.

I looked up at the deputy who had done the shooting and said, "Sorry about what I said."

"Sure." He wheeled around on one booted heel, holstered his pistol in his clamshell holster and clumped toward his car.

I buttonholed his buddy and began jawing like a kid at a picnic. I told him about Leroy snatching Sunshine off the ledge on the bluff, about the case, about Billy Greenlee's murder, about all the things I had been doing the last few days, about what I had seen of Lance's and Leroy's history. I yapped and babbled and blathered, frantic that he understand everything so he could make his partner understand what I had been thinking when I had spoken out of turn—or what I had not been thinking. He listened and nodded. On the ferry on my way back to Seattle with all the weekend tourists, I realized he would never reveal a

222

flyspeck of it to his partner. No matter what I said, to them I was an interloper and Leroy was riffraff.

And who was I to judge? That was exactly how I had viewed things ten minutes ago.

They strapped his body to a slab of a stretcher and slammed it into an ambulance, his family, alternately hysterical and paralyzed, standing around being consoled by neighbors. I debated whether or not to tell Colette or the old lady about the money buried down by the beach. In the end, I told them both. It would give them something to take their minds off the family tragedy.

Leroy wasn't even over the hill when they trudged toward the bluff trail to the beach carrying shovels, a teenaged neighbor girl watching the children.

Colette singing a pop song off-key, her imp-like mother sucking a cigarette to death and the henpecked stepfather bringing up the rear—they went off to look for the end of the rainbow. Moe, Curly and Larry.

Chapter Thirty-eight

DURING THE FERRY RIDE my headache blossomed into something from a nightmare.

Scrapping with Leroy, besides puffing up my lip again until it was as tight as a cooked sausage, had given me a mild concussion. A finger on my left hand had gotten jammed in the scuffle, was stiff, swollen and tender.

Giddy from the rolling action of the waves on the sound, I sat on a bench near the bow. The city was shrouded in a dank, windblown cloud.

A microdot mist, half drizzle and half salt spray, licked at my face. The steady blow sifted through my clothes until I began to feel the onslaught of hypothermia. The chill, along with the accompanying shivers, revived my thinking processes somewhat.

It was almost dark when I wheeled up to Lucy's house.

A tall, thin-boned black woman who looked as if she could have made her living as a fashion model answered the door, peeping past my shoulder. While she eyeballed me, she flipped the collar of her coat up against her pipestem neck, pigeonholing me as something from the wrong phylum. She was dolled up for a party, a ring of cerulean blue spackled with glitter encircling her eyes.

"Is Lucy home?"

"Lucy gone off somewheres. What you want?"

Judging by the atoms of alcohol wafting in the air between us, she had already quaffed a couple of stiff belts.

I told her who I was and explained my working relationship to Lucy. She seemed dubious until one of the twins showed up, puppylike, underneath her posed elbow.

"At's him, Mom. At's him. The private eye we's tellin' you 'bout."

She obviously did not remember being told about any private eye, but she let it pass.

"I'm curious," she said, selecting her words with the care of someone who had always been much too conscious of the impression they were making. "Do you find that being a private detective puts bread and butter on the table?"

"Sometimes." We both stared, each trying to out-tough the other. "Sometimes, I have to make do with cake."

Her eyes folded into slits, like tiny anthracite umbrellas. She was aware of my sarcasm and all that it implied, much more tuned in to the complexities of conversational paranoia than I had imagined.

A car pulled up in front of the house and honked one long and four short ones. The tall woman disappeared from the doorway for a moment, then rocketed out the door, carrying a tiny, useless purse.

"Bye-bye, Momma," said the twin, softly.

She didn't even flick her head. She tapped on spike heels down the steps and faded busily into the dark interior of the car. It sped off, the sound of its mufflers emitting a long soft hiss against the wet streets.

I turned to the twin, who watched his mother speed off with a man I supposed was a stranger.

"What did the ocean say to the beach?"

He gave me a blank look that gave only feeble indications of mutating into a grin. "What?"

"Nothing. It just waved."

It took him almost a minute to calm down. He was P.W. Peckerwood was the laugher. While he rollicked, his twin brother, munching a stalk of celery, showed up at the door, adjusted his taped glasses, gave me a stony look and invited me in.

Flat on her back on the living room couch, their older sister, Cleata, was sawing zzzs, her dress yanked indecorously up around her thick, muscular thighs. Some unknown pixie prankster had jammed the stem of a plastic yellow daisy under the frayed hem of her panties. I had the feeling the boys partially disrobed her every time she got snockered, their own private joke, their own unique revenge for her abuses. I bet they decorated her like a Christ-

225

mas tree, too, when they got the opportunity. Her snores resembled some sort of machine lacking lubrication and on its last legs.

"She out," announced P.W. "Been suckin' up the wrong sort of chemical mixture to support life."

D.W. jabbed at the bridge of his glasses. "She drunk on her butt."

"Been talkin' 'bout inheritin' herself ten million smackers all day. Couldn't stand the 'citement." P.W. dropped one limp hand into the other, making a loud slapping noise, his brilliant imitation of Cleata conking out.

"Maybe we could go into the kitchen and talk?" I said.

"Don' worry. She out!" said P.W., plucking up a cushion from the end of the sofa, flopping it across his sister's face, smirking up at me. The snoring choked off immediately. I expected her to gag, cough, awaken and knock him away, but nothing happened.

We stood like that for quite some time, the boy stuffing the pillow into his besotted sister's face, grinding it with his elbow, her muscular legs jutting out akimbo, unmoving, the other twin standing alongside the affair grinning an identical grin.

I was the first to break. They knew I would be.

Snatching the pillow out from under his elbow, I sailed it across the room onto another sofa. The snoring resumed at its previous cadence and volume, Cleata seemingly undisturbed by their macabre game.

"She out," said P.W.

"She out," said D.W., half in jest, half in mockery of his brother's sober manner.

"I need to talk to you boys about Lance Tyner, and what he said that night when he came here."

The twins glanced at each other. I fancied I saw signals of guilt pass between them. P.W. hitched at his baggy corduroy trousers and said, "Yeah, maybe we should handle this business right now, 'fore it go any further."

D.W. only nodded and avoided my eyes. He went across the room and curled up in a huge tattered armchair. P.W. marched back and forth across the room, his eyes glued to the patterns in the frayed carpet. Cleata's snoring continued unabated. I sat on a rickety straightbacked chair that

226

someone with sticky fingers had abandoned in front of the blank television screen.

"We wasn't exactly truthful wid you the other day, 'bout Lance comin' here in the night . . . you know."

"Keep talking." I tried to keep the excitement out of my voice. If they voluntarily confirmed what I had come here to wring out of them, the case would be over. I had been putting it together all the way back to Seattle on the ferry. I only needed to hear one thing.

"Lance came lookin' for Luce 'cause he was hurtin' real bad."

"Yeah?"

P.W. ceased his tramping and looked at his brother, who nodded. "Lance was hurtin' 'cause some dude shot him. We seen the hole. We got him a clean shirt and he stuffed it in there to stop the bleedin'."

"Cleata's shirt," added D.W.

"He came here so Luce would help him. Only Luce was at dis choir practice. They gittin' ready for some special deal tomorra. We din't know when she be home. Momma never home. Then Cleata show up wid some a her friends an' Lance, he went away. Guess he din't want no one to know about his gittin' shot. Maybe he be embarrassed."

"Bad news," added D.W. "He made us promise not to tell a soul what we seen."

"We promised," said P.W. "That's why we couldn't tell you. Bad news."

"We never even tole Luce. She still don' know."

"Why are you telling me now?"

"Tellin' you," said P.W., " 'cause you been fair with us. You treat us like people, 'stead a couple a nitwits you'd jus' as soon wipe out wid a can a bug spray."

" 'Sides," said D.W. from his perch in the chair. "You a 'tective. You gonna find who kilt Lance and git 'em."

"Punch 'im up," urged P.W., swinging his fist through the air and smacking it into the palm of his other hand.

"You find him, you gonna shoot him?" asked D.W.

"I think I'll do something worse than just shooting," I said. D.W.'s eyes began to swell with imaginings.

"I think you should punch 'im up, den shoot him," said P.W.

"Sorry to disappoint you boys, but I don't usually carry a gun."

"Huh?" D.W. was incredulous.

"You crazy, man?" said P.W. "You and Cleata was mixin' in it, and you never had a gun? You crazy? Cleata carry a gun everywheres." He scooted across the room, dug around in a shabby coat flung on the dining table and pulled a nickel-plated revolver out, bracing it in two hands.

"Whoa, there," I said. "Watch where you're pointing that little machine."

I walked across the room and lifted the revolver out of his hands, flipped open the cylinder and dropped six weighty little blunt bullets into my palm. It was a .357 Magnum, nickel-plated. A Colt. It might have been the mate of the pistol Leroy Hutchcroft had pulled on me this afternoon, the one he had appropriated from the Tyners. Or it might have been a look-alike.

"You boys better learn this about guns right now, hear me?" They both nodded solemnly. "Don't ever point a gun at something you don't want to kill. Understand? You want to kill that wall. Point it at that wall. You want to kill the floor. Point it at the floor. But don't point it at a person, ever, unless you want to kill them. All guns are loaded. You remember that, and you'll be all right."

They nodded.

I made them relive Tuesday night, from the moment Lance Tyner knocked at their door and they told him Lucy was at choir practice, until the moment he left, shortly after Cleata showed up, several toasted cronies in tow. Though they had both ridden in his car in the past, boasted that he had gone over a hundred miles an hour on the freeway with them, neither of them had bothered to look out the window to watch him drive away. It had been dark. It had been late. Had he been alone in the car? I suspected that he had, but it would have been nice to have confirmation.

"Did Lance have anything with him?"

"Like what?"

"Like some papers?"

"Naw."

"Did he say anything about any papers?"

"Naw."

"He did say sompthin," interjected P.W. "He said 'tell Lucy the cowboys got it.' "

"The cowboys got it?"

"Yeah."

"Did you tell her?"

"Yeah. She thought we crazy."

"I don't. You're beautiful."

Lucy arrived in the company of the tall, slim black man I had seen with Cleata several days ago. Their relationship looked tentative, at best.

"Thomas?"

Lucy wore a simple and short brown shift, acres of wiry leg showing. She danced across the living room, hesitated momentarily to give Cleata's sleeping form a disgruntled look, then stopped short of me, expectant. I think she wanted to give me a peck, but wasn't sure.

"Lucy," I said. "One of Lance's former friends got himself killed last night." I cast a meaningful look at her sister on the davenport.

Lucy picked up on my meaning. "What time?"

"The cops figure sometime between nine thirty and eleven."

Shaking her head, Lucy moved closer and said, "Cleata was here until about ten thirty or eleven telling everybody what she was going to do when she got a rich sister."

Lucy didn't look too thrilled at the memory.

"What's the matter?" I asked.

"People are already treating me differently. I had no idea how things would be. Chances are, I'll just be poor old Lucy until the end of time, but people are all different. It's an experience."

The man in the doorway turned on an infectious smile. He was the young man who had given Lucy the desirous glances the first night I had driven her home. He had tried to get Cleata and Mavis and the others to lay off me the other day. With certain reservations, I liked him. Lucy tossed a weary smile in his direction.

"I think I know who killed Lance."

Except for the obscene buzz-saw snoring, the room grew still. Lucy said, "Who?"

"You'll have to bear with me. I'm going to try something I've only done one other time, and that time it turned into a real bust."

"What?"

"I'm going to pull an Agatha Christie."

Chapter Thirty-nine

STAGY, THEATRICAL RIGMAROLE, put-ons for gasping school-girls and the rest of that drawing room razzmatazz had never been my forte.

An evening of exposing murderers in front of an audience was not something I had believed in, or been particularly adept at. The one time I had tried it, it had resulted in a choreographed routine of undiluted slapstick.

Even now, when she thought I was getting too big for my britches, Kathy Birchfield would address me as the noble Nero.

From the Peebles's kitchen I telephoned Kathy and told her what I had in mind.

"You've done it, Thomas," she exclaimed. "You've figured it out. Who?"

"Later. I haven't verified all my facts yet." I gave her detailed instructions. "Not another Nero Wolfe?" she said.

"This one should work out. I've got a handful of puppets to work with. All I have to do is pull the right strings."

"Oh, Thomas. Be careful."

"Thanks for the confidence."

"I do have confidence in you. It's just . . . last time was such a disappointment."

"Not to worry."

I phoned Martin Tyner.

"Black, you bastard. I'll have your hide! I've hired detectives to trace your every move. They'll follow you until you lead them to Lance's last will and testament."

"You're a broken record, old fella. You'll have the will. I know where it is. If you want it, you'll meet Kathy Birchfield outside the offices of Leech, Bemis and Ott in forty minutes."

"You must think I'm a dodo bird to fall for that ruse again."

"Call her up. She'll confirm it. And get your son there, too. If either one of you is carrying a weapon, the deal is off."

"You know damn well that hoodlum stole our guns."

"I'm sending an off-duty Seattle cop with her, understand? Either one of you is carrying anything he shouldn't be, forget the will. I'll light a match to it. And by the way. I located your car."

"Black! No, damn you! Dare to touch that document and you'll be sorrier'n a rat's ass."

"That's an old tune."

I hung up and got hold of Smithers, who I knew was off tonight. Fortunately, he was home, not out somewhere metamorphosing into a third-rate lounge lizard. I told him that if he wanted to meet his blind date, he had better see Kathy outside the offices of Leech, Bemis and Ott. I explained the situation.

After making several more calls, I told Lucy where to meet me and drove to Federal Way.

The drizzle had tapered off. I parked behind the house in the spongy turf in front of the orchard. I needed some time in Martin Tyner's house alone. My plan was to force a door and make myself at home, but I was surprised to discover Babs there.

When the mangy dog snarled and attacked me, Babs Tyner met me in front. She wore a black and white vertically striped jumper and black tights. Her hair needed washing.

"You? Did you ever catch up with Leroy and my father?"

"He didn't tell you about it?"

"No. What?"

"We'll get into that later. I don't have much time."

Together, we locked the barking mutt in the shed in the yard, where he clawed rhythmically at the door. Babs did not seem to mind when I went inside and began searching the house, only traipsed along after me, floating dull stories about various and sundry friends.

I found some of what I needed in a cardboard box that had been shoved under the old man's bed.

It only took a minute to locate both wills in the bookcase, folded into a volume of Frederick Remington reproductions. I turned my back to Barbara Tyner, shimmed them inconspicuously inside my coat and excused myself, sought out the bathroom and sat on the throne perusing them.

I was no whiz at deciphering legal jargon, but it was easy enough to see that Lance had had trouble making up his mind in this, as he had in many things. The two wills were opposite sides of a coin. It was a long while before I took out a wooden match, scratched it on a strip of cement between the tiles in the tub and touched the flame to the bottom corner of one of the documents. When the remnants of the charred document had flushed away in the commode, I went out into the main body of the house and opened the cardboard box I had found under Tyner's bed.

In the box were two hooded sheets, eye holes scissored out. Lucy would recognize them.

The first arrivals were Bill Crum and two officers he had requested from the King County Police. Had I been using my senses, I might have laid it all out for them right then and there, and called off the midnight jamboree.

Then again, getting a search warrant for this place would be no easy proposition. As it was, I thought I could wangle permission from Tyner to stay in his house, and that would be crucial later.

Bill Crum was there as the official representative of the Seattle Police Department in the investigation of Billy Greenlee's death. He was polite and patient, sucking on a pipe, tamping the tobacco down with his almost square thumb. His cohorts from King County were not so dapper or so long-suffering.

One said, "Hey, guy, you got something to give us, fork it over. What is this crap? We ain't got all night to jick-jack around."

Crum spoke softly, then sucked on his pipe stem. "Black knows what he's doing. He's a good man. Let him make his play."

The King County cop telegraphed him a look of consternation, then sat down, twirling his hat in his hands, spinning it onto the floor more than once.

Ten minutes later, Ralph Rasmussen showed up alone, representing the SPD in the Lance Tyner murder. He sat next to Bill Crum and they whispered together. We all waited in the only finished room in the house. I had barricaded chairs across the fireplace and the original painting on the wall. Babs Tyner ogled the plainclothesmen, trying, I think, to spot where they strapped their pistols.

Smithers, Kathy, Martin Tyner and Beulah, the receptionist for Leech, Bemis and Ott, arrived together in Smitty's Camaro. A few moments later Tony Tyner skidded into the yard in Velma's car. Velma was sitting in the passenger seat. When she sauntered into the house she was wearing a red pantsuit that was so snug Crum had to suppress a giggle.

"My own goddamned house," said Martin Tyner, when he got into the living room and saw the congregation arranged on folding metal chairs I had found in a back room. "What the hell is this?"

"You want to see the will, you sit down with the others and wait. One more guest must show up before we begin."

"Give it over, you goddamned pissant!" Martin Tyner made a move toward me. Smithers jumped between us and held up his bare hands. "Mr. Black will show you what he wants you to see in his own sweet time."

"That's for damn sure," chorused one of the King County cops, hunkering with his elbows on his knees, still twirling his hat in his large knuckly hands.

"There's two wills," said Martin Tyner, the veins in his forehead throbbing. "Which one have you got?"

"Why, the one that's signed, of course."

"You seen it? You read it?"

"Yes."

"It's got a signature? Lance's signature?"

"Yep."

He gave out a goatish little snort. "You smartass. If you think you can wrangle some sort of cut for yourself, you better think again. It ain't no good unless it's witnessed. Them damn things ain't no good. We're takin' it to court."

"How do you know you'll need to? Perhaps your son left it all to you, the whole kit and caboodle."

The thought calmed Martin Tyner—momentarily. Then

he got dyspeptic. "I ain't never said none of this scum could come in here. I'm tellin' you that for the record. You people are all trespassing."

I walked past him, heading smartly toward the door. Tyner grabbed at the material of my coat sleeve, pinching it between his remarkably powerful bony fingers.

"Where the hell you going?"

"Me? I'm going home to bed. You just threw me out."

"Okay. Okay. You can stay. The others go."

I shook my head. "It's all or nothing."

"Big deal. Stay. Okay, everybody stay. Jeezus, life is a bitch. Nothing in the last five days has gone right. I been riding this damn roller coaster for the last year, my own damn kid inheriting what I should have got, then having to battle him for it. Then, he turns up dead. Life is a bitch."

"Sit down," I said. "You're going to stroke out if you jack your blood pressure any higher."

It took five finger-strumming minutes before Lucy showed up, arriving in a grimy, mud-spattered cab. Cleata stumped in behind her, glaring at one and all through bloodshot orbs. The silence in the house took on a tangible presence when they arrived, as if someone had slammed down a steel curtain. There weren't enough chairs for everyone, so, ironically, Lucy and Cleata stood at the back of the room.

"We've got a lot of things to clear up," I said, standing in front of the group. "We've had three deaths in the past week. Everybody in here is related to all three of them in one way or another."

Babs Tyner said, "Three?"

"Your brother. Billy Greenlee, who was butchered last night downtown in a vacant building, and Leroy Hutchcroft. You knew him as Lee Scroggs."

She gasped and fell back in her chair, tears dimpling her eyes. "Lee?"

"I'm sorry to tell you this, but he had a misunderstanding with the Clallam County sheriff's office early this afternoon. They shot him."

"Good riddance to bad rubbish," snapped Martin Tyner.

"Noble sentiments," I said.

"Come on, Blacky," said one of the cops. "Get on with it."

"Yeah," prodded Tony Tyner. "Pop said you had the will. Where's our money? Me and Velma's got people waiting on us. We got papers to sign."

"As you all know, Lance tended to be wishy-washy. He couldn't quite decide who to leave his money to. He had his attorney draw up two wills, then he took them both home and tried to decide which one to endorse. All along, I've suspected he was debating whether to leave it to his father and the rest of his immediate family, or to Lucy, his fiancée. Since he was getting the marriage license Wednesday morning, you might see where he felt some pressure Tuesday night to get the will thing cleared up.

"There are potent arguments for him to have left it to either one. He probably felt the family deserved something, because after all, they had been cut out of money they had all figured for years was theirs. On the other hand, he was marrying Lucy, and I doubt if he wanted to leave her out in the cold.

"Lance may even have toyed with the idea of splitting up the inheritance, but I doubt it. He was a purist. And I think, whether he wanted to admit it to himself or not, he held a grudge against his father."

The room was quiet. Finally, Velma Dupont spoke up, her chunky chest swelling with the effort, hitching at her tiny red vest with scarlet painted fingernails. "Lance never was going to marry no colored girl. He was stupid, but he wasn't dumb."

Clenching her fists and whirling them around in wild semicircles at her sides, Cleata said, "You shut ya mouth, you hear? You want trouble, you got trouble. Da boy was gettin' hitched to my sister here. No doubt about it."

Slumping in her chair, Velma retreated into her wig like a snail pulling back into its shell.

"Tuesday night," I continued, "Lance had a big decision to make. But Lance had a hard time making up his mind about anything. He tried to talk to Lucy about it, but Lucy was gone that night. Choir practice."

"Likely story," muttered Martin Tyner.

"So he came here."

"Here?" Tyner looked like he was going to have a seizure. "He didn't come here! Lance never came here. What? Do you think I'm crazy? He never came here!"

"Oh, what a tangled web we weave," muttered Bill Crum around the stem of his pipe.

Kathy watched me and barely smiled.

Beulah nibbled at her lower lip and fidgeted with a handbag.

The King County cops kept their eyes glued on Velma.

Chapter Forty

"UNABLE TO MAKE UP HIS MIND, Lance wanted to discuss the wills with both his father and Lucy. Perhaps he didn't realize just how much emotional wallop the subject packed for his father. Lucy was fairly low-key. She might have been thrilled, but I doubt she let much of it show. Besides, what's a will? It's for when someone dies. And Lance was young and healthy. Who could have guessed he would pass on this week? Who could have guessed he would come here to talk things over with his father and that his father would shoot him?"

The room buzzed. The only mute person in the house was Martin Tyner, who was turning paler and paler.

"I hope you have a good lawyer," said Babs. "Because, buddy, you just put your foot right in it."

I smiled at her and said, "Your blind date is sitting over there. Smithers, this is Babs Tyner. Babs, Smitty." They gave each other evaluating and distracted looks. It wasn't your ideal introduction.

"Get on with it," Martin Tyner growled. "You started, now blow your wad. Let's hear what you got to say."

"My guess is Lance came here, discussed the subject with me, told you he was through negotiating, but that he was considering putting you into his will. You pulled out a pistol, aimed it at him and fired it. Now, maybe you didn't mean to fire. People put their fingers on the trigger of a gun lots of times without actually meaning to fire, then their emotions get the better of them and the darned thing goes off. We've been watching so much TV none of us knows how much respect to accord a gun. Maybe he made you angry and you deliberately blasted him. My guess is, once you did it, you two exchanged harsh words and Lance left—with a good-sized hole in his shoulder."

"Lance died in his boarding house," said Ralph Rasmussen. "How do you place him here? And why did he go to the boarding house?"

"He went there because he was hurt and mixed up. His own father had just fired a bullet through his shoulder. He knew if he went to the authorities his father would be in a heap of trouble. And even though he had been bickering with his father for over a year about this money, he loved him too much to let him get into that kind of trouble."

Kathy spoke up. "Nothing would have happened. Lance would have gotten patched up in the hospital. The police would have spoken to his father. They wouldn't have been able to file charges, nothing that would stick, without Lance's cooperation."

"Lance didn't know that. Lance had lived on the skids so long he didn't trust the law; not cops, not lawyers. He was afraid for his father. He didn't want to see an old man like that end up in prison. Sure, it was stupid, foolish. He did it out of love."

"You'll play hell proving any of that," said Martin Tyner, his face distorting like a sheet of plastic bubbling in a furnace.

"I doubt it." I turned around and removed the western portrait from the wall. "There's a rip in this picture. I wondered why somebody would have an original Remington and not have a tear like this repaired. It's about the size a bullet would make, don't you think? And there's a slug in this wall. You can see it if you shine a flashlight up here. Ten to one it's a slug from a pistol. And ten to one that pistol will be one owned by Martin Tyner. The angle of penetration into the wall will match the wound in your son's shoulder, especially if he were standing right here." I pointed toward a spot in the pile carpeting.

"That don't prove nothing." Tyner was adamant, a rock of innocence.

I knelt down. "Here in the folds of this pile rug you'll find bloodstains. The lab will be able to type it and tell you how recent it is. Tuesday night would be my guess. Oh, yeah, I know. You cut out the carpet where the bloodstain was. You told me this week your dog had puked onto the carpet. But a bleeding wound is a messy affair. There are other spots here. Poking around on my own this evening, I found three of them. The lab boys will find more. Lance's blood type. The bullet in the wall. The evidence is beginning to mount. They'll get the gun and match the bullet."

"Don't prove jack shit. If there's a bullet in that wall, maybe I put it there by accident. Besides that, you'll never match the gun. Leroy stole that gun."

"Which gun? The gun you shot your son with?" Martin Tyner's glibness turned suddenly sour, his eyes squinting flintlike. "Leroy got himself killed this afternoon up in Clallam County. Both those pistols he took from you and your son are in police hands. My guess is the slug in the wall here has bits of human tissue on it. They'll match the slug and they'll match the tissue. How are you going to explain that? Police laboratories are marvelous these days." They weren't all that marvelous, but Martin Tyner didn't know that.

"You ain't gonna prove jack. Besides, so maybe I did shoot somebody the other night. Might have been a burglar. Could have been anybody. A stray cat. I don't let no man sneak in here in the middle of the night and rob me blind."

I pulled the papers out of my coat. "The much sought-after will."

Tyner made a rush to grab it out of my hands, but Smithers interjected his pudgy body and placed his palms flat against Tyner's chest. Reluctantly, Martin Tyner sat down, the wind quitting his sails. Trouble was brewing and he knew it. Sitting next to him, sliding around on one of the folding metal chairs I had set out, Tony was getting more and more agitated. He studiously avoided my eyes. Velma Dupont reached over and patted his thigh near his crotch with one bejeweled hand, four rings sparkling. The King County cops watched her hand. She gave off vibrations like a tuning fork and the cops were violin strings humming into pitch.

"If you don't mind," I said, handing the will across to Kathy Birchfield, "perhaps you can quickly scan through this and put so many of these troubled minds to rest."

Kathy took the will, paged through it quickly, then began reading, bending over to see better in the dim light.

"Where did you find that thing?" Martin Tyner asked

I picked up the volume from his bookcase. "Right here.

240

Lance came in here, no doubt to slip it in for some sort of surprise." I grinned. "If you had known that, you could have saved yourself a hell of a lot of trouble, huh? You might even have saved yourself a son."

"The hell, you say. I been trying for over a year to get my fair share from that kid, and you say he just up and handed it over?"

"He didn't hand over a thing. He wrote a will, to be implemented in the event of his death. He didn't have any idea you were going to shoot him. There's a big difference."

"Horse feathers."

"Lance was just idealistic enough to do something like that, or didn't you know him? He spent a year, maybe two, living on the streets. I've talked to some of the friends he made during that time. He could have come to you, couldn't he, and you would have given him a roof, maybe even a job. But he didn't. He was idealistic. And you mistreated him, didn't you? It would be just like Lance to fight you tooth and nail in court and then hand it over after winning."

Tears began slopping down Martin Tyner's face.

"What about my sister?" It was Cleata, moving to the front of the room. "What about my sister? She mentioned in that thing? I mean, Luce owes me money."

Cleata strutted halfway across the room. Watching her, Velma Pearl Dupont sucked a look of revulsion onto her face that was positively entertaining.

Kathy looked up, her blue locking onto me. When I thought nobody else would see it, I winked. She stood.

"This document is very specific. According to this, and it's signed and dated . . . and notarized, too, by the way . . . According to this, Martin Tyner inherits, upon Lance Tyner's death, all of Lance's personal possessions, all of his poems, his letters, books, and other personal effects, anything he owns that is not in the form of cash."

Martin Tyner stood up and hooted jubilantly, "I knew it! I knew it!"

"But that's all he gets. The money goes to Lucy."

Kathy looked at Lucy in the back of the room, as did everyone else except for one of the King County cops, who leaned over to Bill Crum and asked how much money we

241

were talking about. A new respect for the proceedings was reflected in the way he absorbed that news.

Martin Tyner's voice was growing hoarse. "How much of the money goes to *them?*"

Kathy turned to him. "All of it. Except a few thousand to Beulah for her boutique."

At first he didn't say anything, just gaped at Kathy. "No."

"I'm afraid so."

"That little bastard."

Tyner hollered, stomped his feet and kicked his chair over with a metallic clang. Tony also leapt to his feet. In unison, they said, "That's the wrong will."

They glanced at each other. The old man said, "There's two wills. Where's the other one?"

"Other one?"

"There's two of them. One gives it all to *her* and the other places it all where it belongs, right here in the bosom of his family."

"How would you know that?"

"We saw the copies at Jack Thomas's office."

"And how did you do that, break in?"

"Don't try to confound the issue, Black," said Martin Tyner, flicking a sideways glance at the uniformed members in our midst. "What did you do with that other will?"

I looked Martin Tyner in the eye and said, "You can look all you want. You can even frisk me, if it pleases you, but the only will you're going to find in this house is right here."

"Bastard!" Tony Tyner leaped to his feet again and came at me. "Fifteen fucking million smackers and you hand it to some nigger!"

He threw a hard right to my head. I sideslipped the brunt of it, took the remainder on my cheek. I looked past his shoulder at the King County cops. "I want to prefer charges. Assault and battery."

Tony backed quickly away from me. "I didn't do nothing."

At the back of the room Cleata made some sort of motion, but Lucy moved around and stood in front of her.

"Stupid, stupid, stupid," muttered Barbara Tyner, showering me with the sort of looks you gave a monkey in the zoo when you caught him peeing on the wall. "Lance was such a fool. Why did we have to have a brother like that? And why did Grandfather Rufus have to take such a shine to him?"

Bill Crum stood up, pocketed his pipe and sauntered over to where I was standing, careful to avoid the spots in the carpet I had pointed out, though in the deep pile it would have made little difference. "You got something on the Greenlee case too?"

"Did the coroner find the tip of that knife?"

"Nope. Neither did we. We tossed that building from one end to the other."

"I know where it is."

"Where?"

"Up off I-90. After these two jaybirds came back yesterday, one or both drove back up to where Leroy Hutchcroft set them out of Tyner's car and they picked up their clothes. My guess is they picked up Leroy Hutchcroft's knife at the same time."

"That's a lie," yelled Tony Tyner. "I went straight home. I got witnesses. We was out looking at real estate all day."

Clenching his teeth, he came at me a second time, swinging his left fist in a roundhouse. I put a right into the center of his face. Blood spurted from his nose as he crashed into the chairs, flipping over one of the King County cops.

"You bastard!" Tony righted himself and sponged his bleeding nose with his shirt-sleeve. "Don't you know what you could have had? We would have given you ten percent. Can you think about that for a minute?" He looked around at everyone in the room—Bill Crum; the county cops, one of whom was unholstering a shiny pair of handcuffs; Ralph Rasmussen, who had been scowling throughout; Babs; the two black women in the back. "I want to prefer charges on this fucker."

The county cop who had been ready to cuff Tony shook his head in short spasms and rolled his eyes around in their sockets.

"Sorry, buster. That was self-defense." He wrenched Tony's arms around behind his back and snapped a pair of handcuffs on him.

Bill Crum dug a notebook out of his coat pocket and began scribbling. "Get some good lab people up there and my guess is you'll find where Leroy either buried that blade in

243

the earth, or in a log or a tree or something. I'll bet you'll find the tip up there."

"What does that prove?" Martin Tyner asked, moving in on our tête-à-tête. You could almost see his blood pressure zooming up.

"Nothing, by itself. But you add that together with the fact that Leroy himself had an alibi for Greenlee's murder, that the tennis-shoe print on the outside of the building will match up to your foot, that you were so desperate to find out where the will was you would have done practically anything, and they'll hang you for it. They'll find your footprints up off I-90. They'll find the tip of the knife. That will connect you to the weapon."

"Greenlee?" said Tony, his hands now manacled behind his back. "The cops know Greenlee was iced by Lee Scroggs. They know it."

"That was a dusty building, Tone. Your father's footprints are all over it. Add to that the fact that you two are the only ones with access to that knife, and he's as good as hung."

"Why would he do it?"

"Your father was after the will. He probably thought Billy Greenlee knew where it was, that Lance had left it to him in trust. I don't know where he met Greenlee, but I know Billy was just batty enough to give an impression like that by accident." I turned to Martin Tyner. "My guess is you found him and followed him just like I did."

"You just don't know," said Martin Tyner, suddenly looking very tired. "You just don't know how hard a life can be, do you? I lost everything in the depression. You know that? I lost my job. Went to California to look for work. Work? Hell, I couldn't even find anything to eat. Nearly lost my life in a trucking accident. Then I show up back in Minnesota with some dough to take care of my family and they've all been burnt up in a fire. Neighbors didn't know where to get aholt a me."

Almost in tears, Babs Tyner caught my eye and explained, "His first family. He married my mother in the forties and started another family."

Tyner stood still, his head hanging low, his hunched back looking bonier and bonier.

Kathy said, "The only reason Lance died was because he was trying to protect you. He loved you so."

"God," he said, great elephant tears sliding off his craggy face. "You work and save and try to get something in this world and your own goddamn son tries to take everything away from you. Hell, there's no justice at all."

"Don't be too sure," said Bill Crum, stepping forward.

Chapter Forty-one

"HEY, LITTLE BOY." It was Kathy Birchfield leaning out the driver's window of her Volkswagen bug. "Want a ride?"

"My mother told me never to accept rides from strangers."

"Is your mother watching?"

I got into the Volkswagen and she whisked me off on our date. It was good to clown around with her again. The swelling in my lip had come down nicely and the last of my headache had disappeared during the past week.

Once I was inside her car, she turned serious. Her pooled violet turned on me. "You think they're going to nail Tyner?"

"I think they will. For Greenlee anyway. Maybe not for his son. With a motive, in that messy building, it would have been fairly easy for the lab to formulate a case against someone. With a motive. But they didn't have one until Tyner turned up."

"I still don't understand that."

"You know how crazy with greed those two were. They must have met Greenlee before, when Lance knew him. One or both of them spotted him downtown and followed him to his lair. They might even have followed me, heaven forbid, the other night when I found Greenlee. Either that, or Greenlee tried to get hold of them himself. That's a possibility."

"Why would he do that?"

"Protection. He was scared silly of Leroy. He might have thought the rest of Lance's family was as big-hearted as Lance was."

"Yeah, Lance was a little too big-hearted. I guess his father had wounded a burglar about five years ago. Jack

Thomas told me about it after Tyner was arrested. There was a big stink at the time. You might remember. Lance thought his dad would really get it if he showed up with a bullet in his shoulder and told them it had been his father."

"For a guy his girlfriend called Harmless, Lance was sure the center of a lot of turmoil."

"Amen to that," said Kathy.

We saw a film at the Egyptian, a French movie with subtitles, and spent an hour afterwards gossiping in a bistro on Capitol Hill. "What about the will?" I asked. "Will it hold up?"

"We think so. I still wonder what happened to the other one. It doesn't seem like Lance would have destroyed it. It should have been there, even if it wasn't signed. He probably didn't even know which one he was going to sign until he was in the house. Then his father thought he was a burglar. When his father surprised him, he hid them both in the first place he could find. That's the way Lance was, very tidy and neat. I don't think he would have destroyed it."

"No, I don't think so either."

"Thomas!"

"What?"

"You did something to that other will!"

"Me?"

She gave me one of her looks. "Thomas . . ."

I shrugged. "Don't you think things worked out about the way Lance would have liked?"

Kathy thought on that for a few long moments. "Perhaps. Yes, I suppose so. Do you know what Lucy is planning to do?"

"Before I showed her the Klan sheets at Tyner's house, she was planning to give most of it back to the family. Seeing those sheets scotched that. Now she's enrolling her two younger brothers in a special school. They're pretty sharp kids for a pair of 'retards.' Then she's got some harebrained scheme about a foundation here in Seattle to help down-and-outers like Lance had been."

"Yes," said Kathy, grinning widely. "That is harebrained. I understand from Smitty that you got your TV back."

"They brought it back, all hangdog and apologetic. Said

247

they had been down and out so long the bitterness was beginning to take hold of their reasoning. They asked me to forgive them. He even started crying. Can you believe that? Big sissypants."

"So you helped them move into your basement, didn't you?"

"I might have helped them a little, during the commercials."

"You big sap."

I raised my coffee mug. "To harebrained schemes?"

Kathy tapped her coffee mug against mine. "To harebrained schemes and big saps."

IF IT'S MURDER, CAN DETECTIVE J.P. BEAUMONT BE FAR BEHIND?...

FOLLOW IN HIS FOOTSTEPS WITH FAST-PACED MYSTERIES BY J.A. JANCE

IMPROBABLE CAUSE   75412-6/$3.50 US/$4.50 CAN

INJUSTICE FOR ALL   89641-9/$3.50 US/$4.50 CAN

TAKING THE FIFTH   75139-9/$3.50 US/$4.50 CAN

UNTIL PROVEN GUILTY 89638-9/$3.50 US/$4.50 CAN

A MORE PERFECT UNION

    75413-4/$3.50 US/$4.50 CAN

DISMISSED WITH PREJUDICE

    75547-5/$3.50 US/$4.25 CAN

POLICE THRILLERS by

"THE ACKNOWLEDGED MASTER" *Newsweek*
ED MCBAIN

POISON 70030-1/$3.95US/$4.95Can
"Sums up the hot-wire style that has kept McBain ahead of the competition for three decades." *Philadelphia Inquirer*

EIGHT BLACK HORSES 70029-8/$3.95US/$4.95Can
A series of bizarre clues signals the return of the Deaf Man—who this time intends to exact his full measure of revenge.

LIGHTNING 69974-5/$3.95US/$4.95Can
The compelling new novel in the 87th Precinct series, where the dedicated men and women who wear the gold badge push themselves to the limit of danger.

ICE 67108-5/$4.50US/$5.50Can
"In the rough and raunchy world of the 87th Precinct...a half-dozen murders—including a magnificent piece of street justice—keep nerves jangling." *Philadelphia Inquirer*

DOLL	70082-4/$3.50 US/$4.50 Can
THE MUGGER	70081-6/$3.50 US/$4.50 Can
HE WHO HESITATES	70084-0/$3.50 US/$4.50 Can
KILLER'S CHOICE	70083-2/$3.50 US/$4.50 Can
BREAD	70368-8/$3.50 US/$4.50 Can
80 MILLION EYES	70367-X/$3.50 US/$4.50 Can
HAIL TO THE CHIEF	70370-X/$3.50 US/$4.50 Can
LONG TIME NO SEE	70369-6/$3.50 US/$4.50 Can
DOORS	70371-8/$3.50 US/$4.50 Can
WHERE THERE'S SMOKE	70372-6/$3.50 US/$4.50 Can